RECESS RULES

Jill Vialet

PLAYWORKS

OAKLAND, CALIFORNIA

PLAYWORKS
380 Washington
Oakland, CA 94607

FIRST EDITION

10   9   8   7   6   5   4   3   2

Publisher's Cataloging-In-Publication Data
(Prepared by The Donohue Group, Inc.)

Vialet, Jill.
  Recess rules / Jill Vialet. — 1st ed.
    p. : ill. ; cm.
  Summary: Four friends save recess at their school with the help of
an angel-on-probation named Clarence. Includes instructions for
games to play.
  Interest age level: 008-013.
  Issued also as an ebook.
  ISBN: 978-0-9898487-0-1
  1. School recess breaks — Juvenile fiction. 2. Friendship —
Juvenile fiction. 3. Play — Juvenile fiction. 4. Recess — Fiction.
5. Friendship — Fiction. 6. Play — Fiction. I. Title.
PZ7.V535 Re 2013
[Fic]

Shoes on cover ©2013 New Balance Athletic Shoe, Inc.
Book design by Shannon Bodie, Lightbourne, Inc.
Illustrations by Jann Armstrong

For all the Playworks coaches and
junior coaches — past, present, and future

HEAVEN

The young man had been playing basketball by himself for more than ten minutes before he noticed them. He had just completed a particularly athletic 360° spin-around slam dunk, and he froze himself midair, looking around to see if anyone had witnessed it. He smiled a little self-consciously and waved at the couple before returning gently to the ground and walking toward them.

"You must be kidding." Tim Murphy was seriously questioning his wife's judgment. Why had Helen encouraged him to dress up to impress this guy? Tim was wearing khakis, a short-sleeve pale green shirt, and he even put on loafers. Helen was wearing her favorite cornflower blue sundress, and Tim knew that she was hoping it would bring her luck.

Helen tried to soothe him. "I don't know, honey. He has a certain amount of your bravado." She had an intuitive sense that this was the guy, and she was worried that Tim might do something to derail her plan. She watched anxiously as Tim appraised this person they had come to meet. Tim was still strong and fit, reminiscent of his athletic past, and he could be intimidating. Helen thought the slight hints of gray at the temples of his red hair made him seem more mature than she knew him to be. Her husband would always be a kid at heart. Helen, too, was fit, looking younger than the thirty-six years she had spent on Earth. Her blonde hair was pulled back in a ponytail, and her green eyes shone brightly as she turned to watch the man walk toward them.

"Hey!" the man called out from across the street. He was still bouncing the ball as he walked toward them.

Helen could see that the young man had also put some thought into his wardrobe. He wore a baby blue sweat suit with matching high tops. Even the wristband he wore was color coordinated. Helen noticed that he radiated the energy of an athlete, and she immediately caught a distinct twinkle in his eye.

Baby blue sweat suit guy stuck out his hand to Tim as he approached. Helen read the gesture as a peace offering and felt temporarily relieved. "Hey, I'm Clarence. It's nice to meet you."

Tim was still not certain, even as he shook his hand. "Nice shot," he said, with just a hint of sarcasm. Helen could feel herself getting more and more annoyed with her husband.

Clarence's friendly energy shifted a little, and Helen watched as his guard had come up slightly in response to Tim's tone. "He spent most of the first year in the batting cages after we died," Helen offered, gesturing to her husband with a nod. She really wanted them to connect. Her gut told her they were kindred spirits.

"I guess I couldn't get over being able to see the ball so well. You know?" Tim said.

Helen watched her husband as he spoke. She knew he was making an effort, but she couldn't help but marvel at how uncomfortable he seemed in his own skin.

Clarence made no sign of responding; he wasn't going to help Tim out. Helen thought Tim seemed oblivious to Clarence's reaction as he continued rambling on: "I could see the seams on the ball. I could hit anything the machine threw at me."

"It was heaven," Clarence offered, totally deadpan.

Tim laughed a little at this, but he still didn't seem to relax. "Yeah."

Helen had watched enough of the male posturing and figured that it was probably wise to get right to it. "We wanted to talk with you."

"Yeah," Clarence responded, now clearly a little noncommittal. "Gabe mentioned it."

"It's about our daughter." Tim was suddenly using a more serious tone, and Helen couldn't help but wonder if his competitive nature was kicking in. Did Tim want Clarence to help them more now that he seemed less interested?

"Cassie's going through a rough patch," Helen explained. "We heard that you were still looking for an assignment, and we were wondering if you would consider. . . ." Helen trailed off. Actually talking about her daughter, Cassie, made it hard for her to breathe.

"She needs a reason to believe it's safe to care," Tim came to the rescue. "You know, to believe that she'll get what she needs sometimes. She's not wild about asking for help."

Clarence looked from Tim's face to Helen's and then back again. "She looks like both of you." Clarence could tell that this was hard for them. "She's got your eyes," he said to Helen.

Helen looked down. Talking about her daughter created a physical feeling of missing her, deep in the pit of her stomach. It was almost unbearable. She was surprised that even after all this time, it was still so hard.

"Yeah, I've seen her. And I was impressed," Clarence continued. "She's a good kid. Fierce."

"She's just a little girl," Tim responded abruptly. He could think she was fierce, but who was this guy to be passing judgment?

Helen reached over and put her hand on her husband's forearm to calm him. "I'm afraid we're a little protective. She's an amazing child. And yes, I think you're probably right, a little fierce. She inherited her father's competitive streak. We gather that you and she—and it seems to me, you and Tim—have some things in common."

The two men begrudgingly nodded at one another.

It was clear from Helen's tone that she had intended it as a compliment.

Tim knew that his wife had decided that this was the guy, and he figured he should do what he could to help. "Are you interested?" he asked, cutting to the chase.

Clarence didn't miss a beat. "I'm in. I mean, if you want me. I've never been a parent; I can imagine that it is a huge responsibility. I was a pretty great uncle, but I get that being a parent is different. But if you want me, I'm in."

Helen felt sure this was the right guy. She was also sure that Tim *wasn't* quite convinced. She turned hesitantly toward her husband to assess his comfort with the situation and found him focusing a steady gaze on Clarence, as if he were trying to see exactly what the younger man was thinking.

Helen was about to accept, when Tim interjected. "One question," he said. "You've been a provisional for longer than usual. We saw in your file that you've been assigned to a few other cases but didn't always follow through. Why should we believe that this—that our daughter—will be any different?"

Clarence had known that he was going to ask this. He would probably have asked, too, had the situation been reversed. He thought for a few moments before answering.

"Well, I'm no angel," Clarence began but then immediately regretted it. "No, wait. That came out wrong."

This made Tim laugh out loud. "That's just funny." And for the first time, Tim radiated a warmth and kindness that made Helen certain things were going to work out.

But now Clarence was flustered. "I don't think it's fair to say that I didn't follow through. I did what was asked of me. I just didn't get too emotionally invested. The folks here all seem to want me to make a connection. You know?"

Helen could tell that Clarence had picked up on Tim's changed demeanor and seemed to calm down a little. He continued: "I guess the only thing I can tell you is that I spent most of my life trying to make sure I didn't get hurt . . . as in, getting my feelings hurt. I played it safe. I didn't suffer fools, and I didn't spend a lot of time trying to convince people to like me. I mostly just minded my own business."

Clarence had been looking down at his feet while speaking, but now he looked up. "The only time I really connected with people was when I was playing—basketball, football, whatever. Never met a game I didn't like."

Tim was convinced.

"The assignments I've been sent on—they just weren't me. They were all grown-ups taking themselves too seriously. I don't know . . . I just didn't connect." He stopped again. Sometimes Clarence had a hard time putting his feelings into words. But he really wanted Helen and Tim to understand. So he kept talking.

"But your daughter . . . I don't know. She just struck me as different. When I said that she was fierce, I meant that in the best possible way. I mean, she lost her folks at eight. She's a tough kid. I could relate. I guess your case is the first one where I genuinely feel like I could make a difference."

Helen had heard enough, and she felt confident that she was speaking for the two of them. "We'd like you to do it then."

Tim looked at his wife and wondered briefly how she had known all along that this was the guy. Turning back to Clarence, he said softly, "We would."

"Great!" Clarence allowed his excitement to show through. "I can leave tomorrow." He looked briefly perplexed as to what he should do next. "Is there anything else?"

Helen understood his confusion. It seemed like there should be more to say. "No, I think that's it," she confirmed. "Thanks."

The three of them stood awkwardly for a few more moments until Tim broke the silence. Looking around, it suddenly occurred to him that Clarence's car was the beat-up old avocado green Chevy Nova parked next to them. "That's your car?" he asked in horror.

Clarence turned around to look at the car Tim was referring to, and it was clear that he was immensely pleased with himself. "Yup. It was my brother's. I know it's a little morbid, but it's the car I died in."

Helen shook her head in disbelief. "You could have any car you want. Why . . . ?"

But Clarence interrupted before she could ask the

question. "It's a fuel efficient, flying Chevy Nova. How cool is that? And besides, it would make my brother crazy mad if he knew."

Clarence chuckled to himself as he turned again to walk around to the driver's side of the car. As he reached to open the door, he stopped and looked over to the couple one more time. "Is there anything you want me to tell her?"

Tim looked uncomfortable at the suggestion. "You're not supposed to do that."

"Tell her we knew she didn't mean it," Helen interrupted.

"And tell her we love her," Tim added, his tone softening dramatically.

"Got it," Clarence replied quickly as he opened the car door. "And thanks."

Tim and Helen stood for a while watching, even after he drove away. Helen turned slowly to her husband and kissed him on the cheek. "I love you," she said.

Tim looked at his wife and sighed deeply. "Let's go to the batting cages."

Even at rest, Cassie gave off a low-grade electrical charge. And now, she was fit to be tied. "That's it," she announced, clearly intent upon taking action. "I'm going to get the ball." She headed toward Marcus, who was slowly dribbling the ball back and forth, daring potential opponents to approach.

Marcus was standing in the middle of the Magruder Elementary schoolyard, bouncing a slightly deflated red rubber ball from one hand to the other. He breathed heavily despite standing still and looked around lazily, not expecting to see anyone approach. Marcus was remarkable in his ability to send out a menacing vibe while doing virtually nothing. In no small part, this was due to him being one of the biggest kids at the school. His blonde hair was cut crew-cut short and even though he was only eleven, his neck and shoulders had the muscularity of a teenager.

Cassie's friends, Bryant, Toni, and Zee, followed quickly behind her.

"I really hate that guy," Bryant grumbled, still not looking at Marcus. "I'm not much of a hater, but I reserve some of my best work for this guy."

Bryant Anderson was younger than the rest, still a month away from turning ten. His brown skin, blue eyes, and wild hair made people look twice at him. And much to his dismay, older women universally felt compelled to comment on his extraordinarily long, dark eyelashes. That was the kind of attention Bryant tried to avoid.

Toni sighed, "He's not worth it. He's too dumb to waste good hating on. We deserve a more worthy opponent." Toni Robinson's tiny braids were always absolutely perfect, and today they swung around with bright blue beads at the end of each as she whipped her head to more actively look away from Marcus. Toni was a whole head taller than Bryant and her skin a shade darker. She carried herself with a silent strength that, even at ten, made people think twice before telling her what to do.

Bryant hurried to catch up to Cassie. "*Really?*" he asked, though Bryant's voice was heavy with resignation and it was clear he wasn't actually asking a question. He knew Cassie was going to confront Marcus; it would be the fourth time that week.

As Cassie marched directly toward Marcus, a small, mean smile appeared on his face. Zee, Toni, and Bryant were being pulled in Cassie's wake, not really wanting to go over but unable to avoid being sucked in by their friend's overdeveloped sense of justice.

"What was that thing Ms. Donlon used to say to us in kindergarten?" Zee was setting the others up for the answer they all knew. Bryant and Toni replied in a singsong unison, "Stop, think, make a good choice." Even though things looked bad, the three shared a quick laugh. It had been their joke since third grade when the stopping and thinking part had been challenging, especially for Cassie. And now that they were in fifth grade, it felt like making good choices was that much harder.

Zee, born Miguel Zapata, was the biggest of the friends and at eleven, the oldest of the bunch. Zee's coffee-colored skin, short haircut, and deep brown eyes made him the fifth-grade heartthrob, though he was charmingly unaware of this and wouldn't have believed it if someone had told him.

Marcus stopped his dribbling to more fully enjoy provoking Cassie. "Can I help you?" he asked, his voice dripping with sarcasm as he stared down at Cassie. Cassie was about the same height as Bryant, but she had a wiry strength and fierceness that somehow made her seem bigger than she really was. Her hair was a blondish red, and her pale skin was rich with freckles.

Cassie inhaled deeply as she tried to summon her composure. She was still standing a good six feet away from him, but she knew she was getting close enough to be in harm's way. "Sure," she spoke carefully, trying to sound as though she believed he might cooperate this time. "We wanted to get a game going. Can we use the ball now?"

Marcus snickered. "Of course," he said and then resumed bouncing the ball from his left side to his right.

Cassie could feel herself getting increasingly angry, and she was fairly certain her face was turning red. She had a tendency to turn bright red anytime she ran around—even when she wasn't too tired—and when she was angry or embarrassed. She hated turning red—it made her feel stupid.

"What game do you want to play, carrot top?" Marcus laughed at his own joke and then looked even more pleased with himself as Zee, Bryant, and Toni edged in closer and stood next to their friend.

"C'mon, Marcus, let us use the ball so we can finish up the game of Kickball from yesterday." Zee knew it was useless, but he couldn't watch Cassie go it alone any longer.

"You gonna fight her fight for her, Zit?" Marcus stopped bouncing long enough to lean menacingly toward Zee.

Bryant let out a deep sigh. "*Really?*" he asked again, still not expecting an answer.

"You got something to say?" Marcus's aggressiveness now turned toward Bryant. As he spoke, there was a blur of redness as Cassie launched herself headfirst into Marcus. Bouncing off him, she dislodged the ball in the process.

Cassie hit the ground but jumped up quickly, taking

off after the ball. Marcus was stunned by this unprecedented turn of events. Almost in a daze, he responded with, "What the . . . ?!?"

Zee and Bryant started to laugh at the extraordinary sight of Cassie the human cannonball, which visibly irritated Marcus. He quickly turned his attention away from Cassie and started toward them instead. Realizing that a hasty retreat was their best hope, Zee, Bryant, and Toni all took off running back to the building and the temporary safety of Mrs. Grumble, the head lunch lady who was standing in the doorway.

Flustered by the whole situation, Marcus scanned the area, looking to see who else was watching—and laughing. He made a mental note of the kids he would later terrorize in retaliation.

"Where'd she go?" Marcus demanded of no one in particular. Cassie had managed to disappear into thin air. As he looked around the giant expanse of black top, the bell rang. A profoundly frustrated Marcus shuffled back to the building.

The other students filed in to the building as Mrs. Grumble emerged, looking around for Marcus and the kickball. Mrs. Grumble did not enjoy this job of chasing after balls and such after recess. She much preferred the domain of the school kitchen where she could demonstrate her talent for managing a tight ship and delivering attractive and nutritious food to the student body. "Marcus," Mrs. Grumble called to him. "Where's the ball, Marcus? Didn't you sign it out?"

This was more than Marcus could bear. He began to protest that Cassie had taken it from him, but Mrs. Grumble cut him off. "Marcus, you know the rules. You're responsible for the ball if you take it out. I'm going to have to tell Mr. Unger, and you can work out replacing the ball with him."

This was adding insult to injury. Now Cassie had gotten him in trouble with the principal. And he was going to have to replace that dumb old ball? No way. Cassie was going to pay for this.

For now, though, as there was nothing he could do, Marcus waited while Mrs. Grumble looked around, trying to figure out what to say next. Zee, Bryant, and Toni had lingered just inside the doorway, curious to find out what would happen to Marcus and to figure out where, exactly, Cassie had disappeared to. They inched in close enough to hear Mrs. Grumble say, "All right. Let's go see Mr. Unger." It was only a small victory, and they all knew they'd be better off showing no emotion at all, but Toni emitted a small cheer, and Bryant and Zee both smiled ear to ear.

Marcus glowered at them as he passed by, following Mrs. Grumble inside to the principal's office.

"Man, we are toast," Bryant observed.

"Yeah, but that was the most fun I've had at recess all year," Toni was laughing hard now.

Zee was smiling but also checking around for Cassie. "We gotta get back to class. Where do you think Cassie went?"

The three friends stuck their heads out to scan the blacktop once more, but there was no sign of her. Seeing no other recourse, they headed back to class.

When Zee, Toni, and Bryant arrived, slightly late to Ms. Swanson's class, Cassie was already in her seat.

"How'd you get here so quick?" Bryant glanced over toward the window, half suspecting she had climbed in that way.

Cassie looked pleased with herself. "Ran" she said sweetly.

"Man, you are so glad I didn't get my butt kicked for you," Zee whispered. "I mean, you stunned him, running all seventy-eight pounds of yourself into his big side of beef, but he's furious, and he would have been just as happy to kick my butt as a warm-up for going after you." Even though Zee was chastising Cassie, she could tell he was proud of her.

Cassie's smile faded a little, and she glanced toward the front of the class to see if Ms. Swanson was looking their way. Ms. Swanson was their homeroom teacher, so she taught all their classes except the art elective. It was time for math now, and every math class started with some warm-up problems on the blackboard. The classroom was bigger than most, with the desks set up in the traditional way all facing the front. Cassie looked all around, back to where Ms. Swanson had maps of the world hung alongside pictures by famous artists and portraits of all the presidents. Cassie took it all in now, thinking briefly that she usually looked only at what was on the blackboard. Ms. Swanson didn't like it if the students didn't get right to work.

"He's gonna try and get me back, isn't he?" Cassie wondered aloud.

Toni, Zee, and Bryant all nodded in sync as they settled into their math problems, but none of them said anything.

Ten minutes into class, Marcus shuffled through the door. Bryant marveled at his ability to appear aggressive and menacing even when just shuffling, but he avoided making eye contact. Marcus was looking around as he entered, daring anyone to laugh, and searching for Cassie. He never said a word aloud, but he sent a clear message that he intended to beat up Cassie after school. Cassie tried not to respond visibly, but avoiding Marcus's eye contact seemed to enrage him even more. Halfway through class, he passed a note to Cassie that read simply "Dead Meet." Cassie wondered if it was a pun, as in "When we meet next, you will be dead," but had to conclude that Marcus was simply stupid and had misspelled meat. She shared the note with Toni, who rolled her eyes and passed it to Zee who, unfortunately, laughed out loud.

"Mr. Zapata," Ms. Swanson was clearly frustrated as she addressed Zee. "Is there something funny you'd like to share with the class?"

Zee tried to stifle his giggles as he responded unconvincingly, "No, no, nothing funny, Ms. Swanson."

Ms. Swanson, who was the youngest teacher at Magruder, wore her long brown hair back in a bun. The kids liked her, though Toni thought that she tried to dress and act older than she really was. Today she was wearing a floral dress that reminded Toni of her grandmother.

Marcus was visibly steaming and seemed to sense that he was the object of the joke. "Yeah, what's so funny, Zee?" He never called Zee "Zee," generally preferring to call him Zit, as if it were a brilliant joke.

Zee couldn't resist. "*Meat* is spelled m-e-a-t." And then Zee broke down in hysterical peals of laughter.

"Enough!" Ms. Swanson spoke sharply. She could tell that something was going on, and she didn't like it. "Back to work."

The rest of the class period passed uneventfully and when the bell rang, the four friends stalled as Marcus packed up his books. They waited for Marcus to leave the classroom first, following cautiously. Not surprisingly, they found Marcus lurking menacingly just outside in the hall.

Marcus walked directly up to Cassie and stuck his finger right in her face, not quite touching her but getting just as close as possible. "You are totally dead meat," he said.

Cassie didn't flinch and walked around him, "Yeah, I heard that." Her voice was calm and confident.

Marcus stood a little longer, a little confused by her reaction. "I'm talking to you!" he called out after her.

"And I'm walking away," she replied as though she couldn't be bothered. A cool had descended upon Cassie that blew the others away.

"Man," Bryant whispered to Toni, "She's not even turning red!"

Even Toni was impressed. "You're right. I don't think I've ever seen her act this chill."

"Did I already say that I totally hate this guy?" Bryant laughed a little as he said it. "But I have to admit, it is entertaining to watch Cassie put him to shame." The three smiled broadly as they followed after Cassie to their last class of the day: art.

Marcus wasn't in art with the other four, so that class passed quickly. Mr. Street, the art teacher, allowed the students to talk while they were working on projects, but none of the friends had much to say in this class.

"Do we have a plan?" Zee finally asked as they cleared the project table in preparation for the dismissal bell.

Cassie looked composed. "I'm thinking I run. You got something better?"

Bryant and Toni nodded their approval. "Sounds about right to me," Bryant had been thinking the same thing. Cassie was faster than Marcus, and he figured the key was to avoid getting caught.

"I don't know," Zee couldn't help but think there had to be a better way. "Marcus is as dumb as a post. Don't you think we can outsmart him?"

The four of them sat quietly for a few moments considering the possibilities. "I know!" Toni exclaimed. "We get Sarah Hechtmeyer to walk with us wearing Cassie's sweatshirt. We get a few blocks away and then reveal

18

she's a decoy. He'd never be stupid enough to pound on the police chief's daughter."

Cassie looked hopeful and Bryant was smiling in approval. Only Zee looked uncomfortable because they all knew the real reason it would work: Sarah could pass for Cassie because of her size and her red hair, but Sarah would be willing to help only because she had a massive crush on Zee.

"Dude," Bryant turned to Zee, "this is such a no-brainer. You don't have to kiss her or anything."

Zee shot Bryant a withering look. "You are so completely lame." But Zee knew he had no choice.

Cassie pulled her sweatshirt over her head and held up a high five to Zee. "I totally owe you."

Toni took the sweatshirt from Cassie. "Where do we meet?"

Zee shook his head in resignation. "All right. Let's meet at the park, over by the Grove."

They discussed Cassie's route for a bit longer and then split up, Cassie heading toward the back exit while the others headed to Zee's locker. Sarah had the locker right next to his and was in the habit of waiting for him at the end of the day to say good-bye.

When Zee, Bryant, and Toni arrived at the locker, Sarah was there waiting as anticipated and excited to be a part of anything Zee-related. While Zee and Toni filled Sarah in on the plan, Bryant went off to do some reconnaissance. "He's outside already," Bryant offered upon his return. "Some of the other kids said he is so mad that he just couldn't stop talking about how he was going to catch Cassie a few blocks from school and teach her a lesson."

"I hope she's already half way home." Zee's tone conveyed his concern.

"Man, I hope he doesn't catch her," Toni was starting to regret her idea now, wishing instead that they had all stuck together.

Cassie jogged down the hallway, heading for the girls' locker room. She had decided to exit through the back of the school near the gym. If Marcus were standing out there, she would at least have a wide open space to make a run for it.

Cassie was surprised by her own mixed emotions: she felt a little scared, but she felt so much better at the same time. She had finally done something, finally stood up to that bully Marcus. Maybe it was going to get worse from here, but at least recess hadn't been so boring today.

The girls' locker room was empty as she crossed through it. She came to the back door and pushed it open slightly, sticking her head out just enough to look all around. The coast seemed clear. Cassie figured it was best just to go for it. She wasn't very big, but she'd always been fast. She counted to three and took off running for the Grove.

As expected, Sarah had been pretty easy to convince. Toni and Bryant stifled any teasing comments they could have made and only exchanged one pained look between them when Sarah gushed: "Oh, Zee! I bet this is your idea. You're amazing!" Zee had winced, knowing he would inevitably hear about that one later.

"No, no!" he protested. "This was Toni's idea." Sarah did not notice the defensiveness in his voice.

With the sweatshirt on, Sarah was the right size to pass for Cassie, and the little bit of red hair that peeked out from under the hoodie was enough to complete the disguise.

"You think he's gonna want to kick one of our butts when he realizes he doesn't get to kick Cassie's?" Bryant was going through all the possible outcomes in his head.

"He's most definitely going to be mad," Toni confirmed.

Sarah seemed to suddenly consider the danger she had put herself in. "You think he's going to be mad at me?" Sarah's tone quavered a bit as she spoke, making Toni and Zee instantly feel guilty. Bryant was too preoccupied thinking through all the different scenarios and trying to imagine one where things worked out well.

"Oh, no, no, no," Zee insisted, but he didn't sound as though he really meant it.

"Because I've made him look foolish?" Sarah was sounding more and more anxious as the implications of their plan dawned on her. She suddenly felt incredibly uncomfortable wearing Cassie's sweatshirt.

Sarah's obvious change of heart made it hard to continue vehemently denying the possibility of his wrath.

"Well, maybe . . . ," Zee admitted. "But we'll be there."

The four of them took a collective deep breath and emerged from the school into the afternoon sunlight.

As they stepped outside the school, everything seemed normal. Kids were all heading off in the various directions home, the sun was shining, and the air felt crisp and autumnal. For a moment, their fears allayed, and it seemed as though they had all worked themselves up unduly. Until Eddy Zellerbach walked by.

"Man, he is going to kill you," he said to Sarah, clearly thinking she was Cassie.

"Well, the disguise works," Toni observed drily.

"What now?" Sarah wasn't yet hysterical, but she was heading that way.

Zee took her hand and summoned his bravest tone. "Let's walk home." As the oldest of his siblings, Zee's parents had taught him to step up and take responsibility. With three younger sisters and a little brother, he was used to having people look to him for a sign of what was OK to do and what wasn't.

"Drop her hand, Sir Galahad. Cassie would never let you hold her hand," Bryant was nervous, but he hadn't lost his sense of humor.

Zee dropped Sarah's hand, suddenly embarrassed. He considered being mad at Bryant, but he was used to Bryant's wisecracks. It was Bryant's way of fitting in, being the smallest and all. And Zee knew it was also the best way Bryant had found to get along with his older

22

brother who was eight years older and about three feet taller. Teasing was just the way the Anderson family showed the love.

Bryant immediately regretted having called Zee out. He turned to Sarah, summoning his most reassuring voice, "We got this."

The four walked the usual route toward Toni's house. She always peeled off first. Then Cassie, then Bryant, and finally Zee, whose house was right next to the Grove. The Grove was a stand of old beech trees adjacent to the city park. The canopy of trees stretched a hundred feet or so in either direction, and underneath small hiding places were interspersed with bigger openings. Beneath the tree cover there were well-worn paths that ran between the trees and the biggest clearing, The Room, where kids had held meetings for generations.

Outside the Grove where it met the park stood a line of basketball hoops where older kids played and a big field that stretched out through the middle of the park that played host to football and soccer games on the weekends. Most of the time, though, the field had a strip of orange tape lining the outside, with big signs explaining that the grass was being reseeded, or aerated, or something that required people to keep off. So, usually, the only place the younger kids felt like they could really play was in the Grove.

Piles of autumn leaves lined the side of the street, and on a normal day, one of Cassie's group would have been inspired to jump in or kick a pile or two, but today they were all a little too distracted. Instead, they were looking all around as they walked and talking only a little. Sarah had stopped talking all together.

Increasingly, their anxiety was mixed with a growing sense of confusion. Why was there was no sign of Marcus or for that matter, Cassie? When they finally neared Zee's house, he looked across the park toward the Grove.

"Should we go see if she's there?" Zee asked uncertainly, pointing over at the trees.

Toni shook her head: "No, let's get Sarah home first. I feel bad about coming up with this idea. I want to make sure we get her home safely." Toni could be pretty stubborn about "doing the right thing." This plan she'd come up with, she realized now, was questionable. She knew her mom and dad wouldn't be so happy about it—if they found out. Either way, she was determined to make it right now and led the way to Sarah's house, not waiting for group consensus. Sarah's house was back around the corner from Bryant's, so they doubled back, still looking for Marcus, but now thoroughly confused about his plan, or lack thereof.

"Man," Bryant said. "You think he's really this dumb?" The other three just shook their heads. They were all feeling pretty dumb themselves.

Back at Sarah's house, Zee walked her up the stairs of the front porch, and they all watched to make sure she was safely inside. At the door, she handed Cassie's sweatshirt to Zee a little hesitantly. "Zee, will you call me and let me know Cassie's alright?" she asked.

"Promise," Zee was trying to sound sure of himself. He stood awkwardly at the door for a moment and then turned abruptly and headed back down Sarah's front steps. "Thanks for helping, Sarah. You were great."

As soon as Zee was down the steps, the three friends turned and jogged back toward the Grove.

"She's pretty cool," Toni puffed out as they ran.

"Yeah, I might wait till tomorrow to tease you about how amazing you are," Bryant added with a laugh.

Back at the Grove, the park was just as empty as it had appeared when Zee and the others had scanned it earlier. They looked around again for Cassie, but to no avail. The place was desolate, and the open grassy area had grown brown and stubbly, an early sign of winter's imminent arrival. The stand of beech trees was largely leafless and contributed to the depressing feel, the limbs jutting out in every direction like arthritic fingers. No one said anything, but the worry that Marcus was pounding Cassie somewhere else, out of sight, weighed heavily on all of them.

They walked across the field and slowed as they approached the edge of the Grove.

"What's the plan?" Zee asked, sounding more than a little hopeless.

And just as he asked, they all heard a blood-curdling scream and saw the blur of Cassie's red hair go flying into the woods, followed closely, though clumsily, by Marcus's lurching form.

"I am so going to nail you," Marcus yelled, his voice filled with rage, in the general direction of the red blur.

"No time for plans!" Bryant shouted as he headed straight for Cassie and Marcus.

"I go left; you go right," Toni instructed and took off, flanking Bryant.

What followed was five minutes of sheer chaos with kids running through branches, jumping over tree stumps, and ducking under fallen limbs. Legs and arms were scratched by twigs, shins were bruised, and toes stubbed. Every now and then, the air was punctuated by a Cassie scream or a Marcus grunt. The bedlam continued this way for what seemed like an eternity until, suddenly, all five of them arrived simultaneously in the small opening in the middle of the Grove that had held so many gatherings of kids before.

Marcus was slightly bent over, breathing hard and snorting like a bull. Cassie was clearly winded and bright red in the face, though she definitely looked fresher than Marcus.

"C'mon, Marcus, give it up," Zee tried to reason as he caught his breath.

"Yeah, you don't want to beat her up; she's like one third your size. That's just incredibly uncool." Bryant's voice was dripping with disdain.

"Shut up, little man. I'm coming after you once I finish with her." Marcus's reply managed to match Bryant's disdain despite his exhaustion.

"Man, I was feeling bad about hating on you earlier, but the 'little man' comment just cemented it."

Cassie cleared her throat. "You know what makes me the maddest?" It was a rhetorical question. She didn't really care if anyone else had a clue. "I don't hate you, Marcus. You're not worth it. But you've made me hate recess. How messed up is that?"

And at that Marcus roared and lunged at Cassie. What happened next would be debated by the four friends for many years to come. Bryant insisted there was a flash of light, but the other three remembered smoke. Cassie said she saw a puzzled look cross Marcus's face as he froze midair. Zee insisted he heard Marcus fart, but Toni said that Zee was just being immature. They all agreed, though, that Marcus momentarily froze midair before crashing to the ground and that, suddenly, standing right next to Marcus's statue-like body, appeared a man in sweats.

"What the . . . ?" Zee spoke first.

Bryant and Toni immediately backed up, as if to take in the situation from a little distance. Only Cassie stood stock still. "Hi," she said uneasily.

The man walked over to Marcus and knelt down next to him, "Aw, man, I am so busted." He poked at Marcus's lifeless form and rolled him over so that he was face up. Then he looked up at Cassie. "Hey," he said. And then in a tone that was clearly meant to be reassuring, "Don't worry; he's OK."

The man was dark skinned and looked to be in his

midtwenties and athletic. He wore sneakers and had a little bit of a beard going. Toni thought to herself that he looked like he was trying really hard to look casual. It also occurred to her that she should be very concerned about a random strange man suddenly appearing in the Grove, but at the same time, she couldn't shake the feeling that there was something bizarrely serene about this guy.

"C'mon, Cass. We should be going," Zee urged. He shared Toni's concern and was backing up now, willing Cassie to come with him even as she was moving in the opposite direction.

Cassie wasn't picking up on the hints. "You sure he's alright?" she quizzed the stranger.

"Yeah, he's fine. I just stunned him a little. He looked bigger from far away; I should have gone a little easier. I didn't think he was going to lunge like that. He startled me, you know?" And then he stopped and chuckled a little as he turned to Bryant. "I thought you were going to lose it after the 'little man' comment."

"Far away?" Serene or not, this guy was giving Toni the creeps.

The man turned to look at Toni, and Zee thought he sounded a little defensive, "Well, yeah, you know . . . "

"Not really," Toni wasn't giving an inch, and once again Zee marveled at her ability to make grown-ups uncomfortable.

The man looked around at the faces of the four fifth graders and seemed to make a decision as to his next step.

He nodded his head slightly and five logs moved into a semicircle of seats without being physically touched. "I can explain," he said, gesturing for the kids to sit.

Zee, Bryant, and Toni all looked at one another in complete disbelief and confusion, but Cassie was avoiding eye contact. "Aw man," Bryant said, voicing what the others were thinking. "This is too weird."

After hesitating for a moment, the four sat slowly down on the logs. Zee was watching Cassie closely, and he had a nagging sense that she was strangely unsurprised by the situation. She had been acting weird all day; could it be that she was in on this? Did she understand what was going on?

The man waited for them to get settled. It did not escape him that Toni was staring at him in a way that conveyed profound distrust.

"OK, OK," he was trying to begin again. "I admit that I owe you an explanation. This was not the way the protocol says an initiation is supposed to go down."

Cassie leaned forward. "An initiation?"

"You know," he tried to explain, "making contact."

Toni shook her head, her tone forceful. "What are you talking about? We are *not* making contact with you!"

"No, no, no, let me start over. My name is Clarence. I died six months ago."

Bryant was up and off his log immediately, heading quickly for the street when Clarence nodded toward him, freezing him, though not with the intensity that he had frozen Marcus who still lay immobile on the ground.

31

Bryant, in his frozen state, could still move his lips a little and manage to speak.

"Man, that is so way out of bounds, freezing a dude you hardly know. Do you know what I'm saying?" Even frozen, Bryant could work up a good head of indignation.

Clarence conceded the point: "You're right, but this is a sensitive situation. I overfroze a guy from an extreme elevation, and I've disclosed my metaphysical limbo to you, so I need you not to run off. Can you appreciate my position?"

Toni seemed to be weighing this information with an unusual open-mindedness, perhaps because she was not the one frozen. She didn't trust this guy, but she had to respect the directness with which he stated his case. "He's got a point, Bryant. I'd say offer not to bolt if he unfreezes you."

"Done," Bryant confirmed.

And with that, Clarence nodded and Bryant thawed.

"So what's the deal?" The only possible explanation was that this guy was crazy, but Toni needed more information. "You died six months ago? Does that make you an angel?" She sounded unconvinced even as she pronounced the word.

"A fallen angel?" Cassie added. She hadn't spoken in a while, and her tone conveyed that she had something invested in believing in Clarence, that she wanted it to be true.

Clarence gave her a sideways glance. "It's not exactly like that . . . ," he started.

"I cannot believe you are even having this conversation!" Zee erupted. He was having none of it and was overwhelmed by both impatience and worry. "This is nuts."

"Well, maybe, but my butt was frozen," Bryant offered. He was still tingling in a weird way, post-freeze, and while he'd be the first to acknowledge this was unbelievable, he was nonetheless a believer.

Bryant's conviction slowed Zee down a bit. "Oh, yeah, right. . . . Still! This dude is so not an angel!"

"I think I should resent that comment." Clarence was mildly taken aback by the vehemence of Zee's accusation, but he didn't seem annoyed.

"So, tell us then," Cassie insisted. "What's the deal? Are you an angel? A ghost?"

"OK," Clarence began again, "here's the deal. I was killed six months ago. It was an accident, and while I'd like to pretend I had nothing to do with it, I was pretty much to blame. Anyway, I end up in heaven. Not a full pass, but I'm there provisionally. And it's not at all what I was expecting." Clarence looked from Toni to Bryant to Zee to Cassie. He had never talked about this with anyone, and he wasn't sure how to explain it. He needed them all to understand, but only Cassie seemed to be following.

"I mean, it's incredible. Don't get me wrong. It's incredibly beautiful. The design of the place is not to be believed. But I guess I was expecting something different. Like, there isn't a clear answer. Not a right and wrong the way I was thinking there would be. Like, you'd finally know—something, anything.

"Nope, everyone is still holding on to their opinions about how it all works—I mean, there are Muslims, and Jews, and Christians, and everybody, all still believing what they believed on earth. They all just agree to disagree—everyone's a whole lot nicer about it in heaven.

"It just turns out that whatever got you through still works—if that makes any sense. I guess I was just hoping to know something for sure. But I guess not knowing got me through on earth, so that's what I got in heaven."

Clarence sat and thought about that for a while, seemingly forgetting where he was and that others had been listening to him. His wary audience watched quietly.

After a while Cassie asked softly: "You said something about 'metaphysical limbo.' What's that?"

Startled from his reverie, Clarence looked around a little surprised to find himself sitting in the woods. "Well, you know how you asked if I was a fallen angel? You weren't too far off. I mean, I didn't exactly do anything wrong, but I haven't done quite enough right either. I guess you'd say I had some 'unresolved issues.'"

"No way. We got an angel with 'unresolved issues?' That's just messed up." Bryant was still not pleased with having been frozen and was not going to pass up the chance to give the freezer a hard time.

Clarence appreciated Bryant's hazing for what it was, and Zee began to suspect that they were kindred spirits.

"Fear not, Bryant, it's your lucky day. I've been sent here to help you!"

Marcus stirred just slightly as Clarence said this and then the crumpled bully made a very faint moaning sound.

"You did a good job on Marcus, that's for sure." Toni was peering over at the big lump of him on the ground in between sideways glances at Clarence.

"You're not sure about me, huh?" Clarence had a strong feeling that winning over Toni would be critical to his success.

"Most definitely not," Toni confirmed. And even as she spoke the words, she was aware that while still uncertain, she was indeed warming to the newcomer.

"And you?" Clarence turned to Zee.

"I'm with Toni," Zee replied. Zee was more entrenched in his distrust. His basic desire to protect his friends made it almost impossible for him to relax around this new guy. None of it made any sense.

"How about you, Bryant?" Clarence's tone lightened as he addressed Bryant. He had a good sense that he was already convinced.

"I gotta admit that while I wish it wasn't so, you know my name and somehow froze me mid-stride. I'm a believer."

Finally, Clarence turned to Cassie, even though he already knew what she thought. "And you?"

Cassie looked down at her feet. "I'm why you're here. Aren't I?"

The other three turned and stared.

"Huh?" Zee demanded. He had suspected something was going on.

Clarence had wondered if Cassie had mentioned anything to the others. Now he knew for sure she had not. "It's not that simple," he wanted to protect Cassie from the others feeling mad or left out. "Though your saying you hated recess got my attention."

"You *knew* about this? About him?" Now Toni seemed annoyed.

"No, not exactly." Cassie was feeling defensive; she hadn't expected the others to react the way they were reacting. She wasn't sure how best to explain. "I mean, well, I had this dream. I mean, I thought it was a dream."

"It happens all the time," Clarence interjected. "I met Cassie when she was out on a dream one night. We played this amazing game of Capture the Flag with all these other kids who were out on a dream as well." He looked around to see if the others knew what he was talking about. Seeing no looks of recognition, he turned to Cassie. "How'd you get there?" he asked.

Cassie looked from Zee to Bryant to Toni, willing them to believe her. "It was last week. We all just went home after school that day. I think you had practice, Zee. Anyhow, nothing unusual happened. I fell asleep that night and then had this dream. I remember because it started the way a lot of my dreams start: I'm on my Dad's shoulders at this grown-up party and then all of a sudden I take off flying. At first I'm not too high, and I can see the lights at the party. But

I keep getting higher and higher and then I'm flying over the city and up in the clouds." It was a dream she had been having ever since her mom and dad had died. But this time it had been different. Usually she just flew around for a while and then returned to the safety of her father's shoulders.

"This time, though, the dream felt like it was going on forever. And I was up in the clouds somewhere I'd never been before."

"You were in my neighborhood," Clarence spoke softly.

Cassie paused for a moment to take this in. She had never considered that there might be an actual geography of heaven. "And that's when I saw him." She turned to Clarence. "That's when I saw you; do you remember?"

Clarence remembered distinctly. "Yeah, I asked if you wanted to play."

Cassie hadn't thought about it much in the past week, but it had been one of the most vivid dreams she'd ever had. There had been hundreds of kids, all wearing red or blue shirts to designate their team. Cassie remembered looking down to see that she was wearing a red shirt. She remembered how the boundaries had been marked out with a white cloudy line that you could wave your hand through. The game had started out in a cloud—it had been bouncy to stand on, like the rubberized mats that they installed in the new playground. And as the dream progressed, she saw hills and a lake that reminded her of a game she had once played with her father's family when she was younger, before her parents had died, though the colors were brighter than usual. The blues bluer and the greens so bright they were almost neon.

Clarence had assigned Cassie to a defensive stretch on what felt like firm ground guarding the red flag for a while. A girl from the other team appeared then, trying to steal the flag. Although Cassie caught only occasional glimpses of the girl, she was struck by her long flowing hair and unusually large emerald green eyes that peered out from various hiding places. At one point, the girl made a break into the clearing, but Cassie managed to chase her down, only then realizing that she was really a horse, or that she had turned into a horse while Cassie was chasing her. Cassie hadn't been entirely sure. But once caught, the horse-girl gave Cassie a ride to a giant celebratory feast where Cassie got to the meet the team captains.

Cassie looked at the faces of her friends, somewhat embarrassed and entirely confused. She wasn't sure if she should tell them any of this or not. "There was a big feast, and everyone seemed so happy to be there. People were laughing and telling stories. It seemed like we ate for a long while, and then we went back to the game for a bit longer till it started to get dark." Cassie turned to Clarence. "That's when you told me I had to go home."

"Right. And do you remember what else I said?"

"You said I could be this happy playing at home." Cassie remembered Clarence looking her straight in the eye when he said that, willing her to believe the words. But she couldn't. Even as she spoke the words now, she knew that it couldn't possibly be true.

Toni, Bryant, and Zee all looked at Cassie. It was clear to all of them that she was telling the truth about the dream and about Clarence. They had no reason to doubt her. And she still seemed unnaturally calm, which for Cassie was particularly unusual. Maybe Clarence wasn't crazy. Maybe what he said about heaven and all that was true.

Marcus stirred again.

Clarence turned his attention to Marcus. "I suppose I should wake him up," he sighed. He wasn't looking forward to the demerits he'd receive from the celestial authorities on this one.

"Is he still going to want to clobber Cassie?" Bryant was wondering how lasting the effects might be.

"We can fix that. Well, I mean, I can make it so he doesn't remember being mad at her for now. It's going to take something more to make him not want to clobber her in general."

The others agreed; this was most definitely true.

Zee was still feeling a little uncertain about everything going on, even as he was adjusting to Clarence's presence. Still, he felt compelled to ask his standard question: "Do we have a plan?"

"I got nothing. My last plan was a disaster," Toni volunteered. She was not feeling confident in her own decision making at the moment and was just as happy to take a backseat until she felt her natural self-assurance return.

"Not me," Bryant was also at a loss.

"Clarence?" Cassie asked. She was OK with an angel with 'unresolved issues' as long as he was an angel with a plan.

Clarence looked around, relieved that they had made it this far. "Yeah, I can help. That's what I'm here for. How about we get Marcus home and then we start making recess a little more fun tomorrow?"

The kids all nodded, although Zee was a little less enthusiastic than the others.

Clarence stuck his hand out to the group to shake, "Deal?"

Bryant hesitated for a second but then shook Clarence's hand. "You're solid," Bryant observed. "I thought you might be, like, vapor or something."

"Like a rock." Clarence was smiling broadly now. "All right then, let's get Marcus home. Then we'll figure out a plan to make it so that Marcus doesn't want to clobber Cassie."

"That's going to take a miracle," Toni sighed. And she was willing to believe in miracles only up to a point.

"I don't do miracles," Clarence corrected, "but I know how to play some awesome games."

As promised, Clarence was able to get Marcus revived, and he seemed too groggy and unclear of his whereabouts to focus on being mad at Cassie. Still,

Cassie kept her distance as Clarence and her friends escorted Marcus down the tree-lined street and back to his small, ranch-style house.

Toni was fairly convinced that people were looking out their windows and discussing the unlikely scene. "Aren't you worried people are going to see you and wonder what you're doing with a group of kids, especially when one of them looks like he just got his bell rung?" she quizzed Clarence.

Clarence was unfazed. "They can't see me."

"What do you mean?" Zee needed more information. "How come we can see you?"

"Well, I had to make a decision. It occurred to me to let only Cassie see me, since we'd already met. But I was watching all of you today, and it seems like you're rarely apart. Letting all of you see me seemed like the most practical decision. You know?"

Nothing about any of this felt practical to Zee.

Clarence continued: "Other people can't hear me either. So if you're talking to me, and someone else is nearby, they'll think you're nuts."

"Or that you're talking on your cell phone," Bryant corrected.

Clarence seemed genuinely impressed. "That's brilliant! I can't believe I hadn't thought of that. Do you all have those little ear piece doodads?"

"Nope. You're not allowed to have cell phones at school. If you get caught with one of those ear pieces, the principal, Mr. Unger, confiscates it." Bryant was mostly telling the truth. None of the four actually owned a cell phone, but the rule was still the rule.

By the time they were a few houses away from Marcus's house, he seemed almost back to normal, only a lot more mellow. He didn't seem angry with anyone, and while a little disoriented, he actually seemed to be in a pretty decent frame of mind. When they walked him to his front step, he actually said, "Thanks. See you tomorrow."

Bryant's jaw literally dropped open. "No way," he said as the front door closed behind Marcus. "Marcus did not just say 'Thanks. See you tomorrow.' Did he?"

At this, even Zee broke into a big smile. Maybe this guy was for real. Zee turned begrudgingly to Clarence. "Man, I have no idea what's going on, but I'm starting to like you."

Cassie was encouraged to see Zee softening toward Clarence. She wanted to nail down the next steps. "I'll ask this time: What's the plan?"

They gathered in a circle, and Clarence took the lead. "I'll meet you at recess tomorrow to do an assessment. We'll take it from there."

Cassie had been hoping for more. "Be prepared to be disappointed," she said. "Our recess is lame."

"She's right," Bryant confirmed. "It's pretty bad."

"Nothing that can't be fixed," Clarence insisted. He was feeling positively victorious at this point. "I'll see you tomorrow at school." And with that, he vanished.

Everyone stared at the spot where Clarence had just

been standing. After a long moment, Zee spoke, "Did that really happen?"

The other three only managed nods.

"I'm sorry I got you all into this," Cassie said regretfully. She wanted to believe that Clarence could help, but she didn't like the feeling that she was dragging her friends into something so completely crazy and risky.

"Are you kidding?" demanded Toni, completely incredulous. "This is the most interesting thing that has happened in my whole life. I wouldn't miss this for the world."

"Me either," Bryant agreed. He seemed positively energized by the whole experience.

"Just seeing Marcus get his clock cleaned like that was worth the price of admission."

"And seeing you get frozen?" Zee was addressing Bryant now. "I mean, I can't tell you how many times I've wanted to freeze you." They all laughed. The day had proven to be the most bizarre experience that any of them had ever been through, and Cassie was still fairly certain she was dreaming.

"He seems like a good guy," Cassie said tentatively. "He was totally cool in the Capture the Flag game in my dream. Maybe we just wait and see what he does tomorrow?" She wanted to believe that it was possible to make recess better, but she couldn't quite let herself. "I mean, if he doesn't show up, then that's OK. At least I didn't get pummeled today. And if he does show up, well, maybe we can have some fun?"

Toni was far more hopeful. "We'll see what happens. And it's our secret for now, right?" Zee and Bryant nodded their heads in agreement. The whole scene in the Grove was too much to comprehend just yet anyway; no one in the group felt like talking about it beyond the four of them.

No one was ready to head home yet either, but the sky was growing dark. It was October now, and the days were getting shorter. The longer days of summer felt distant. With some hesitation, owners reunited with their backpacks, everyone said their good-byes and turned toward his or her respective home. Even as they walked away, they each knew that it would be hard to fall asleep that evening; even now they were wondering what would happen tomorrow when Clarence showed up at recess.

Cassie woke up fifteen minutes before her alarm went off the next morning, anxious to get to school. The weather had turned colder overnight, and she knew most of the kids would be sporting new puffy winter jackets. Cassie, however, was wearing three sweatshirts, one over the other. She alternated wearing them in a different order, the Georgetown sweatshirt, the New Balance sweatshirt, and the Washington Mystics sweatshirt. She knew her Aunt Marilee and Uncle Steve didn't have a lot of extra money to be buying her new clothes, and she hated to impose, so she hadn't told them how cold she was walking to and from school. She also hated to stand out, and she worried that the other kids would notice that she didn't have a new coat. She couldn't help but envy Clarence's ability to simply disappear or to make himself invisible. She imagined it would be an ability that would come in handy.

Cassie flew through her aunt and uncle's kitchen, grabbing a banana from the bowl on the counter, rushing out the door, and yelling out a quick: "I'm leaving. Love you! Bye."

She arrived at school a full fifteen minutes early. Cassie was never early to school. Not immediately seeing her friends, she made her way to her locker, noticing a few of the other kids staring. She figured they were probably a little shocked to see that she was not only still alive but also that she bore no visible bruises. When Cassie passed Marcus in the hallway, a hush fell over the students standing nearby as they waited to see what would happen. Cassie herself wasn't entirely clear what to expect, so she was relieved when Marcus only grunted menacingly as he passed her. He seemed to be back to his old self, although with a minor memory lapse.

"I don't think he remembers what happened," Toni whispered as she walked up behind Cassie. "But I think some of the other kids asked him if he beat you up, so his little snake brain knows he has some reason to be mad at you."

When the morning recess rolled around, all four of the friends were feeling as if the events of the day before had been a dream and that it was unlikely that Clarence would actually show up. They headed out to the schoolyard with a mixture of anticipation and dread. Zee marveled at his own ability to want Clarence to show up while simultaneously hoping that he wouldn't.

It was a confusing feeling that left him a little sick to his stomach.

The day had warmed a little as they walked out to the side of the field, next to the jungle gym where they usually hung out during recess. Cassie felt particularly awkward just standing there, waiting and observing the nonexistent recess.

"He's not going to show," Bryant said, his status as a believer fading.

"I don't know," Toni hedged. Toni had noticed Cassie's discomfort, and she shot Bryant a look encouraging him to be more positive.

"He's coming." Cassie tried to sound more certain than she actually was, willing it to be true.

Zee peered at Cassie suspiciously. "You didn't hang out with him in your dream last night; did you?"

"No!" Cassie answered indignantly and started to turn ever-so-slightly red. "I would have told you guys if I'd seen him!"

Zee immediately felt bad for having asked. "No, I didn't mean . . . sorry."

"I don't think he's coming," Bryant said again. Toni wasn't sure if he had missed her look or if he was just being difficult, but Bryant was starting to make her mad.

Almost on cue, Clarence appeared. He was wearing a far spiffier tracksuit than the one the day before: today his sweats were forest green, with matching sneakers, and he had a whistle around his neck.

"Well, you look ready," Toni remarked a little sarcastically.

"I wasn't expecting to go out yesterday. Those were my stay-at-home sweats." Clarence was excited to get to work.

The kids looked at each other, and then Zee shrugged and asked his standing question: "What's the plan?"

Clarence looked around: "Well, when recess starts, we'll map the yard. You know, diagram where different games are happening and what the flow is."

Cassie cleared her throat. "Recess *has* started," she corrected him.

Clarence looked at her quizzically and then looked around again. "What? Where is everyone then?"

The schoolyard was a massive, largely empty expanse of asphalt with cracks in which the dandelions struggled to pop through and survive each year. At the moment, a clump of kids were hanging close to the building, and it sounded as if another, smaller group had gathered around the other side of the portable classrooms that had been "temporarily" plopped onto the blacktop twelve years before. The field lay adjacent to the jungle gym and wrapped around the back of the school. A six-foot fence ran around the perimeter, too low to keep balls from escaping out into the street but high enough to make climbing over it a challenge. Today the playground stood completely empty of kids and the large expanse of dirt was growing only slightly more vegetation than the blacktop.

"I don't see Marcus," Bryant observed. "He's usually standing out in the middle of the field terrorizing people. I guess he's not completely himself since you froze him."

Clarence seemed genuinely shocked and turning toward Cassie, said apologetically: "Wow, no wonder you're cranky. This is beyond lame."

He paused to consider the scene. He was flummoxed. "Has it always been like this?"

"We used to get some good games of chase going last year," Zee reflected, sounding almost wistful.

"I didn't think they were so good," Bryant contradicted.

"That's because you were always the one being chased." Toni's analysis, as usual, cut right to the heart of the matter. "We have three recesses a day: morning, lunch, and afternoon. They're all pretty much like this. They last for fifteen to twenty minutes, and most people just wait for them to be over."

"This is hopeless!" Cassie turned in frustration and started walking back toward the school.

"Wait, wait, wait," Clarence called out. But Cassie kept walking. So, true to form, Clarence froze her.

"Are you supposed to keep freezing people like that?" Bryant inquired. It was clear from his tone that he thought that that particular technique should have some sort of limitation. "I'm just saying . . ."

Clarence shot Bryant a warning glance, as if to say "Do not mess with me at this moment," and Bryant pursed his lips together to signify he understood.

"Cassie, you cannot just stomp off every time things do not go your way," Clarence was trying to be patient, but he sounded a little exasperated nonetheless. "We're going to fix your recess; it's just going to take a little more effort than I thought. When we first met, and you described your school, I thought you were just being dramatic, but your assessment of the situation was dead on. People here need to be reminded how to play, and I am the man for the job."

Even frozen, Cassie was able to communicate an amazing degree of frustration.

"Can I unfreeze you now?" Clarence asked. He had calmed down a bit, and his tone now sounded genuinely empathetic.

There was no reply from Cassie, so Toni answered on her behalf. "She gets it."

Clarence nodded and Cassie's form eased a little bit, though she neither continued walking away nor returned to the group. Cassie wasn't at all sure there was anything Clarence could do. She wasn't convinced there was anything anyone could do. But the worst part was that since yesterday she had let herself start to believe he could help. That little bit of believing just made her feel mad at herself, and mad at him, all at the same time. She glared back at him waiting to see what he would say next.

"You know where I stand on being frozen, correct?" Toni raised her eyebrows and cocked her head slightly, just in case her stance wasn't crystal clear.

Clarence didn't even look at Toni as he confirmed, "Yes, I believe I do."

Zee shook his head at Toni in dismay. To his mind, she had never been a regular kid. She had never been afraid of grown-ups, and now she didn't even seem to be intimidated by angels. Initially, he had wondered if it was all an act, but now he didn't think so. He had never seen her back down from anyone.

Clarence was ready to get to work. "First thing, we need to map the yard. Who's got some paper?"

"*Really?*" Bryant sounded incredulous.

Clarence stopped for a second, looking somewhat thrown by the question. "Say that again," he asked with a slight hitch in his voice.

"What?" Bryant asked, now thoroughly confused.

"What you just said," Clarence replied.

"What'd I say?"

"You said 'Really?' like you always do," Zee explained.

"Yeah," Toni agreed, "There's this way you say it, like you can't believe someone means whatever they just said . . . '*Really?*'"

"Oh," said Bryant.

"Say it again. Will you?" Clarence seemed genuinely off balance.

"*Really?*" Bryant repeated. It wasn't entirely clear if he was questioning the request or cooperating.

"Yeah, that. Uncanny," Clarence narrowed his eyes and stared at Bryant more intently.

Cassie hadn't spoken during this entire exchange, so

busy was she watching Clarence's expressions. He had shown a wide range of emotions, but finally she thought he looked a little sad. "You OK?" she asked.

"Yeah," replied Clarence, "He just reminded me of someone." Clarence paused, deep in thought. "Hey," he said to Cassie, returning to the present. "I'm sorry I froze you just now. I get mad like that, too, when I'm frustrated. Well, I mean, I used to. I guess it's different now."

"Cause you're dead?" Bryant inquired bluntly.

"Wow, you have no grace." Toni was visibly appalled by Bryant's question.

Being called out left Bryant uncharacteristically flustered. "Sorry. That was a total brain fart. I just said out loud what I was thinking. My bad."

"No, no worries. It's cool. I mean, it's been six months, I'm getting used to it." Clarence gave Bryant a reassuring look to show him it was OK. "All right, paper. We need to draw out the space we have to work with."

"Want me to run to the school office?" Cassie asked, trying to shift her own attitude back to hopeful.

"No need," he replied and pulled a piece of paper out from behind his back, placed it down on the ground, and began drawing the map of the schoolyard using his finger. A misty white line emerged from his finger, and the trail left a mark on the paper that looked like a fine, dark pen mark. Clarence moved his finger back and forth, gracefully creating shading and an almost topographical representation of the playground with all the major land-marks and the surface rendered in an image that was both simple and detailed. The kids looked on in awe.

"Sometimes we try to get a Kickball game going there," Zee pointed to an open space at the corner of the drawing. Seeing that space and remembering how much fun Kickball could be gave Zee just the slightest flash of hopefulness. Maybe this was possible.

"Remember how in kindergarten we'd get to play Duck Duck Goose right next to the cafeteria?" Toni added. "I used to love that game!"

Looking down at the map, Cassie started to get that feeling she had in her dream, the feeling she'd had playing Capture the Flag—like she was exactly where she was supposed to be and that everyone else was, too. She looked from Toni to Zee to Bryant. She always knew that she could count on them, but now, even just for the moment, it felt like she might be able to count on something bigger.

She turned to Clarence. "What do we do with the map?"

Clarence looked at the group. "Now we need to make copies for everyone in the school."

"How come?" Cassie wasn't following.

"We need to get everyone involved in imagining the perfect recess: where they'd play different games, where they'd borrow equipment, and how it would flow. You know?"

"Not exactly," Cassie thought she understood what

he was saying, but she wasn't at all convinced he was right. "You think they'll have any good ideas?"

"I know they will," Clarence insisted.

"Hand it over then." Bryant was resigned to his fate; if anyone was going to get the map copied, he was the man. "I can go ask Ms. Houghton to let me use the mimeograph machine."

"She likes him," Toni explained drily.

"Your school still has a *mimeograph machine*?" Clarence sounded genuinely surprised.

Bryant looked a little defensive. "It's Ms. Houghton's. She says it's a solid machine, and there's no reason to get rid of it."

"Who's Ms. Houghton?" Clarence asked.

"The school secretary. I'm her favorite discipline problem." Bryant might be trouble, but he was good at it.

"All right then; we're in business." Clarence started walking toward the school, and the four fell in line behind him, Bryant holding the map. As they got closer to the building, Toni noticed Marcus heading their way. "Uh-oh. Can Marcus see you?"

"Nope," said Clarence.

"He looks mad," observed Cassie. She felt fairly certain his ire was aimed at her.

"I don't know," said Zee. "That's kind of how he always looks."

Marcus walked straight toward them and clearly couldn't see Clarence as he just narrowly missed bumping into him.

"Would you be like vapor if he ran into you?" Bryant asked Clarence, completely ignoring Marcus as he spoke about him. Not surprisingly, since Bryant was speaking in Marcus's direction and Marcus could not see Clarence, Marcus assumed Bryant was being a smart aleck. Taking all of this in, it occurred to Toni that Marcus wasn't that far off.

"What are you talking about, butt head?" Marcus shot out. Marcus could not believe these clowns were disrespecting him like this. First Cassie, and now the little man.

"*Really?*" Bryant winced almost immediately after he said it again, and Cassie noticed that once again it had that same unsettling effect on Clarence.

Toni made the executive decision that nothing good could come of this conversation. "Sorry. No time to stay and chat," she said to Marcus. "We have to go to the office." And she hustled the group along, leaving Marcus standing alone, looking confused.

Bryant cleared his throat as he stepped up to the counter in the office.

"Hey, Ms. Houghton," Bryant greeted the school secretary warmly. "How's it going?"

Ms. Houghton looked up at Bryant over the top of her glasses. She wore them low on her nose and attached to a chain that hung around her neck. Bryant wasn't sure he'd ever seen her actually look through the glasses instead of over the top of them, squishing up her forehead and crinkling her nose. Ms. Houghton had worked at the school forever—she'd been there when Bryant's older brother had been in kindergarten—and Bryant figured she was about the oldest person he knew.

"Good morning, Bryant. What have you done this time?"

"Nothing, ma'am," Bryant said, flashing a charming smile. "I . . . I mean we," and he gestured back to his three friends (and Clarence, though Bryant knew Ms. Houghton couldn't see him), "were wondering if we could use the mimeograph machine to make some copies."

Ms. Houghton had returned her attention to the work on her desk and nodded as she listened, "How many copies do you need to make, dear?"

"One for every student," Bryant replied.

Ms. Houghton looked up, shocked. "You want 378 copies! Oh, dear, I'm afraid we don't have the resources to just copy willy-nilly like that."

Bryant felt a thud next to his feet. He looked down and saw a ream of paper lying on the ground. Definitely Clarence's work.

"Oh, of course, Ms. Houghton. We have our own paper," Bryant said and leaned down to pick it up and show it to her.

Again, Ms. Houghton looked surprised—and just a little skeptical. "Well, there's the ink, you know," she muttered. "What is it you want to copy?"

Zee held up the sketch of the playground. "It's a map," he explained. "Just an outline of the playground. We want to get some ideas from the students on how to make it better."

Ms. Houghton tilted her head and reached for the map, "Bring it here." Bryant came around to the other side of the counter and handed her the drawing. Ms. Houghton looked at it for a moment and then looked up at the kids. "This is quite good. Who drew it?"

It was one of those times that they should have thought to get the story straight ahead of time: all four of the kids said a different name—Toni said Bryant, Bryant said Cassie, Cassie said Zee, and Zee said Toni. "We worked on it together," said Toni, vainly trying to explain away the confusion.

Ms. Houghton still seemed unconvinced, but she wanted to get back to work so she waved them through. "Go on, then. Bryant, you should know how to work the machine after all the time you've spent helping me when you've been in detention." And the kids (and Clarence) headed quickly to the copy room before she had time to change her mind.

The mimeograph machine was big and with its giant drum and a crank, looked like a machine from an old-fashion science-fiction movie. The room had clearly been a utility closet at one time, with water pipes running from the ceiling and the circuit breaker on the wall. The space was cramped and crowded with papers stacked everywhere. And up against the wall opposite the mimeograph machine sat the equally old and comparably big Magruder Elementary PA system. Emerging from the system was a tangle of wires that fed under the little desk and to the microphone from which the principal, Mr. Unger, broadcast his daily message. Taken as a whole, the room was a fire hazard.

"Wow," Clarence was clearly overwhelmed by the chaos and surprised by the vintage equipment. "This is seriously old school."

"Be careful not to let the door shut all the way," Bryant warned as he moved the brick that sat there for just this purpose into position as the door jam. "It locks from the outside."

Bryant had clearly spent a considerable amount of time with the mimeograph machine. The others watched with no small degree of admiration as he loaded in the drawing, created the stencil on the electrostencil machine, and then wrapped it around the drum of the mimeograph machine. The five took turns working the crank until, in a matter of minutes, the 378 copies were made.

"It's old," Bryant said, "but it still works well. Ms. Houghton says it's the only thing that she can count on around here. And she says that when the mimeograph machine goes, she goes too."

Toni shook her head, "I don't know how she can stand Mr. Unger. He has got to be the most boring person on the whole planet."

"Speaking of Mr. Unger," Cassie said. "Shouldn't we ask him about giving these maps out first?"

Clarence thought about this for a moment. "Well, you know the old saying? 'It's easier to ask for forgiveness than to seek permission'? I'd have to say, I think this is one of those situations."

Bryant seemed comfortable with that approach, but Toni, Zee, and Cassie were still uncertain. Bryant was more fluent with seeking forgiveness than the others.

Seeing their uneasiness, Clarence tried to figure out a middle ground. "Do you have a teacher who, you know, is a little cooler than the others? Someone who doesn't always follow the rules exactly?"

The four knew exactly who he meant.

"Mr. Street," they said in unison.

"What's he teach?" Clarence asked.

"He's the art teacher," Bryant explained. "He's the one who got my brother to go to art school."

"Perfect," Clarence replied. He started to say something more, but Toni interrupted.

"I got it!" said Toni. "We ask Mr. Street for help, and then we can distribute the maps as part of an assignment."

"Now you're thinking." Clarence was starting to enjoy himself, and Cassie flashed back to that first time she'd met him. She remembered how Clarence had been deeply engaged in the game of Capture the Flag—she had been struck by this grown-up taking the game so completely seriously, while also being so visibly happy to be playing. She remembered how during the dream it had occurred to her that being so competitive sometimes got in the way of her having fun. But she had dismissed the whole idea when she woke up. After all, it was only a dream, she'd told herself. He hadn't been real. Now she didn't know what to think.

The five filed out of the PA room, thanked Ms. Houghton, and were headed directly for Mr. Street's classroom when Zee reminded them that they should probably get back to English class before they got into trouble. "We can meet in Street's at lunch. He's always in his classroom then."

Cassie turned to Clarence to check on his plans, "Where are you going to be?"

Clarence smiled mischievously, "Gotta do some research."

And he was gone.

First thing, Clarence decided, was to check out Mr. Unger. His experience of school had taught him that if you wanted to understand how a school worked, you had to get to know four people: the principal, the school secretary, the lunch lady, and the custodian.

Ms. Houghton seemed pretty solid, and the fact that she liked Bryant was a good sign. He would observe the other three and then go check on Marcus to make sure he wasn't suffering any lingering effects from their encounter the day before.

Clarence headed first to Mr. Unger's office, but he wasn't there. The office was less chaotic than the PA/mimeograph closet, but it had a similarly disorganized energy. Clarence checked out the jumble of framed photos on Mr. Unger's desk and seeing no pictures of a family, guessed that Mr. Unger was a bachelor. He did, however, have a picture of himself prominently displayed that provided Clarence with an important visual clue for his manhunt: Mr. Unger sported a serious comb-over. It took Clarence only a moment to consider the assorted possibilities of where Mr. Unger might be before going directly to the men's staff bathroom. Bingo! Mr. Unger was alone in the bathroom, standing in front of the mirror combing his hair over the very prominent bald spot on the top of his head. He seemed cheerful as he did so, and Clarence felt only a little embarrassed to be watching him as he sang and talked to himself.

Initially, this sudden intimacy with strangers had been one of the weirdest things to adjust to in the afterlife. Clarence didn't come down to earth too often, but when he did, he found that being invisible put him in situations in which he saw how people act when they think they are all alone. In the beginning, it had made him horribly uncomfortable. Now that he had seen it a number of times, though, he'd adjusted, and his whole attitude about it had changed. It just seemed like this was the human condition, with people being vain and insecure and scared and lonely, all mixed in with people feeling happy and proud and hungry. He'd always known it, but being dead had really driven home the point: people were, simply put, human.

Mr. Unger swiped the comb over his head one final time and then headed out of the bathroom and down the empty hall toward the cafeteria. He bent down a couple of times to pick up garbage from the floor, and he stopped briefly to look at the graffiti that someone had written in felt-tipped pen on one of the lockers. Mr. Unger scowled at the writing, and Clarence wondered about the content of what was written, so edged up closer to look over Mr. Unger's shoulder.

Clarence couldn't quite make out what was written, and he was a little slow when Mr. Unger turned around quickly, giving the principal the unsettling experience of brushing against someone he couldn't see. "Huh?!?" Mr. Unger sputtered.

Clarence backpedaled quickly.

A little flustered, Mr. Unger nevertheless continued on his way to the cafeteria with Clarence in his wake. As they passed through the doors to the cafeteria, they walked into a wall of noise. The cafeteria was full with the first lunch period, and kids were literally bouncing off the walls.

Despite the chaos of the students, the Magruder Elementary cafeteria was a picture of efficiency and cleanliness. The light blue linoleum floor shone brightly and the beige-colored tile walls sparkled, the grout between each tile bleached a brilliant white. Foldable tables with attached chairs were lined up perfectly along one side of the room, from the front where the students entered to the back where the double doors led out to the recess area. The serving area included three stainless steel-and-glass tables, located just in front of the kitchen and across from the students' lunch tables. The doors to the kitchen swung open and shut frequently as the cafeteria workers streamed in and out, revealing momentary glimpses of stainless steel prep tables, sinks, and two giant industrial stoves, all of it busily in use and gleaming with a perfect polish.

"Girls and boys!" Mr. Unger exclaimed as he entered through the front. He repeated himself several times more, but to no avail. "Boys and girls!"

Frustrated by the general lack of response, he began calling students out by their individual names, and while this was slightly more effective, the din continued. Clarence watched this exercise in futility until he could bear it no more. He knew he wasn't supposed to interfere, but this was just too much. So he nodded at Mr. Unger who, much to his own surprise, clapped out a rhythm. A couple of students looked over at him, and Mr. Unger felt himself clap the rhythm again. This time, a number of kids repeated the pattern. Finally, Mr. Unger clapped the pattern, and the entire cafeteria repeated the rhythm. Clarence watched with delight, wondering which surprised Mr. Unger more: the possessed clapping or the effect it had on the students.

"Well," Mr. Unger said, altogether flustered. "Much better." And he strode quickly to the kitchen.

Mrs. Grumble, the head of the cafeteria, did indeed run a very tight ship. The kitchen was immaculate, and the staff was crisply dressed in standard-issue cafeteria staff garb: white dresses or white shirts and pants, with aprons on every employee and a pristine hair net on every head. Mr. Unger looked around the kitchen for Mrs. Grumble—it was sometimes difficult to easily identify her given that they were all dressed identically—and spotting her, headed in her direction.

"Mrs. Grumble! So good to find you. I've just gotten a call from downtown that the district superintendent is coming here next week. Magruder Elementary is being recognized."

Mrs. Grumble turned quickly, and her white tennis shoes squeaked on the floor. Clarence noted that her expression turned immediately from dour to pleased. "Oh, Mr. Unger! That's so exciting! Is it the ACE Award?"

Mr. Unger replied seriously, "Indeed. Achievement, Cleanliness, and Efficiency."

Clarence stood by listening with a combination of horror and fascination.

"Well, you know," Mrs. Grumble saluted as she spoke, "I stand ready to serve."

"I do so appreciate having you on the team for this," Mr. Unger returned the salute and then fumbled briefly, not entirely clear how he should communicate his desire to achieve "at ease." "I'm afraid not everyone is as enthusiastic. But the woman from the superintendent's office was extraordinarily encouraging. She said we positively 'had it in the bag!'" He paused for a moment. "Though she also mentioned something I found somewhat troubling about 'student leadership'—not sure exactly what she meant." He paused for a moment to remember exactly what she had said. "I suppose we could have a Clean Team or something. . . ."

Mrs. Grumble jumped right in: "Well the students *are* so positive about recycling. We could always reconstitute the Recycling Team."

Mr. Unger sighed with relief: "Well, yes, of course. That is so authentic."

The two nodded some more at one another and when it seemed that no more nodding was necessary, Mr. Unger turned and walked quickly away.

Mrs. Grumble called out as he left, "Mr. Unger, you'll speak with Mr. Rodrigues?"

"Oh, yes, of course. He's a good man."

"Oh, indeed," she agreed, though it was clear from her tone that she didn't agree at all, "but he can be lax. . ."

Mr. Unger made no response.

"And Mr. Unger?" Mrs. Grumble hated to nag, but she sensed that this was the opening she'd been hoping for.

"Yes?" Mr. Unger had no doubt that the next request would be more challenging.

"The PA room?"

"You mean my announcement command center?" Mr. Unger was working hard not to sound defensive.

"Yes. It's going to require some attention before the superintendent arrives." Mrs. Grumble had anticipated some resistance, but she felt she had a duty to stand firm.

Mr. Unger pondered this for a moment. "It's my creative space, you know."

Mrs. Grumble waited patiently. She knew better than to say anything else.

"If you're willing to work on it with me personally, then I'm sure we can make things right." Mr. Unger had intended the statement to sound sporty, but felt immediately self-conscious, worried that it sounded almost flirtatious instead.

Mrs. Grumble looked at her feet as Mr. Unger walked quickly away.

Clarence followed after Unger, trying to make sense of the whole interaction. He looked up at the clock in the hall and realized he needed to hightail it to Mr. Street's classroom. He wanted to follow the principal, since he figured Mr. Unger was on his way to meet with the aforementioned Mr. Rodrigues, but that would have to wait.

Clarence loved Mr. Street the moment he laid eyes on him. He had the requisite cool teacher's gray ponytail, and his classroom was extra large and had a warm and welcoming vibe. Clarence arrived before the kids did and got to watch as Mr. Street turned on the classical music and pulled out his own sketchbook to draw. There was a giant mural of the solar system on the wall behind Mr. Street and concert posters from the 1960s along the opposite wall. Clarence sat for a while in the classroom with Mr. Street and briefly considered making himself visible to him, but ultimately decided that there were enough people involved and that he would leave well enough alone. Clarence had a good feeling that Mr. Street would be an ally no matter what.

Clarence eased himself out the door to meet the others. They arrived within moments of one another.

"How'd your research go?" Cassie asked, looking Clarence over for clues.

"Interesting." Clarence was still uncertain of what to make of what he'd seen. "I followed Mr. Unger around for most of the time. Apparently your school is up for the ACE award: Achievement, Cleanliness, and Efficiency. I didn't make that up. " He watched the kids' faces to see if any of them thought this sounded as nuts as he did. They seemed unfazed.

"Honestly, it makes no sense. I mean, what about Learning and Independence? Creativity and Engagement?"

Toni looked at him as if he were crazy. "Clarence, that spells LICE. There's no way the superintendent's going to offer a LICE award."

"Right. There's that. And who is Mr. Rodrigues?" Clarence was interested to find out who this person was who had disappointed Mrs. Grumble so.

"He's the custodian," Cassie offered up. "He's a good guy. He used to play with us at lunch sometimes, but Mr. Unger made him stop."

Zee followed up with a little context: "Instead of playing outside at recess, a bunch of boys were hiding in the bathroom and writing on the walls. Unger assigned Mr. Rodrigues to watch the bathroom to prevent it."

"Bummer," Clarence sighed.

Zee agreed. It had been a whole lot more fun having Mr. Rodrigues playing with them.

"Yeah, tell me about it."

"Let's go talk with Mr. Street," Bryant pressed. "Then we can take you out to see the yard during lunch."

When the five of them walked into the art room, Mr. Street looked up from his sketchbook: "Welcome, fellow travelers. What brings you here this lunch period? Aren't you usually out running around?" He tilted his head toward the big window that looked out on the schoolyard. "I think of you four as the keepers of the recess flame."

Cassie responded immediately. "The recess flame has been basically snuffed out. That's why we're here."

Bryant held up the pile of map outlines. "We had this idea," he started somewhat hesitantly. Bryant definitely sounded a little unconvincing claiming the plan. "We want to get everyone in the school to help us design the best possible recess."

Toni continued, "So we were wondering if you could help us."

The corners of Mr. Street's mouth raised just slightly, "Pray continue."

"We want you to make it an assignment," Zee explained. "You give the mapping idea to us as an assignment so that we can go to the other classes and have all the kids fill in the map."

"Why couldn't you just do it on your own?" Street asked, though his tone suggested he knew the answer.

Cassie responded with obvious exasperation in her voice, "The other kids would just think it was stupid."

"And they won't think it's stupid if I assign it?" Street asked.

"It'll be a different kind of stupid," Toni explained.

"And they'll do your stupid thing, and that will get them thinking a little about the possibility of making recess more fun," Bryant added, connecting the dots.

Street paused to consider the idea: "It's quite brilliant. I'm impressed that you four came up with the idea."

Cassie looked at the other four and then blurted out, "It wasn't our idea."

"We read about it," Toni said quickly, shooting Cassie a sharp glance. Once again it was apparent that they were going to have to work on getting their stories straight.

"Well, still . . . I'm happy to help if I can. I'll let Mr. Unger know I'm assigning this." He looked at the pile of papers Bryant was holding. "Are those the maps?"

Bryant paused slightly. All four of them were in Mr. Street's art class, and he would know immediately that none of them had the skill to draw the map outlines he held in his hands.

"Yes, sir. My brother helped us with them and then Ms. Houghton let us run them through the mimeograph machine." Bryant's brother Paul had been one of Mr. Street's star students. It was a stretch, but it was the best story Bryant could come up with on the spot.

Bryant handed them over and Street looked at the drawing appreciatively. "These are quite wonderful," he said. "I'll distribute them in class. We'll see if your class-mates get interested in the project as well." Bryant made a note to himself to use Paul as an excuse more often.

Mission accomplished, they filed out of the classroom. Toni turned to Clarence, seeking some clarification. "Is there something magical about those drawings?"

Clarence smiled and shrugged a little. "Not in the way you're thinking. You look at an open map of a play space and the possibilities are endless, but there's nothing extra special about the maps."

The four kids looked at one another and then back at Clarence and all wondered yet again about what they had gotten themselves into.

Out on the schoolyard at lunch recess, it was the usual scene: Marcus standing in the middle of the field with a few boys listening to him brag about beating people up, and most of the other kids just trying to stay out of harm's way. Marcus's followers were a motley crew. The six regulars, all fourth and fifth graders, were Andy, Carl, Ray, Eli, Matt, and Sam.

They weren't bad kids, but they shared a certain insecurity with one another and seemed to follow Marcus mostly as a strategy for avoiding being the object of his humiliation. None of them did particularly well in school, but taken individually, Zee thought they were all basically decent human beings. Occasionally a couple of other kids joined the group—kids like Kevin Sweeney—but it was usually an uneasy truce. Marcus offered full indemnity only to his most loyal followers, so the occasional hangers-on were often the butt of jokes if there were no other available targets.

As the four friends and Clarence walked out into the sunshine through the doors at the back of the cafeteria, Cassie noticed a shorter, dark-haired boy with glasses heading toward the basketball hoops with a ball. Cassie had seen Aaron Zimmerman before and noticed that he often brought his own basketball to school, but she'd never actually spoken with him. He seemed like a nice enough kid, and generally he was able to shoot around without attracting much attention. Today he wouldn't be so lucky. Marcus spied him and was looking back and forth between the four friends and Aaron, unsure of where to start.

Bryant made a snorting noise. They were all thinking the same thing. "I'm guessing he takes the ball first and then comes over here to hit us with it."

Clarence laughed. "Let's head to the courts then, to make it easier for him."

Marcus looked pleased when he saw the four walk

toward the courts, and he rallied the boys around him to follow as he made a beeline for the unsuspecting Aaron.

Cassie could feel herself getting more agitated with every passing moment. Just watching Marcus moving toward Aaron made her furious, and she could feel her face starting to turn red. Zee noticed, too. "Steady there, Tiger," he said gently to Cassie.

Clarence sensed her energy as well. "I got this, Cassie. You just focus on breathing."

Cassie realized that he was right: she had been holding her breath.

Marcus and company and the four friends all arrived at the basketball courts about the same time. "Pass the ball here," Marcus called to Aaron as he stepped onto the court.

Aaron was startled to find himself suddenly at the center of a crowd. He held the ball and hesitated. "Uh, you want to play HORSE or something?" He clearly wasn't wild about the idea of sharing his ball with Marcus.

"Tell him it's cool to pass it to Marcus," Clarence instructed Toni.

"Go ahead, Aaron. It's OK." Toni tried to sound convincing, but she wondered if it was true, even as she said it.

Aaron looked doubtful as well, but it was also pretty clear that he didn't have a choice, so he bounce-passed the ball toward Marcus.

Marcus laughed a mean laugh. "Sucker!" he taunted Aaron. Clarence nodded in Marcus's direction, and when Marcus reached to grab the ball, he missed, his hands bobbling it uncontrollably. Marcus looked confused and bent over to retrieve the ball, but again it was as if he had buttery mittens on, and he was incapable of actually holding onto the ball. The kids in his posse laughed. "Marcus, stop messing with Aaron!" Carl cried out, thinking that he was only pretending to be unable to pick it up.

"Shut up!" Marcus yelled. Suddenly he was beginning to feel frightened by his inability to grasp the ball. He turned and looked at Cassie. "What did you do to me?" he demanded, his voice quavering with both anger and fear.

Even Bryant knew better than to laugh and in fact, Marcus sounded so genuinely frightened that he almost felt bad for him. Not quite, but almost. Cassie responded in a serious tone, "It's not me, dude."

Marcus chased the ball around the court for a few moments more and then stomped off in frustration, leaving his gang still standing there in confusion. Aaron walked back to his ball, picked it up effortlessly, shrugged, and returned to shooting around. He looked over at the others, "You want to play?" he asked.

Toni started to say "No," but Clarence interjected again. "Tell him 'Yes.' Let's play Three-Lines Basketball."

"Do I look like a puppet?" Toni asked, putting her hands on her hips.

"Uh, no." Aaron replied defensively, worried she was talking to him.

Zee stepped forward, "Sure," he said. "Let's play Three-Lines Basketball."

Aaron was relieved to have the focus back on the game and excited to play something new. He passed the ball enthusiastically to Zee. "How do you play?"

Zee caught the ball and then looked momentarily confused. "That's a good question."

Not wasting a moment, Clarence walked immediately toward the court. "All right, just repeat after me. Everybody needs to line up in three equal lines at the top of the key." Clarence showed the three places where the lines should form and then gestured to Zee that he should follow him.

Zee repeated: "Everybody needs to split up into three equal lines. Here, here, and here." Zee pointed to where they should all line up, and quickly the assembled kids filled in the three lines.

"The first group of three is going to start out on defense, so they stand right here facing out." Clarence walked to mid-court and showed where the first three players should stand, facing the others with their backs toward the basket.

Zee followed in Clarence's footsteps. "OK, the first three of you are on defense. Come stand here." And he showed the first three—Cassie and two of the kids who had been following Marcus around, Andy and Eli—where they should stand.

"And the next three are on offense. Once everyone has touched the ball, you can shoot. Each round lasts for sixty seconds. Whoever scores becomes defense, the folks who are defeated go to the back of the line, and the next group of three becomes offense. If no one scores, they Rock-Paper-Scissors to see who stays."

Zee repeated the directions again and passed the ball to Bryant who was standing in the middle of the next group of three. Bryant was in a group of three with Aaron and another of Marcus's followers, Carl. Bryant passed the ball to Aaron, who passed the ball to Carl. Carl dribbled, and Cassie came in close to cover him. Carl passed it to Aaron, who took a shot and missed. Cassie rebounded the ball and shot it up right away, scoring.

Clarence said, "Nice basket, Cassie, but everyone on the team needs to touch the ball before the basket counts."

Before Zee had a chance to say anything, Cassie was complaining: "That's not fair. You didn't say that!" The other kids gave Cassie confused looks.

"Who didn't say what?" Aaron asked. He liked playing with these kids, but he didn't think they made a lot of sense.

Bryant picked up the ball and handed it to Cassie. "Your ball. Let's keep playing."

Cassie considered protesting but passed the ball to one of her teammates, the red-headed fourth grader named Andy, who started to shoot, but Zee yelled out, "Everyone on your team needs to touch it before a basket counts." Andy passed the ball to Eli who began running around dribbling frantically, his long hair hanging across his face, evidently making it hard for him to see. Cassie was open underneath, but the boy wasn't passing it.

"Start counting down from ten," Clarence instructed. Zee began counting down "10, 9, 8, 7 . . ." When he got to three, Eli managed to pass the ball to Cassie who immediately put it into the air but missed the shot.

"Rock-Paper-Scissors." Clarence spoke the words as though they were orders from on high, and while Zee recognized that Clarence did indeed possess celestial authority, he didn't think the suggestion was going to go over big.

Zee looked at Clarence unclear as how to proceed. Specifically, Cassie was not going to be happy. "You don't know how to do Rock-Paper-Scissors?" Clarence knew what the problem was, but he wasn't going to make it any easier for Zee.

"Well, yeah, OK." Zee couldn't see another alternative, so he turned to the two teams, "Cassie and Bryant, do Rock-Paper-Scissors to see who stays."

Cassie looked annoyed, and Bryant looked amused. The two squared up and chanted out in unison, "Rock, paper, scissors." Bryant threw scissors and a visibly frustrated Cassie threw paper.

"Have the teams give each other high fives, say 'Good game,' and bring in the next three," Clarence instructed.

Zee parroted Clarence: "Both teams high five and say 'Good game.' Bryant's team stays on defense, Toni your team is on O."

The two teams exchanged slightly awkward high fives and self-conscious "Good games."

Cassie's team got back in line, and the game continued. After the first bumpy round, it got smoother. And when Cassie's team got up again, they stayed on the court for three wins in a row, notably improving Cassie's mood. They had just been defeated when the bell rang signifying the end of lunch.

"High fives all around," Clarence said, and Zee started to repeat it, but it was unnecessary. The high fives were happening on their own.

"That was cool, Zee," Aaron was happily bouncing his ball as he walked back toward the cafeteria, having almost completely forgotten his earlier Marcus-induced terror. "Thanks for organizing."

A couple of other kids also said thanks to Zee, and Toni and Bryant just stood next to him making him feel self-conscious about the attention. Toni mumbled something about a ventriloquist, but in a good-natured way. Only Cassie was quiet.

"You OK?" Zee asked her.

Cassie wasn't quite sure how to answer the question. She felt foolish for having gotten so worked up and embarrassed that she had made a scene like that. It was just another thing that made her feel so different from everyone else. "Yeah, that was fun, I guess. Sorry I got kind of worked up in the beginning."

"No worries, Cassie, you've always been intense like that." And Zee knocked her lightly on the shoulder.

"I guess so," Cassie said and turned and headed back toward the school on her own.

"Is she always that competitive?" Clarence asked Toni and Bryant when Cassie was out of earshot.

Toni thought for a second, "Usually worse."

"I don't think she means anything by it," Bryant added almost protectively. "She's just never been particularly good at losing."

Clarence continued watching Cassie as she walked away from the others. "I know the feeling."

By midafternoon, practically everybody at school had heard about Marcus's sudden inability to catch the ball and the game of Three-Lines Basketball. Through the telling and retelling, the basketball incident had become as big an event as the time the third-grade class snake got loose and ended up in Mrs. Grumble's kitchen.

When Cassie and her friends arrived for Mr. Street's class, he passed out the blank maps and gave the instructions for a schoolwide project to redesign recess. The buzz in class was palpable. Everyone wanted to be a part.

Mr. Street had his students break into small groups and assigned each group two to three different homerooms. They would be responsible for distributing the maps, explaining the process, and then collecting the creatively enhanced maps in two days. Mr. Street had gotten Mr. Unger's approval for his students to go classroom to classroom that afternoon. Much to Mr. Street's surprise, Mr. Unger had been positively excited about the project and was hoping that Mr. Street's class would send some representatives to discuss the best ideas with him toward the end of the week when the superintendent was to make his visit in honor of the ACE Award nomination.

The enthusiasm for the project left the four friends feeling a little taken aback. They hadn't anticipated other kids being so excited about it, and they certainly had not imagined that it might be embraced by the school administration. They had mixed feelings about all this newfound interest in recess.

"I suppose it's a good thing," Zee said, valiantly trying to sound positive.

"I guess so," Toni agreed halfheartedly. "I mean, I didn't want to do all that work alone. It's just . . ."

"It's just that they're totally going to mess it up!" Cassie was having none of it. It made her mad that no one had shown any interest in recess whatsoever until now. And now that recess was suddenly cool again, they all wanted to be a part. What a bunch of phonies!

"Whoa. Hold on, all of you. This is exactly right. This is the way things change." Clarence explained. He was genuinely surprised by the group's reaction.

"Yeah, but no one will ever know *WE* did it," Bryant sounded even more put out than usual.

Clarence laughed out loud. "Getting credit for stuff is way overrated," he observed. "And it's almost always connected to taking the blame."

The four looked at him quizzically. "You only make sense about half the time; you know that, Clarence?" Toni asked.

Clarence considered her statement for a moment before answering. "I suppose that's better than usual. I can work with that."

"So what do we do about the mapping project?" Bryant was more concerned with the matter at hand.

"We'll see what the other kids come up with," Clarence offered. "And then we move on to the next phase of the plan: Operation RoShamBo!"

The next day when the four friends arrived at school, the maps were everywhere. Missy Davis had gotten her father to make even more copies at his office, and everywhere you looked, kids were checking out one another's ideas. Toni saw students talking about their drawings on the front steps and noticed some kids had hung them up in their lockers. The four friends were all still shocked and more than a little put off by the interest the project was generating.

Clarence had promised to meet with them again at recess.

"You think this is Clarence's doing?" Zee was truly surprised by what he was seeing: virtually everyone they passed was either holding a map or talking about one.

"No doubt," Cassie said, slowing down to take a look at a map that two pigtailed second graders were heatedly discussing. She had expected them to have childish drawings of fantastical jungle gyms, but instead the taller of the two had drawn a very detailed picture of a baseball diamond and was conferring with her friend, "Can we have a big kickball field close to the building?"

Cassie was flabbergasted. She hurried to rejoin her friends.

"They're over the top about this thing. It's just not right," Cassie said to her friends. "No way this is happening without Clarence's voodoo."

Bryant wasn't convinced it was Clarence. "Don't worry; it won't last. In the meantime, just enjoy it. You're always complaining that everyone is too cranky to make time to play. Now you've got a whole army of teammates!"

But when recess rolled around, it seemed that the interest in the mapping project had not yet translated into actual interest in playing outside on the yard. The scene on the playground was as desolate and depressing as it had been initially the day before, only slightly worse because Aaron hadn't brought his basketball to school with him.

Marcus was standing all by himself and hanging close to the school building. He was a little spooked by the ball incident and still had a lingering sense that he was mad at Cassie, although he was fuzzy on the details.

Clarence appeared just when the four friends were starting to wonder if he was coming. He seemed to be in a particularly good mood, whistling and walking with a noticeable bounce in his step. He was wearing yet another fancy sweat suit. This one was red with black stripes down both the pant legs and on the sleeves, and he was wearing matching high tops and a red-and-black flat-brimmed cap bearing the Los Angeles Angels logo. Bryant was just about to ask him if the hat was a joke when Clarence proposed teaching them all RoShamBo Relay.

Clarence deputized Zee to round up some additional kids to join in the game, so he headed over to the courts where Aaron was talking with three other fourth graders—twin sisters Haley and Camille, and Ryan, a boy who had just transferred to Magruder this year. Looking around to see who else he could enlist, Zee waved at Sarah and her friend Megan Hanawalt. They were standing near the school but at a healthy distance from Marcus, and they quickly walked over to Zee when he waved at them to do so.

Clarence looked around the field, "Bryant, can you walk over to the fence and get the equipment bag?"

Bryant looked over at the fence but saw nothing. He started to ask, but then just shrugged and started walking. "I suppose I'll see it when I get there." Having Clarence in his life was teaching Bryant a lot about going with the flow.

The nine kids assembled in a circle, all staring at Zee expectantly. "What are we going to play today, Zee?" Aaron asked, his enthusiasm radiating from a smile that extended ear to ear.

Zee looked around at the group. "RoShamBo Relay," he announced proudly.

The mood shifted immediately from excitement to

skepticism. Megan voiced what they were all thinking, "A relay?"

"Yeah. Wait till you see it," Zee was suddenly a little less sure of the idea himself. He was beginning to feel as though Clarence might have thrown him under the bus, when Bryant ambled up, and as promised, he carried an equipment bag.

Bryant slowly dumped out the contents—a few cones, a couple of red kickballs, and some chalk. "Seems a little skimpy, given it's magic." Bryant observed.

Aaron was adapting to the nonsensical comments, and the other kids were all pretty used to Bryant saying random things anyway, but Ryan hadn't been at Magruder long enough to know all this. He simply stared at Bryant trying to understand.

"No magic necessary," Clarence assured him. "Just set the cones up in a big horseshoe shape."

Bryant and Cassie jumped up eagerly to follow his instructions, and Clarence continued. "OK, Zee. First have everybody who has birthdays in January through June line up behind the end cone on the left side. Then have everyone who has birthdays July through December line up on the other end."

Zee repeated the instructions and Cassie, Ryan, Megan, and Aaron went to one cone, and the remaining six kids to the other.

"Bryant, switch sides so the teams are even," Clarence instructed. So Bryant moved from the cone with six people to the cone with four.

Aaron looked at the two teams: "Hey! That's a cool way to make teams," he said out loud. "Way faster than picking with captains!" Cassie was really starting to like this kid.

"When I say 'Go,' the first person from each team racewalks around the outside of the horseshoe till they meet up with the other team. They stop and throw RoShamBo—it's the same thing as Rock-Paper-Scissors—to see who continues around the horseshoe. As soon as a winner is determined to that match, she or he continues toward the other team, and the other team sends out the next player to try and stop the person. The first team to send someone all the way around the horseshoe and to the other team's home base wins the relay."

Zee repeated the instructions.

"Now remind everyone how Rock-Paper-Scissors works," Clarence prompted.

Zee looked around the group: "You all know how to do Rock-Paper-Scissors, right? Rock crushes scissors, scissors cuts paper, and paper covers rock. You throw on three."

"And now ask if anyone has any questions."

"Does anyone have any questions?" Zee asked.

All the kids shook their heads "No."

"Remind them to racewalk and not run."

Zee was starting to get impatient with all the instructions: "Remember, we're racewalking, not running. Ready, go!"

Aaron took off racewalking with abandon, his hips wiggling as he stepped quickly in a straight line. Toni took off on the other side and looked just marginally less silly. They met at the halfway mark of the horseshoe and put out their open palms and both threw out rocks. "Again!" everyone cheered. The second time, Toni threw out a scissors, defeating Aaron's paper. She continued racewalking toward Aaron's side and quickly met up with the taller twin, Camille. Camille threw paper, covering Toni's rock, and immediately started racewalking toward Toni's side. Toni's team responded slowly, partly because they were all laughing at the silliness of the racewalking, and by the time Ryan took off racewalking, Camille was most of the way around. Ryan and Camille both threw paper, and then Ryan threw scissors to Camille's repeated paper effort and forged ahead to meet Haley at the top of the horseshoe. Ryan defeated Haley, Megan, and then also Aaron, who had gotten back in line. Ryan ultimately crossed over into Aaron's team's home base amidst cheers and laughter.

Toni noticed Mr. Rodrigues, the custodian, standing beside his supply cart and watching.

"Mr. Rodrigues, you want to play?" she called out.

Mr. Rodrigues smiled: "Not today, Toni, but thanks. That's a good game. I've never seen it before."

Toni looked over at the kids all laughing and jostling each other as they set up for another round. It seemed like they had known this game forever, not just a few minutes.

RoShamBo Relay continued until the bell rang. Mr. Rodrigues had stood by watching for the final minutes, and when the bell rang, he returned to pushing his cart loaded with all the trash cans and supplies back toward the cafeteria entrance near where Marcus was standing. Toni and Cassie jogged to catch up with him and walked alongside Mr. Rodrigues as they headed back in to school.

"Hello, Marcus," Mr. Rodrigues said as they passed by.

"Hello, Mr. Rodrigues," Marcus replied, looking down at his feet.

One of the kids standing near Marcus, Kevin Sweeney, snickered. "You hanging out with the custodian now, Marcus?"

"Shut up," Marcus replied. He looked up and saw Toni and Cassie looking at him and starting to blush, looked back down at his feet.

Kevin was not infrequently the object of Marcus's teasing, and he resented Marcus for making him look stupid. Sensing weakness, Kevin proceeded to push his luck. "Better watch out, Marcus, or Cassie might beat you up again."

And then, like a blur, Marcus lunged for Kevin. He managed to knock him down, but Mr. Rodrigues was surprisingly quick and had pulled Marcus off Kevin before he was able to do any harm. Clarence and Bryant and Zee were over in a flash to see what had happened.

"Nothing to see here, kids. Back to class," Mr. Rodrigues said matter-of-factly. "Marcus and Kevin, you're coming with me to the office. And Toni and Cassie, you come along, too." Cassie started to protest, but Toni shot her a look. Bryant and Zee clearly wanted to come, but Mr. Rodrigues firmly waved them off. "Back to class, I said. Let's go."

Clarence turned to Zee and Bryant, "I'll come tell you what happens." Begrudgingly, the two boys turned and walked away.

In the school office, Mr. Rodrigues seated Kevin and Marcus across the room from one another and had Cassie and Toni sit in the two seats near Marcus. Mr. Rodrigues went to Mr. Unger's office and Clarence sat down next to the girls. Ms. Houghton peered over her glasses and looked at Toni. "Well. I'm not so surprised to see the other three here, but what did you do to get yourself hauled into the principal's office?" she asked.

"Hey!" Cassie protested.

Toni was wryly amused: "I think Cassie and I are just witnesses. We were standing right there when these two idiots got into it." Marcus briefly stopped glaring at Kevin to shift his glare to Toni, but even Marcus didn't glare too much at Toni.

Mr. Unger and Mr. Rodrigues emerged from Mr. Unger's office and walked toward the students. "Boys, I am very disappointed," Mr. Unger began. "Mr. Rodrigues has told me that you've been fighting."

"*We* weren't fighting!" Kevin declared indignantly. "He jumped me!"

"You deserved it," Cassie interjected in disgust.

Now, generally, a comment like this would have been condemned by any of the grown-ups in the room, but the very act of Cassie standing up for Marcus was so extraordinary that it frankly shocked everyone into silence for a moment.

Marcus finally broke the spell. "What'd you say?" he asked, the suspicion evident in his tone.

"I said Sweeney deserved it. He was being a jerk to you. I would have jumped him, too."

Toni smiled at this, and Mr. Rodrigues did his best to not smile. Kevin just scowled.

"Jeez, Cassie, I can't believe you're sticking up for him," Kevin said.

"I'm not sticking up for him," Cassie spoke dismissively. She wasn't wasting any energy on Sweeney. It was clear she had decided the kid was a jerk and unworthy of her attention.

Mr. Unger could see this was going nowhere. "All right, that's quite enough. Girls, I think you can go back to class. Kevin, I'm going to call your parents. And Marcus, I'm afraid you're going to have to be suspended. We will not tolerate hitting here."

Cassie and Toni were standing to leave when Clarence whispered, "Ask Mr. Unger if Marcus can be a recess coach instead."

Toni was wondering why Clarence was whispering,

but more importantly, why he'd suggest helping the bully out. Cassie, on the other hand, didn't miss a beat, "Mr. Unger, would you consider letting Marcus do his time serving as a recess coach instead?"

"Well, it's hardly 'doing time,' Cassie." Mr. Unger was a stickler with words.

"Tell him that as part of the mapping assignment, the class needs students to help monitor the playground, handle equipment, and teach the other kids games," Clarence coached.

"Marcus would have to miss his own recess to help the other kids and distribute balls and teach games and keep games going. But he wouldn't get to miss school the way he would if he was suspended."

Mr. Unger seemed to consider this for a moment. "Cassie, I must tell you that I'm quite surprised by your sudden loyalty to Marcus. It's no great secret here at school that you and Marcus rarely see eye to eye on anything."

"Yeah," agreed Toni, weighing in despite her better judgment to stay quiet in front of the principal. "Quit it already!"

Cassie just stood her ground, saying nothing. So far Clarence had delivered on his promises. If this was a way to make recess work again, she was willing to give it a shot.

"Very well, then," Mr. Unger agreed.

Mr. Rodrigues smiled. Clarence did a quiet, but dorky, victory dance. And Toni shook her head. "You're going to regret this," she said to Cassie.

The full weight of her action seemed to hit Cassie all at once, and she physically rocked back as Mr. Unger agreed to her proposal. "I know," Cassie said, the instant remorse evident in her voice. "I know."

Zee and Bryant were puzzled when Cassie and Toni came in late to Ms. Swanson's language arts class. Cassie refused to make eye contact and appeared deflated, Toni was rolling her eyes and seemed annoyed, Marcus looked stunned, and Clarence trailed behind looking simply ecstatic.

Clarence walked right to the boys in the midst of Ms. Swanson's lecture on research projects and burst out, "Cassie was awesome!"

Toni ignored him, trying to get seated and focus on Ms. Swanson. Cassie was absolutely and completely disengaged.

Bryant was looking back and forth from Cassie to Clarence to Toni, totally perplexed by the scene.

"Can I help you, Bryant?" Ms. Swanson asked, noticing him looking all around.

"Huh? Oh, no, sorry. I'm good." Bryant tried to regain his focus on Ms. Swanson, or at least to keep looking forward while he listened to Clarence.

"No, really, she was extraordinary!" Clarence pressed on, oblivious to the teacher at the front of the classroom who fully expected her students' undivided attention.

Toni made a noise of derision through her nose. She had not found Cassie's valiant performance quite so heroic.

"Toni, you don't get it. It was exactly what we needed. Guys, you should have seen her. You know what happened, right? Nod if you know what happened." Clarence was moving back and forth between Zee and Bryant, bouncing up and down in their line of vision to the teacher. Zee shook his head just slightly—almost imperceptibly—no.

"So here's what happened," Clarence continued, talking right over Ms. Swanson. "Marcus was just standing there, right? And then that other kid . . . what was his name?"

"Kevin Sweeney," Toni mumbled.

"Toni?" Ms. Swanson demanded. "I would appreciate it if you would settle down."

"Sorry, Ms. Swanson," Toni answered, casting an annoyed look in Clarence's direction.

Ms. Swanson had lost her train of thought. "Now what was I saying?"

Clarence paused briefly, shook his head and continued. "Right, so this kid, Kevin Sweeney, starts dogging Marcus out because Marcus and the custodian exchanged hellos. Totally uncool. Marcus doesn't react at first, right, but then the Sweeney kid signs his own death warrant by talking even more smack to Marcus about how Cassie was going to kick his butt."

Cassie started to protest but then caught herself before actually saying anything when she noticed Ms. Swanson staring right at her.

"Did you have something to add Cassie?" Ms. Swanson asked, her frustration with the class now at full bore.

Cassie just shook her head.

So Clarence continued. "Marcus totally blew a fuse, and he just completely lunged at the kid. Mr. Rodrigues was quick though. For an old dude, he moves like a cat, you know?"

Getting no response, he continued. "So Rodrigues drags Marcus and Kevin into the office, and he has Toni and Cassie come along because they had been standing right there. When Mr. Unger came out, he was all set to suspend Marcus. That's when Cassie stepped up! You know? I mean, she was a rock star! And she convinced Unger not to suspend him."

Zee was literally incapable of controlling his reaction to the news that Cassie had somehow intervened in Marcus's suspension. His head whipped around to look at Clarence, and Ms. Swanson audibly sighed. "I have no idea what's going on today, but perhaps we should spend the rest of class reading quietly." And then she sat down at her desk and began grading papers. Ms. Swanson had had enough.

"I thought she'd never stop!" Clarence sighed. "So you're wondering how Cassie managed to get him out of suspension. It was awesome. She suggested that Marcus be a recess coach with you guys, basically helping out on the schoolyard at recess. She convinced Unger that this would be more of a punishment than just suspending him. And it's perfect, you know? Because the way I see it, Marcus is one of our biggest obstacles, so if he's helping out, I mean, if he's on our team, then we've got a much better chance to win!"

Cassie put her head down on her desk in despair. Zee and Bryant had so many questions and were doing all they could not to blurt them out, when the loud, piercing, siren-like noise that Mr. Unger made before every announcement, came blasting out over the PA system.

"Boys and girls," he said. "I have an exciting announcement! As you may have heard, Magruder Elementary has been nominated for an ACE Award—Achievement, Cleanliness, and Efficiency. Dr. Kardashian, the superintendent of schools, will be visiting us next week. To prepare for this important visit, I am asking that you all join me for an assembly next period to review the school plan and our expectations for student involvement in the application process."

"Staff," he continued "if you could walk with your classes to the auditorium when the bell rings, we will begin immediately so that we don't cut too deeply into your instructional time. Thank you for your cooperation."

And with that, the bell rang.

"This is perfect!" Clarence positively cheered.

"I really don't think it could get any worse," Cassie said, incredulous that Clarence seemed so pleased. When Clarence threw the recess coach idea at her in Unger's office, she thought he had a plan, as in something he knew would work. Now she was absolutely convinced that if he had a plan, it was the worst plan in history. And when it didn't work, it would be all her fault.

"Never say that," Toni advised. "It can always get worse."

By the time Ms. Swanson's class arrived, the auditorium was complete chaos. The big open hall was one of the nicest spaces in the school, having been renovated by the PTA only a few years before. The theater seats all had cushions and leaned back extravagantly, meaning that most assemblies were punctuated by the sounds of squeaking chairs as students rocked restlessly back and forth. The stage had been redone, with stairs on either side, an expensive curtain, and real stage lights that hung from rigging up above. The order and official appearance of the stage was in marked contrast to the bedlam that filled the space.

Clarence was looking around in amazement. "I haven't been in an elementary school for a while, I admit. But I swear my teachers did a better job of controlling things."

Mr. Unger was standing on stage and speaking into the microphone trying to get everyone's attention. The students, however, ignored him and continued talking loudly among themselves. Clarence watched for a while and then, unable to take it anymore, made a slight head gesture in Unger's direction.

Recognizing the nod, Cassie, Bryant, Toni, and Zee looked up expectantly at their principal to see what would happen next. Quite suddenly, he walked to the front of the stage, put both of his hands on his head, and said in a loud, but not-too-forceful voice, "Match me."

A good number of kids looked up, and a couple put their hands to their heads. And then Mr. Unger did it again, this time touching his index finger to his nose, "Match me!" More students quieted down to watch, and most of them were touching their noses. And then finally, Unger moved in a way that created an image that Bryant was worried might be permanently burned into his retinas: he swiveled his hips in a slow motion hula-hoop swivel while saying "Match me!" And while no one actually matched Mr. Unger, everyone was completely silent.

Mr. Unger then seemed to snap out of the trance that had held him during Match Me, and his attention shifted quickly to the quiet and attentive audience. He looked briefly confused but then forged ahead. "Well, then, excellent!"

Zee turned to Clarence, "Dude, that was reckless."

Clarence was pleased with himself, "I thought it was a nice touch!"

Toni just closed her eyes and shook her head.

Mr. Unger spoke with an almost military sense of urgency. "Students. As you know, our school has been nominated for the ACE Award. This is truly something that every principal dreams of. And while I am, of course, very honored that the school should receive such acknowledgment under my leadership, this is an honor that shines upon us all."

The students began to stir as Mr. Unger continued to talk, though a few watched in a stunned silence that hung on from the earlier slow-motion dance move.

"Next week when Dr. Kardashian arrives, we are going to need a 100 percent team effort to make it through to final consideration by the school board. I am so pleased to have Mrs. Grumble heading up preparations for the visit, along with Mr. Rodrigues (there were a smattering of cheers for Mr. Rodrigues) working hard to make sure that the school itself is as bright and shining as our students!" There were some groans from the shining students.

Mr. Unger continued on in this vein for a while, going into excruciating detail on the ten-point scale for each of the categories—achievement, cleanliness, and efficiency—with specific examples of ways students could help Mr. Unger in his pursuit of a perfect score.

"OK, this has gone on long enough," Clarence declared.

"There's something about Clarence reaching his limit that makes me feel both excited and terrified at the same time, you know?" Bryant whispered to Cassie.

Cassie knew exactly what Bryant was talking about.

"There is one final thing," Mr. Unger was mercifully beginning to wrap up. "This year the ACE Award has a special emphasis on student leadership. I have decided to exemplify our proud abundance of said leadership by including a special presentation by Mr. Street's class on their playground map project." Mr. Unger's eyes darted around as he spoke, and Zee, Cassie, Bryant, and Toni knew for a fact that these were not his own words, but that Clarence was somehow responsible.

"What are you doing?" Zee whispered frantically in Clarence's direction.

"Operation RoShamBo is in action!" Clarence was grinning maniacally.

The four looked around and found Mr. Street sitting in the back of the auditorium. He shrugged in their direction; this was news to him as well.

Mr. Unger continued looking confused as he gestured to Cassie, Zee, Toni, and Bryant, "Could you four join me here on stage?"

Zee turned to Clarence, more shocked than outraged. "You have got to be kidding!"

Clarence was openly enjoying himself now "Come on! It'll be fun!"

Cassie turned to Toni: "You were right. I never should have said earlier that the day couldn't get worse."

"Apology accepted," Toni replied. "You think a person can whoop a ghost if she catches him when he's not expecting it?"

Clarence turned and looked at Toni in a way that clearly conveyed she was next.

"Oh, no you don't!" she said, but she knew that he had decided that she was going to be his ventriloquist's dummy for this most humiliating moment.

Mr. Unger again gestured for them to join him, and the four of them, followed by a more enthusiastic Clarence, walked slowly to the stage. Once on stage, the kids could see clearly that Mr. Unger was having a total out-of-body experience.

"Why doesn't one of you tell the school about the project?" Mr. Unger instructed, his face bizarrely contorted, presumably because Clarence was speaking through him. The kids looked at one another, and then finally Toni stepped forward. If she was going to do this, she would do it on her own terms.

"We've been working with Mr. Street and the fifth-grade art class to distribute a map of the playground. I think many of you have already submitted your ideas for improving recess, so thanks for that. We'll be pulling together the best ideas for a presentation to Dr. Kardashian next week when he visits."

Toni looked over at Clarence with a look that screamed: "There! Are you happy?" But Clarence looked back in a slightly mischievous way that let her know he wasn't quite done, and thus neither was she.

"And you wanted to lead the group in a game before we all go back to class?" Mr. Unger asked in a strangled voice that was unmistakably someone else talking through him. Toni thought he sounded more like Mickey Mouse than anything else.

"How about RoShamBo Rockstar?" Clarence suggested helpfully.

Toni took a deep breath. And then she repeated Clarence's words, "How about RoShamBo Rockstar?"

Bryant and Zee and Cassie all clapped supportively. "You got this," Bryant encouraged. Toni turned to look and see if he was mocking but quickly surmised that he was genuinely appreciative that she was stepping up in these adverse conditions.

Remarkably, the students in the auditorium were all watching in stunned silence. They were going to play a game during an assembly? Led by other kids? Nothing like this had ever happened at Magruder Elementary School before.

The game was a simple one, essentially a giant Rock-Paper-Scissors single-elimination tournament. Clarence explained quickly to Toni that everyone needed to find a partner to kick off the game. When she said, "Go," they'd all play a round of Rock-Paper-Scissors.

The person who was defeated would then become the winner's cheering section, with the victor going immediately to find another victor for another round of Rock-Paper-Scissors, their respective cheering sections all cheering them on. Clarence did a little dance and sang a little "Go, Toni!" song to illustrate. Zee wondered briefly how Toni was going to figure out a way to exact revenge on an angel. He didn't doubt for a moment that she would find a way.

Toni repeated the instructions, and Clarence continued: "So the cheering sections keep getting bigger and bigger, and ultimately there should be just two winners left representing all the other students in the room, and everybody should be cheering for them in the ultimate Rock-Paper-Scissors contest. In the end, only one person is left. She or he is the rock star, and we all cheer!"

Toni took another deep breath, finished relaying the instructions, asked if anyone had a question, and seeing none, shouted, "Go!"

All four kids turned to look out into the audience. Initially there was no reaction, and Toni shot Clarence a withering glance. Clarence smiled serenely, though, as the entire student body suddenly stood and began playing. The four friends watched in amazement as their fellow students engaged in a giant, simultaneous Rock-Paper-Scissors tournament. Students from different grades were asking each other's names so that they could cheer one another on, and the winners happily went looking for other winners to compete against, their new-found cheering squads enthusiastically in tow as they made their way around the auditorium.

And then, just as quickly as it had started, they were down to two final players: Jimmy Driscoll, a fourth grader who talked endlessly about superheroes and spoke with a slight lisp, and Mary Chen, a fifth grader who was known as the school's best speller.

Mary and Jimmy began the final round with both of them throwing out rock. The two teams of cheerers went wild. "Rock-paper-scissors!" everyone cheered, and again the two both threw rock. The crowd went nuts. "Rock-paper-scissors!" And with that, Mary threw rock once again, with Jimmy throwing scissors, and the crowd erupted into cheers of "Mary! Mary! Mary!" with Jimmy laughing and clearly unfazed by his defeat at the hands of Mary Chen.

Mr. Unger looked completely stunned. "Thank you for your cooperation," he said meekly into the microphone. "You may all go back to class now." And he walked down the steps from the stage and out the side door, leaving the teachers to do what they could to restore order.

The rest of the day was a continuous stream of kids coming up to the four, asking to be a part of the recess coaches. Apparently Marcus had been telling other kids that he was the captain of the coaches, and that they were going to be in charge of recess.

Bryant felt compelled to tease Cassie just a bit, "It seems you've created a monster."

But Cassie was still not talking about it.

"C'mon Cassie, you're the one who wanted to get more kids participating in recess in the first place," Zee noted.

"And so far Clarence hasn't made you stand up in front of a big group of people and repeat after him," Toni added.

"No, only small groups for me," Cassie corrected. She wanted to believe that Clarence had spoken through her when she interfered in Marcus's suspension, but she knew she had done it of her own volition.

Meanwhile, Clarence couldn't understand why they all seemed so frustrated with him.

From his perspective, things were going exactly to plan.

"I don't get it," he said at last. "What did I do?"

No one said anything at first.

"Didn't you want my help? Didn't you want to make recess fun?" He was genuinely exasperated now.

"The problem," Cassie said finally, "is that none of it's real. It's all magic. The way the kids got excited about the map. Mr. Unger saying those things, Marcus being frozen, the kids playing RoShamBo Rockstar and Three-Lines Basketball. None of it would happen without you, and when you leave, nothing's going to be any different!" She had turned bright red, as though she'd just been running, and Zee wondered briefly if she was about to cry.

"Hey, now!" Clarence protested. "That's not true! Well, I mean, I did make Unger do those things, and I did freeze Marcus. I froze Bryant, too; you forgot that part." Bryant shot Clarence a dirty look. "But all that other stuff? That's just regular magic. The kind of magic that you can make happen same as me."

Toni wasn't quite believing it. "Even the map?" she pressed. "There wasn't anything hypnotic about the way you drew it or the magical paper it was copied on?"

"It was a nice drawing," Clarence conceded, "but I was a great artist when I was alive, too. This is just a different medium. Nothing magical about the paper, though I did think that the way Bryant charmed Ms. Houghton into letting you copy it was a little other-worldly." Clarence was shamelessly trying to win his way back into Bryant's heart.

"Look. Tomorrow we'll start working with the other kids about being recess coaches. I won't be so bossy. I can teach you the games now if you want, or I can work with you so that my teaching the games and having you repeat the rules doesn't feel so fake. I swear, once we get the kids all playing Rock-Paper-Scissors and the playground all mapped out and the recess coaches on board with how they can help games get going and how to keep them going, it's all going to feel 100 percent different." Clarence looked imploringly from one face to the next.

No one said anything for a few moments until Zee cleared his throat. "OK." Zee had been the most uncertain about Clarence to start, but he had been won over, and Zee was nothing if not loyal.

"I'm in," Bryant agreed.

Toni shook her head at Clarence, "I cannot believe you did that to me today!"

"I'm sorry, Toni," Clarence apologized. "But you were great up there. And that whole first piece was all you." Toni looked just slightly pleased by this acknowledgment. Not entirely forgiving but not quite so peeved either.

"Cassie?" Clarence asked. "Do you believe me?"

Cassie bit her lower lip, "I really want to believe you, Clarence. I really do."

"Are you willing to try?"

She nodded, though Zee and Bryant and Toni all knew that she wasn't entirely convinced.

It had been a long day, and the four friends were all a little exhausted from the week, so it was agreed that they would meet up at the first recess to begin working with the prospective recess coaches. They would break up into groups, and Clarence would circulate among them, helping out. Tomorrow would just be about teaching some Rock-Paper-Scissors games, and then maybe they'd get a game of Kickball going at lunch. The goal was to keep it simple.

They walked the regular route home: Toni's, Cassie's, Bryant's, and then Zee's. It was almost dusk as Clarence started to walk away from Zee, but before he'd gone very far, he turned back, "Hey, man," he said to Zee. "Thanks for stepping up just now. It meant a lot that you were the first to say you were in. The other kids look to you, and I appreciate it."

"Clarence," Zee said, "I'm a little worried about Cassie, you know? She cares so much and well, I really don't want her to get hurt."

"I got it, Zee. That's why I'm here."

"So you know that Cassie lives with her aunt and uncle?" Zee was hesitant to talk about Cassie's family. He had known her since they were in kindergarten, and he felt very protective of her, even if she could be stubborn and difficult.

Clarence nodded "Yes."

"And you know that her parents were killed in a car crash?"

Clarence nodded again.

Zee shifted from foot to foot, looking uncomfortable. "Thanks, then, I guess."

Clarence smiled at Zee, "You're a good kid, Zee." And then he disappeared.

7

Friday proved to be bright and sunny, one of those fall days that feels like summer. It made the worries of the day before harder to summon, especially with the prospect of the weekend.

The four made their way to the playground for the first break of the school day and were amazed to find a group of almost forty kids waiting for them. All of the kids from the previous day's RoShamBo Relay were present, Marcus and the basketball bunch, Mary and Jimmy of Rockstar fame, the pigtailed second grader, Missy Davis. Even Kevin Sweeney was standing near enough to get involved, should he be invited.

Clarence was already there and wandering around among them, seemingly assessing their potential as recess coaches.

Sarah spotted Zee and made a beeline for him immediately. "Hi, Zee!" she called out as she

111

approached. "Isn't this great? Everyone is so psyched that you're doing this. I can't wait to be a coach. What are we going to do first?"

Zee looked embarrassed by Sarah's attention and turned to Toni. "Well, Toni's actually in charge," he stammered.

Toni couldn't help but laugh a little, but she jumped right in, not wanting to leave Zee hanging. "All-righty then! C'mon Sarah; let's go get this thing organized." And she led Sarah over toward the group of kids. Bryant followed along after Sarah and Toni, whispering loudly to Zee as he passed, "You are incredibly smooth."

Toni stood near the front of the group, with Clarence standing just to her right. "So, thanks, everyone, for coming. We're excited that so many people want to help. And there's going to be something for everyone to do." She paused and looked in Clarence's direction.

Clarence waited for a moment and then explained the delay, "I didn't know if you wanted me to make a suggestion."

Toni had mixed feelings; she wanted to do it on her own, but she wasn't entirely sure about what to say, so she just continued talking. "We want everyone to be included." Having nothing else to say, she raised her eyebrows in Clarence's direction.

"I'd suggest you circle everyone up and have them go around and say their name," Clarence gently offered.

Toni sounded relieved as she repeated the instructions, and the kids all moved toward making a big circle.

Clarence coached Bryant on coordinating a name game in which everyone said their name aloud and made a movement that everyone else then repeated. Bryant embraced the game with his usual enthusiasm, dubbing it the "Move Your Booty Game" and kicking it off Bryant-style with a "riding the pony" dance that was so supremely silly that everyone was immediately put at ease. Cassie was shocked as the kids around her seemed to visibly relax. Kids imitated lawn sprinklers and dunked themselves under imaginary water and shimmied and hopped. Cassie could not believe these were the same kids who had all seemed so preoccupied with looking cool not even twenty-four hours before. Even Marcus made a flexing super-Hulk pose that made people giggle.

Once everyone had been introduced, Clarence wandered over next to Zee. "You need to explain that the idea behind the recess coaches is to make sure that all the kids understand how the games work and how to keep the games going. If we're going to have enough kids to actually get a lot of games going, everyone needs to be having fun. The big idea is that the more fun we make it for everyone, the better."

Zee looked a little anxious as he took in everything that Clarence was saying. He wanted to say the words in a way that sounded like his own ideas, but he wasn't sure how to start. He hesitated just for a second and looked over to Cassie for help.

"Here's the deal," Cassie said, jumping in to fill the void. "Recess hasn't been any fun. And nobody else is going to make it fun for us. The goal out here is to have fun, but we also have a big responsibility. We need to make sure that all the other kids are having fun, too. We're going to talk a lot about different games: how you get them started, how we make even teams, how we handle it when there's a disagreement. But all the rules in the world won't help us if we don't understand one big thing: we need each other to play."

Clarence was nodding and smiling the whole time Cassie was talking. "Hallelujah!" he shouted when she was done.

The group was quiet for a bit, taking this in. Most of the other kids were only aware of Cassie as this super-competitive girl who seemed pretty independent. The other kids were shocked to hear her sound so passionate about the whole issue. Zee looked around the circle, waiting to see who would say something in response. Marcus started to speak, and Zee felt himself get angry in anticipation of what he might say.

"What do we do first?" Marcus was ready to go.

Clarence looked from Cassie to Toni to Bryant to Zee, "Who's up?"

"Hit me!" Bryant said, stepping forward and once again mildly confusing the other kids around him.

"Have them go around the circle and count off 1-2-3-4" Clarence instructed. The kids counted off per Bryant's instructions, and he assigned Zee the 1s, Cassie the 2s, Toni the 3s, and he took the 4s.

"You're going to start off by having them play

RoShamBo Relay and Rock Star. And then I'll come around to teach you all Switch. And you can explain that all next week we're going to be focusing on Rock-Paper-Scissors so that the students have a way to resolve their own conflicts. You should also let people take turns teaching each other how to do Rock-Paper-Scissors so they can teach the younger kids. OK?" Clarence was really making an effort to offer instructions and guidance without being bossy.

The four friends all went to their respective groups. Toni ended up with Marcus in her group, which proved to be fine. Clarence checked in on all four groups and showed them all how to lay out the cones with four corners and a center for Switch. Switch operates on the same principles as musical chairs: one more person than spots. The game starts by having someone in the middle and then four people on each of the corner cones. When the person in the middle yells "Switch," everyone abandons their cone to race for a new one. Once the person has the left the middle cone, it's no longer available, and thus, suddenly, there are four cones for five people. In the event of a tie, the two disputants use Rock-Paper-Scissors to determine who stays.

For some reason, Marcus had a mental block about the game. He would yell "Switch" when he was in the middle and then stand stock still. Toni thought at first that he was kidding, but then it became clear that he was just having some weird brain short circuit. Clarence was standing with them, wondering if it was all going to go horribly wrong. And on the third time that Marcus stood in the middle, seemingly anchored to the center cone, Toni started to laugh. Really laugh. Out-of-control hysterics.

And everyone else just stood there, waiting to see if this was going to make Marcus go nuts. Marcus looked at Toni and then down at his own, stuck feet, and he started laughing hysterically too. The group let out a collective sigh of relief and joined in on the hysteria.

When Toni was finally able to pull it together, she suggested that Marcus start from one of the corner cones instead of the middle and somehow this made all the difference in the world. When the person in the center cried out "Switch!" Marcus took off running for the next corner. He spent the next ten minutes basically running counter-clockwise around the Switch square, periodically laughing at himself as he recalled his inability to get off the center spot.

After the four groups had gone through all the games and almost everybody had had a chance to offer up the basic Rock-Paper-Scissors instructions, Clarence walked back over to Zee and enlisted him to bring everyone back together using the clapping signal that Clarence had gotten Mr. Unger to use in the cafeteria on the first day. Zee clapped out a rhythm that everyone immediately repeated. "Can I get everyone to circle back over here?"

As the kids were all gathering, Clarence stood next to Toni. "You want to wrap it up?"

"What's the basic idea?" she asked in a hushed toned, intended for only Clarence to hear.

"Thank them for being a part of it. Remind them that next week we're all about Rock-Paper-Scissors, and that once we've got that going, we'll go over some more games."

"Got it," she said and then addressed the bigger group. "That was great today. Thank you all for helping to make recess better. Next week we're going to start out by just focusing on Rock-Paper-Scissors. Once everyone is using that, then we'll start adding other games. But we need to start by showing Mr. Unger that we have a plan." She turned and looked at Zee and Cassie and Bryant, who were all agreeing.

"Anything else?" Toni was much happier speaking in her own words.

Marcus spoke up, "My football team usually ends practice with a cheer."

Cassie did a double take. She had been thinking the same thing as Marcus.

"Recess rules!" Bryant shouted. "On three!"

And then Marcus counted out "1-2-3," and the whole group yelled in unison, "Recess Rules!"

When everyone but the four friends and Clarence had gone back into class, they sat quietly for a few minutes.

"I know what you're wondering," Clarence said, breaking the silence. "You're wondering if I used any magic."

No one responded at first. And then Cassie stood up, brushed the grit off her knees, and saying simply, "Nope," she headed back to the building alone.

The three remaining kids looked at each other and then started to laugh. "He really could not get himself off that center cone!" Toni said, giggling again at the thought of Marcus standing in the middle of the Switch court.

"But he was being a good guy today," Bryant observed. "Wasn't it weird?"

"Totally weird," Zee agreed. "But I'll take it."

Clarence was pleased. "You haven't *seen* weird yet!"

The next morning, Saturday, Clarence had planned on going to Zee's soccer game on the field adjacent to the Grove to watch with the others. On his way to the game, however, he stopped by the school and found Mrs. Grumble approaching the front door just as Mr. Unger was unlocking it.

"Yahtzee!" Clarence exclaimed. He had a strong sense that these two were worth following.

Mrs. Grumble was carrying a clipboard with her, and Mr. Unger realized as she approached that it was the first time he had ever seen her not in her cafeteria uniform. Instead she wore neatly ironed blue jeans and a matching blue-jean shirt. Mr. Unger was wearing his usual coat and tie and wished immediately that he had thought to dress more casually.

"Thank you so much for coming in early on a Saturday, Mrs. Grumble. I do hope it wasn't an inconvenience to your family."

Mrs. Grumble swatted the clipboard at him, "I wouldn't have missed it, Mr. Unger. This is such a tremendous honor. And besides, there's no one at home to worry about—the kids all moved out ages ago, and you know that my husband passed away going on three years now."

Mr. Unger did recall that Mr. Grumble had passed away. "Yes, yes, of course. I'm so sorry. He was a bus driver?" Mr. Unger inquired politely.

"He worked for the transit authority, but he stopped driving a few years back." She stopped and seemed to be thinking of her husband for a moment, so Mr. Unger waited respectfully for the moment to pass.

Clarence watched all this and felt an almost overwhelming urge to meddle. He had been so good the day before, not using any magic to manipulate the kids and trying to give only the most necessary instructions to Cassie, Zee, Bryant, and Toni. But here, with Mrs. Grumble and Mr. Unger, he had a situation that just called out for celestial intervention.

Mrs. Grumble snapped back to reality while Clarence was plotting her fate. "Oh, dear, I seem to have gotten distracted for a moment. Excuse me, Mr. Unger!" Mrs. Grumble flushed with embarrassment.

"Oh, please, no. And if it's all right with you, I'd like it if you would call me Harold."

Mrs. Grumble smiled. "That's so kind, Harold. Please call me Erma."

Clarence stood on the steps outside after he watched them pass through the doors. He could hear Cassie in his head, and he knew he shouldn't meddle. There was already a lot of natural magic in the world. He also knew he shouldn't get involved because that was the instruction from HQ: "Members in metaphysical transition should use their skills only in an emergency." But Clarence had been in "transition" for longer than most.

He had to admit to himself that his limbo wasn't that surprising. He hadn't ever been a bad kid, but he had flirted with bad. He had been fiercely independent and insanely competitive. In regard to that, he saw a lot of himself in Cassie. But he went beyond Cassie, as he would have done almost anything to win. And his guidance counselor in high school had observed that he had "trust issues." Clarence figured he probably wasn't going to be sprung from the metaphysical transition phase until he could show that he was able to let people in. He just wasn't sure where to begin.

So, standing there on the school steps, he decided to hold off on messing around with the emotions of Mr. Unger and Mrs. Grumble . . . at least for the time being. And then he passed through the doors without opening them, a novelty that still amazed him even six months after having left his earthly body behind.

Mrs. Grumble and Mr. Unger (a.k.a Erma and Harold) had made it as far as the office. Mrs. Grumble was making notes on her clipboard as they walked through the hallway. Clarence came up behind them just as they were heading into Mr. Unger's PA room.

"Mr. Unger!" Mrs. Grumble positively exclaimed upon entering.

"Please, Erma, call me Harold." Mr. Unger knew that the room was a mess, but he felt protective of the space nonetheless. He knew he shouldn't, but he associated the messiness of the room with the creative flair he tried to bring to his morning announcements. He considered describing this connection to Mrs. Grumble, but he feared she might think it silly.

"Harold, this room is a disaster!"

Mr. Unger looked around and shook his head ruefully. "I'm afraid things are somewhat in disarray," he agreed.

"And that machine," Mrs. Grumble waved her clipboard at the mimeograph machine. "It's the antithesis of efficiency, Harold."

"Oh, I wouldn't go that far, Erma. It still works well. And it doesn't break down all the time like those expensive copy machines. Ms. Houghton swears by it, and she's the one who has to run the papers through."

Mrs. Grumble just shook her head. "Now you know I'm not one to value form over substance, Harold, but appearances are important! You know how I feel about surfaces, Harold. And that machine just sends the wrong message, if you know what I mean."

Mr. Unger suspected the superintendent would agree with Mrs. Grumble, but it pained him to get rid of a perfectly good—and frankly more dependable than most—piece of equipment.

"I'll clean out the room, Erma, and we'll figure out what to do with the machine."

Mrs. Grumble considered pressing more but figured that she had gotten as much of a concession from him as she was going to get. "Very well." And then she made some more notes on her clipboard.

Mr. Unger and Mrs. Grumble made their way through the entire school with Clarence following behind them all the way. When they came to the door in the cafeteria that led out to the playground, Mrs. Grumble lowered her clipboard and looked concerned.

"Harold, I think we need to discuss your plans for the student leadership component of our presentation," she began.

"Well, yes, we should." The whole subject made Mr. Unger somewhat anxious. The assembly had been a bizarre experience, and when he tried to recall what had happened exactly, he was unclear on the details.

Nonetheless, Mr. Unger tried to sound confident about the process. "The students have been collecting schoolyard design plans, and Mr. Street is working with them to cull out the best. I've spoken with him about the importance of the plans being both practical and efficient. He was very impressed with the students' efforts so far. The plan is to have the students review the key ideas with the superintendent after he's completed the cafeteria inspection."

"And what about these new *recess coaches*?" Mrs. Grumble was not a big fan of change.

Mr. Unger looked momentarily confused. "You mean Marcus and Cassie?" That had been an unlikely development last week. And he was mildly unclear on the details of that as well. He remembered that Mr. Rodrigues had come to him, but Mr. Unger was a little fuzzy on the intervening steps that had led to him agreeing to let Marcus serve out his detention as a recess coach.

"It's not just Marcus, Harold. I was watching them yesterday. At least three dozen students have been recruited as recess coaches."

"Well." This was news to Mr. Unger, though he was reticent to admit it. "I don't know what to tell you, Erma. But it certainly sounds like student leadership."

Mrs. Grumble was not convinced. "I hope you'll keep an eye on it, Harold."

"I will, Erma. I will."

"Wouldn't it be better if we just had them organize a recycling project?" Mrs. Grumble was making one last-ditch effort. "The students seem to like recycling."

"Erma, listen. I understand your concern. I want to win this ACE Award as much as you do—maybe more. And I think these students can help us. From what I've seen, they genuinely care about improving recess. Cassie Murphy was willing to stick up for Marcus Mackey. I think it's serendipity, Erma, and I think we'd be foolish to stand in its way."

Mrs. Grumble was still reluctant, but she was inspired by his vision. "Oh, Harold. You're such a dreamer. Just promise me that if it starts to feel too out of control, we can highlight the Magruder Recycling Club instead."

"Of course, Erma. Of course." Mr. Unger was feeling quite pleased with himself; the confusion about the assembly had faded, and he was energized by the sense that he was leading a truly great school.

Clarence watched in fascination and was pleased with himself as well. He had shown tremendous restraint with Mr. Unger's and Mrs. Grumble's affections, and they seemed quite enamored with each other nonetheless.

8

onday started out slowly as usual, but when the bell rang for recess, there was a virtual stampede to get to the playground. Not only did all the students rush out to be a part of the new and improved recess, but the school staff were equally intrigued by the rumors of the extreme recess makeover; Mr. Unger and Mrs. Grumble, Mr. Street, Ms. Swanson, and Mr. Rodrigues were all in attendance. Just having so many more people out on the yard, not to mention a mix of kids and grown-ups, made recess feel a little bit like a carnival. The buzz was electric.

The newly minted recess coaches broke off into pairs around the schoolyard, setting up cones for Switch and RoShamBo Relay. The other students headed directly to the different stations, filling out the groups. Within a few minutes, the yard was overwhelmed by the happy noise of deeply engaged kids. In place of the desolate yard of the week before was a lively space filled with well-organized, kid-led play everywhere you looked.

Even Mrs. Grumble was impressed. "Heavens, Mr. Unger!" (They had reverted back to using last names.) "This is remarkable!"

Mr. Unger was beaming and happily taking full credit for the transformation.

Not too far away from where Mr. Unger and Mrs. Grumble stood, Toni and Marcus were managing a game of Switch. Two of the fourth graders, Carl and Andy, had reached the cone at the same time, but Carl was refusing to do Rock-Paper-Scissors to resolve the dispute, insisting that he had arrived there first.

Marcus was getting frustrated. "Listen, Carl," he was trying to maintain an even tone, but Marcus was not used to having his authority questioned so blatantly. "The whole point of the game is that you play Rock-Paper-Scissors when you can't agree."

Carl was not having it. "Marcus, the point is that you do Rock-Paper-Scissors when it's not clear who won. It was totally clear that I won, and he's just cheating!"

Toni started to say something, but noticed that Clarence was walking toward the stalemate, so she waited a beat while the other three continued arguing.

"How's it going?" Clarence asked Toni, though he could see for himself that it was not going well.

Toni didn't think that offering a reply was necessary.

"You want me to do something?" he asked.

Toni thought about it for a moment and then shook

her head. She turned to the three disputants, leveled a gaze that left no doubt who was in charge, and then cheerfully announced, "New game!" And she picked up the cones and rearranged them in a horseshoe to play RoShamBo Relay.

"Hey!" Carl shouted. But he sounded more off balance than angry. "But. . . ."

Marcus's whole demeanor toward Toni shifted in that moment, and he spoke to her in a tone of genuine respect, "Great idea. I'll count off people." And Marcus went around the circle designating people as either "ones" or "twos."

Clarence watched with open admiration. "Wow, you are amazing!" he said to Toni. "I hate to say it, but I couldn't have done it better myself." And he headed off to see how the others were doing.

By the afternoon recess, a few of the recess coaches were getting a little bored with the various Rock-Paper-Scissors games, and they started clamoring for new games.

"I can teach you how to play 'Wahl!'" Clarence offered.

"I'm up for it," volunteered Cassie, and she headed over to the group playing on the jungle gym. The kids were mixed in age, and Cassie's pigtailed second-grade friends were managing to keep up with some of the more rambunctious fourth-grade boys. Cassie figured they could use a distraction, but she wasn't convinced they'd be willing to leave the thrill of the structure.

Nevertheless, she tried to drum up some business, "You all want to learn a new game?"

Much to Cassie's surprise, the kids enthusiastically jumped at the chance. She had turned and was walking back toward Clarence when she felt one of the little girls, Caroline, take her hand. Clarence jumped right in to describing the set-up once they made their way back to him, "You're going to need everyone to circle up."

Cassie had just started to get the group in a circle when Clarence had an idea about how to convey the rules to Cassie. She was clearly sick of parroting back the instructions, and he wanted a way to show her rather than tell her. The first time he ever played Capture the Flag in heaven, the team captain had drawn the strategy for approaching the flag right in the middle of the air using his finger. He had thought it totally cool at the time. Now he couldn't imagine why he hadn't thought to do it before.

"Hold on," he exclaimed. "Check this out." And just as he had drawn the original playground map using his pointer finger, Clarence quickly drew out a picture of a person standing like a tree with her hands over head, only this time the misty cloud line that emanated from his finger just held its shape in midair.

"The way the game works is that one person puts their arms up over their head, hands touching, and then they lower their arms to point at someone across the circle, yelling 'Wah!'" Clarence continued drawing in the air, now showing three people, a new person raising her arms up over her head flanked by two others. "The person who is pointed at then raises his arms over his head and says 'Wah!' and then the two people on either side of her move their arms like they are karate-chopping her in the middle, though they don't really touch, while also saying 'Wah!'" The two figures in Clarence's sky drawing acted out their parts as instructed. "Then the person with her arms over head points at someone else, saying 'Wah!' and the whole thing repeats. When someone messes up—a person doesn't respond when pointed to, or makes the wrong gesture—he or she steps outside the circle and cheers the other folks on."

Cassie shook her head and laughed. She wasn't sure what was more improbable, Clarence's fingertip cloud sketching or the preposterous idea that her schoolmates might actually cooperate. "You're not going to believe it, but here's how it goes. . . ." Toni and Bryant jogged over to stand on either side of Zee so that they could demonstrate and sure enough, once they started playing, the game took off, with people giggling and yelling 'Wah!' in all sorts of unlikely and ridiculous ways. Cassie watched in amazement as her fellow students once again defied her expectations and were willing to be silly.

When it was down to four people, Cassie clapped and said, "Great job, everyone, I wasn't sure that was going to work." By this point, the yelling of 'Wah!' had captured a lot of people's attention and Mr. Unger, Mr. Street, and Mr. Rodrigues were all standing nearby.

Even Marcus had gotten into "Wah!" Almost everyone in school had noticed a transformation in him in the past couple of days. Bryant and Zee and Toni all thought it was the aftereffects of having been frozen by Clarence. Cassie wasn't so sure. But everyone agreed it was nothing short of miraculous.

"I have a game," Marcus announced in the lull. Everyone turned and looked at him, though Bryant, Toni, and Zee were a little concerned about the possibilities. "It's called Ninja Tag."

Toni looked over at Clarence and raised her eyebrows. "I know it," he said a little hesitantly. "It's a good game, though it's usually better for older kids." He stopped to consider it a little longer and then offered a qualified endorsement. "I suppose it's probably all right." His judgment was still in limbo, just like him.

Marcus looked around the group, suddenly seeming more self-conscious than usual. "Well, the way I remember it, you go around the circle and assume whatever pose you want."

Clarence was demonstrating some poses so that the four friends, at least, would know what they were supposed to do and be able to support Marcus's effort. Clarence froze in a karate stance and then modeled an Egyptian pharaoh, finally jumping into something reminiscent of a genie emerging from a bottle. They got the idea.

"And then," Marcus continued, "you go around in the circle and try to hit somebody else's hand."

Toni cringed a little; she had the sinking feeling that this could be dangerous.

Marcus noticed Toni's cringe and began to explain "Not really hard or anything. You know, you just sort of slap it." And he demonstrated by lightly slapping his own hand. Marcus was getting increasingly anxious about having stepped forward to do this now and feeling more than a little defensive.

"Anyhow, the person whose hand you're trying to slap can move it out of the way, but he has to stay frozen where he ends up, and the person who has tried to slap has to stay where he is. Once your hand is slapped, you put it behind your back, and you can't use it. You're out when both hands are slapped."

He stopped, unsure if he'd said everything he needed to say, but not sure what else the other kids needed to know. "Does that make sense?"

Zee wanted to be supportive, so he said, "How about if we try it, just a practice round to start, and we'll go real slow to make sure everyone gets it?"

Marcus seemed happy for the support. "Yeah, good idea. OK, everyone assume a warrior pose."

The four friends led the way by jumping into poses like the ones Clarence had modeled, and everyone else followed suit. Once everyone was set, they went around the circle, flailing slightly, albeit slowly, as they swung at one another's hands. Sarah Hechtmeyer managed to hit Zee's hand and then wouldn't stop apologizing.

When it came to Cassie's turn she asked, "Can I hit any hand, or just the person who's next after me?"

"Any hand you can reach," Marcus answered, and

Cassie sprung almost instantly like a cat across the circle hitting Kevin Sweeney's hand.

"Hey!" he exclaimed but then quit complaining almost immediately after Marcus shot him a look.

Cassie was now stuck in the middle of the circle, with both her hands over her head. Marcus made a high to low chopping move for her hands, and she swung her hands down and back, leaving her face exposed, which Marcus, meeting no resistance from her now-moved hands, managed to chop. Blood spurted out of Cassie's lip, which instantly swelled up, and Cassie slumped down to the ground.

Mr. Rodrigues was over immediately, with Mr. Street right behind him. Mr. Unger was a little less quick to respond and had a hard time making his way through the circle of kids who had instantly surrounded Cassie. "What's happened?" he demanded repeatedly, his voice rising in pitch as he pushed his way through.

Kevin Sweeney didn't miss a beat, "Marcus hit Cassie."

Clarence was in close enough to get a good look at Cassie's face, "Serious ninja lip," he diagnosed.

Marcus was crouched down right next to Cassie. "Cassie, I'm so sorry" he said, his voice quavering a little as he spoke the words.

Cassie's lip hurt, and she thought that maybe her front tooth was loose. At first she was incredibly mad at Marcus—he had swung way too hard. She had known she shouldn't trust him. But now he seemed so genuinely sorry, it was hard to believe he had done it on purpose.

She took a deep breath. "It's OK, Marcus. It's a cool game. I think I get it now—you don't want to put your hands near your face." Her eyes were watering, but she tried to smile. "I want a re-match."

Having gotten a close look at Cassie's lip herself, Toni turned to Clarence. "I'm totally cool with you using magic so she can avoid stitches." Toni wasn't squeamish, but she wasn't a big fan of blood.

"Huh?" Sarah Hechtmeyer had been standing just next to Clarence and Toni and was confused by the comment.

"Just something my grandmother used to say."

Zee was crouched down right next to Cassie, on the other side from Marcus, "You sure you're alright?" he asked. Cassie nodded.

Mr. Rodrigues helped Cassie get up. "Zee, you help get Cassie to the nurse's office," he directed.

By this point, Mr. Unger had finally pressed his way to the center of the circle, "Marcus, I'm very disappointed."

Marcus had felt terrible about hitting Cassie, but this caught him off-guard. He was used to being in trouble when he deserved it, but this felt completely unfair. "But it was an accident!"

"Enough!" Mr. Unger said firmly. "Follow me!" And he turned and began marching toward the office with Marcus in tow.

Cassie tried to wriggle loose from Zee to protest, but he held on tight. "C'mon, Cassie. Let me get you to the nurse's office, and then we'll go check on Marcus."

Zee, Clarence, and Cassie made their way to the nurse's office. Cassie's lip was cut deeply, and she was now quite certain that her front right tooth was seriously loose. Mrs. Davenport had been the school nurse at Magruder Elementary for twenty-four years and had seen every possible contusion, but this one made her shake her head. "Not good," she muttered as she left the three of them to get some bandages and supplies. "Definitely going to need some stitches."

Clarence looked from Cassie to Zee. Zee's eyes were wide with encouragement, and Clarence nodded at Cassie. She felt a warm buttery sensation on her lip, and gingerly rubbed her tongue over the area that had only moments ago been a gaping wound. Her lip was completely healed, her tooth securely in position.

The nurse returned with a tray of implements and set them down next to Cassie. "It feels a lot better," Cassie said meekly. Mrs. Davenport started to offer reassurances but then went completely quiet when she saw that indeed the cut on Cassie's lip had disappeared entirely.

"Well, I never," she finally managed and wandered back out of the room.

Quickly Clarence and Zee bustled Cassie out of the nurse's office and almost ran headlong into Bryant and Toni.

"Is she all right?" Bryant, who was squeamish, had to look away from the sight of Zee's bloody T-shirt.

"I'm fine. Mrs. Davenport's a little freaked out, but she'll probably recover quickly as well."

Toni peered more closely at Cassie's uninjured lip and gave Clarence a high five. "Right on!"

Clarence high-fived Toni back, but maintained a very serious face. "I have no idea what you're talking about," he deadpanned. "That's my story and I'm sticking to it."

Cassie turned to Bryant and Toni. "Did you have a chance to see what happened to Marcus?"

Bryant shook his head, "Nuh-uh. I heard Unger came down pretty hard on him, and I saw Mr. Street following them, but we didn't follow them all the way to the office. We could go check."

"Would you?" Cassie asked. "I feel really bad. He didn't mean to hit me. It just seems messed up that he should get in trouble when he's finally acting nice."

"Was it a madhouse on the playground after we left?" Zee was picturing a complete zoo.

"You know, I expected it to be out of control," Toni responded. "But a bunch of kids just started playing Switch until the teachers got it together to bring everyone back in to class. And Sarah and Kevin gathered all the cones."

And with that, Toni, Clarence, and Bryant headed to the office to try and help Marcus.

Mr. Unger was standing just outside the office door when the three arrived.

"May I help you?" he asked, though the question conveyed a clear level of annoyance and impatience, and absolutely no desire to help.

Bryant spoke first. "Cassie wanted us to let you know that it was an accident."

"That may well be," Mr. Unger said, clearly irritated. "But we can't have students hitting one another in the face. As you might imagine, it creates a serious liability issue."

Toni thought a different approach might be more effective. "Mr. Unger, you know I've never been a big fan of Marcus. But it would be seriously unfair if he got punished when he was finally trying to do something good. He was leading a game, and it was actually a kind of cool game, you know? And Cassie got hurt because she didn't quite get the game. Accidents are going to happen. That's all it was."

Mr. Unger spoke slowly. "Yes, Toni, I understand this. Marcus's mother is on her way in. I will take your perspective into consideration, but I do not think you fully appreciate the situation. I have a responsibility to ensure the safety of our students—to make sure that nothing happens to them."

And then Bryant, despite his own better judgment, heard himself saying, "But how are we going to learn anything if you make sure that nothing happens to us?"

Even Clarence winced at this bold statement. Toni grabbed Bryant's arm and thanking Mr. Unger for his time, turned immediately and walked away, pulling Bryant with her before he said anything else likely to get them in trouble.

"Dude, has anyone ever told you that being too smart can get you into a world of hurt?" she asked as she dragged him away.

"I didn't mean to . . . And I cannot believe that you, of all people, are giving me this lecture. You are the original Queen of not being afraid of grown-ups!" Bryant protested.

"There's a difference between not being afraid and talking back. And it's a difference, in my experience, that grown-ups take very seriously." Toni looked back, just to make sure that Unger hadn't decided to follow them and give Bryant detention. He hadn't. Mr. Unger was standing next to a very tall woman, with very tall hair, wearing high heels and a gray business suit. But even the height of her hair was less striking than the way she was animatedly talking on her cell phone while gesturing with her index finger for Mr. Unger to wait. And just in case Bryant and Toni had missed how rude she was being, there was Clarence, standing right next to the two of them, pretending to be on the phone and mocking the gestures of the woman.

"Check this out," Toni pulled Bryant over to the side of the hall so that they could watch Mr. Unger from behind one of the locker doors. "I bet that's Marcus's mom. What is Clarence doing?"

The two watched as the woman continued to talk on her phone and Clarence continued to imitate her. Mr. Unger tried to interrupt her a couple of times, but she waved the "just one more moment" finger, surprisingly close to his face. Both Toni and Bryant felt a little uncomfortable watching the scene; there was something profoundly disrespectful in the way the woman was interacting with Mr. Unger, and it was impossible to miss it with Clarence's simultaneous mimicry.

"Ouch," Bryant said, wincing a little. "Definitely Marcus's mom."

Mr. Unger opened the door to the office for the woman, who entered while continuing to talk on the phone. Clarence stood in the hall for a moment and then vaporized through the closed door to follow.

"Whoa," Bryant marveled. "I've never seen him do that."

"You don't think he's going to do anything bad, do you?" Toni worried aloud.

"Clarence? Distinctly possible," Bryant replied. "Likely even. Poor Mr. Unger, he's so busy trying to make sure nothing happens to us, and he doesn't have a clue."

"We should probably go back to class." There was nothing left to see, and Toni knew that they'd have a stronger alibi if they were in class. She didn't know what was going to happen, but she could feel a storm brewing. "The more distance between us and whatever happens next, the better."

Marcus stood up the moment he saw his mom walk into the office. "Mom!" He immediately began pleading his case, "It was an accident!"

But Mrs. Mackey continued talking on the phone. Seeing this, Marcus slumped back down into the chair looking hopeless and dejected.

Mr. Unger held the door open to his office and Mrs. Mackey walked right in, still talking. Mr. Unger gestured for Marcus to follow and Clarence slipped in behind. Mrs. Mackey and Marcus sat down in the chairs in front of Mr. Unger's desk, and Marcus slouched down in his seat. Mrs. Mackey made a big production of ending her call. "Charles," she spoke the name dramatically, drawing it out: "I absolutely have to get off the line now. I'm at my son's school. I'll call you back as soon as I can break away." And she hung up. "Well!" she said, turning toward her son. "What have we here?" she looked from face to face, blinking repeatedly as she took in the situation.

Mr. Unger absentmindedly straightened the papers on the desk in front of him. "Thank you for coming in, Mrs. Mackey. I realize that you're quite busy."

"Well, yes, of course. What's he done this time?" Mrs. Mackey turned to look at her son and then back again to the principal.

"Mrs. Mackey, as you are undoubtedly aware, I have a responsibility to the school community to keep everyone safe."

Mrs. Mackey's phone rang, the ring tone a series of bird calls that started off somewhat charming, but quickly grew tiresome. She reached immediately for it, holding up her hand to Mr. Unger signifying that he should put that thought on hold.

Marcus let out a loud, exasperated sigh as his mother answered, "Carol Mackey."

Mr. Unger tried to interject, but Mrs. Mackey continued, "Gary, I'm going to have to call you back." She looked up at Mr. Unger and gestured again for him to wait while she continued listening to Gary. "Absolutely. I don't think we can let him just walk away."

Mr. Unger stood up, "Mrs. Mackey!"

Mrs. Mackey held up her hand again, "Gary, I'll call you right back" and she ended the call, stuffing her cell phone into her purse. "Really, Mr. Unger. I was trying to get off."

"I would ask that you not get on, Mrs. Mackey."

And Marcus made a small, snorting noise of derision. "Not likely" he said under his breath.

"As I was saying, Mrs. Mackey, I have an obligation to the *entire* Magruder Elementary School community when it comes to safety."

"Did Marcus get in another fight? He is a rambunctious boy, you know, Mr. Unger."

Mrs. Mackey smiled in the direction of her son, but he refused to meet her gaze.

"Mrs. Mackey," Mr. Unger began again, but he was interrupted by the bird calls on Mrs. Mackey's cell phone once more. Mrs. Mackey started to reach for her purse, but Clarence simply could not bear it and he nodded in her direction, rendering her incapable of reaching for the phone. Mrs. Mackey spasmed slightly as her body refused to do the will of her brain, which was uncontrollably drawn to respond. Her arm jerked toward Mr. Unger's desk, where she grabbed onto a pencil and promptly snapped it in half. Marcus watched in fascination as his mother struggled. The tweeting of the phone continued for a few more seconds and then stopped. Mr. Unger was confused, but decided it best to forge ahead. "Thank you for not answering your phone, Mrs. Mackey."

Mrs. Mackey nodded meekly as Mr. Unger continued: "Marcus did not get into a fight today, but he did make some bad choices, and I am gravely concerned, as we have discussed before, that he is not getting the support at home that he needs.

"Marcus is a very strong young man, and I am not always sure he understands his own strength. He hit Cassie Murphy in the face today. . . " Marcus started to protest, but Mr. Unger continued. "It was by accident, but nonetheless, it was very a serious blow to the face, and she was quite a lucky young lady not to need stitches."

Mrs. Mackey tut-tutted Mr. Unger's assessment. "I'd hardly call Cassie Murphy lucky, losing both her parents in that car accident. I sold them their insurance policy, and it couldn't possibly have been enough to cover the costs of the funerals. I tried to convince them to buy more coverage. . . ."

Mr. Unger interrupted Mrs. Mackey sharply,

"Mrs. Mackey! I do not think this is appropriate in front of Marcus."

Mrs. Mackey looked from the principal to her son and then back again, "Well, of course, Marcus knows better than to go blabbing anything he hears from my work."

Marcus just shook his head in disbelief.

Mr. Unger took a deep breath. "I have asked you in, Mrs. Mackey, because I'd like to know how the three of us—you, Marcus and I—can work together to support Marcus in making better decisions."

Mrs. Mackey turned to her son. "Well, what do you have to say for yourself? I don't have time to be called into school every time you make a bad decision. What do you suggest?"

Marcus looked down at his hands. Clarence eased in closer to him and stood right behind him, trying to be a supportive presence. Marcus looked up and spoke directly to Mr. Unger: "I'm sorry about what happened to Cassie today. Up until that moment, today was one of the best days I've ever had at school." He stopped and looked expectantly at his mother.

"I don't think I made a bad decision, Mom. I think I tried something new that accidentally went wrong. I think there's a difference. I'd like the chance to try again." He started to say more but decided instead that he had said enough.

Mrs. Mackey looked genuinely surprised by her son's response. She turned to the principal. "What would you like me to do, Mr. Unger?"

Mr. Unger thought briefly and then had the odd sensation of speaking words that hadn't even crossed his mind. "Dr. Kardashian, the superintendent of schools, is coming in tomorrow to assess our school as a candidate for the ACE Award. I've asked the students, including Marcus, to make a presentation on their efforts to enhance recess. I'd like you to be in attendance for the presentation."

Mrs. Mackey started to reach for her phone. "Let me check my schedule." But again she found that her arms were uncooperative as she tried to reach for the device. She twitched and strained for a few moments, and then ultimately gave up, saying: "I'll make it work. What time?"

"The presentation is scheduled right before lunch. It would be best if you could arrive around 11:30." And with that Mr. Unger stood. "You can go back to class now, Marcus."

Marcus rose quickly and headed out of the office, not saying anything to his mother or Mr. Unger as he left.

Mrs. Mackey hesitated before reaching for her purse, uncertain that she would be able to actually lift it. Mr. Unger watched her and walked around to the front of his desk, bending down to pick up Mrs. Mackey's purse for her. As he handed her the purse, he said, "Marcus is not a bad child, Mrs. Mackey, but I worry that he could come to see himself as one." Mrs. Mackey accepted the purse with some hesitation. She looked at Mr. Unger in confusion, thanked him, and promptly left the office, her phone twittering with bird songs again as she walked out the door. Clarence couldn't help but hope that she might be a little hesitant about trying to answer it.

That afternoon, Mr. Street asked Toni, Zee, Cassie, and Bryant to stay after class. The four of them had been wondering about Clarence's whereabouts, and were a little surprised to see him when he appeared with Marcus, walking into the classroom just as Mr. Street picked up the stack of maps on his desk.

Mr. Street seemed like a less energetic version of his usual self as he explained that Mr. Unger had asked that the five of them make a presentation to the superintendent, Dr. Kardashian, who was scheduled to visit Magruder Elementary School the next day. Mr. Unger had asked that they walk Dr. Kardashian through some of the best recess maps and to talk a little about the recess coaches and the new games they'd been teaching the other students. Mr. Street explained that the presentation would be short, only five minutes, and that he was sure that they would do a great job.

Toni had the distinct sense that something was bothering Mr. Street. "Is there something wrong, Mr. Street?" she asked.

Mr. Street's look was a mix of bewilderment and fatigue. "I don't know, Toni. I've been truly impressed by the real change I've seen here at the school in just the past few days." His words didn't match the exhaustion in his voice.

"But . . . ?" Like Toni, Bryant sensed there was more to the story.

Mr. Street handed the papers to Zee. "It's nothing. You kids have done an amazing job. I sincerely hope you get the credit you deserve. That you can make it work."

Street turned and faced Marcus: "I don't think you intended to hurt Cassie, Marcus, but I don't think the group was ready for that game. It's been fascinating for me to watch what you've been doing because it never occurred to me before how much childhood has changed. I mean, when I was a kid, we played every day outside after school and on weekends and all summer long. But now, well, you all have had a very different experience of being a kid from what I can see. And I've been watching the five of you, and all I can think is 'Wow!' It's like you're having to recreate the idea of play for everyone here."

Street stopped and looked at all of them. He couldn't see Clarence agreeing vigorously. "Sorry, I don't mean to lay a heavy trip on you. I think what you're doing is great. And tomorrow is your chance to let the real powers-that-be know about it. I mean, wouldn't it be amazing if the superintendent heard about it and realized that every school should be doing this?"

Bryant thought he was following Street, but he had his doubts. "So what's the plan for tomorrow?"

"Right. The plan is that Dr. Kardashian arrives at 10. Mr. Unger and Mrs. Grumble are touring him around the school, and at 11:45, the five of you will show the superintendent the drawings in the cafeteria. Then we all head to the auditorium where the chorus sings him a song, and that's it." Mr. Street looked from face to face to see if it all made sense to the kids.

"So you want us to figure out what we're going to say?" Toni asked.

"Right," Mr. Street confirmed. "Just five minutes worth."

Zee was enormously relieved to hear again that it was only supposed to last five minutes.

"And why am I involved?" Marcus asked.

"Mr. Unger asked me to include you, Marcus. I gather your mother will be there at the presentation?"

Marcus shifted uncomfortably from one foot to the other.

"Besides," Toni added. "You're part of the whole thing now." She shook her head in resignation. "It's way easier with you on our team than against us."

Marcus looked over at Toni to confirm that she meant what she was saying in a kind way, and seeing that she did, he felt himself flush with embarrassment. He was used to attention, but not the positive kind.

The next morning classes flew by. Ms. Swanson seemed aggravated that the five students would be leaving early for the ACE Award site visit. She did not appreciate having anything prioritized over her instructional time with the students. The five students weren't overly excited about missing class, either. Marcus was worried his mother wouldn't show, Zee was worried about what they would say, Cassie was worried it wasn't going to work, and Toni and Bryant were just worried.

Bryant had spotted the superintendent arriving, and between classes Zee had seen him sitting in the library with Mr. Unger, Mrs. Grumble, and Clarence. Zee couldn't help but wonder what mischief Clarence was going to cause on this visit, though he had noticed that with the exception of fixing Cassie's busted lip, Clarence had been showing an increasing amount of restraint with regard to his use of otherworldly power.

At 11:30 precisely, the four friends and Marcus walked down to the cafeteria.

"I'm a little nervous about this," Marcus confessed.

"Man," Bryant said. "You never cease to amaze me. I mean, have you been like this all along?"

"Like what?" Marcus was confused by the question.

"Real." Toni replied in a tone that was altogether too straightforward and frank for an elementary school student.

"Huh?" Now Marcus was utterly befuddled. In his mind, he had always been acting this way. They were the ones who had changed.

"Dude," Cassie tried to explain, "You've been a jerk since third grade. And now you're just normal. What happened?"

Marcus just stood there and said nothing. Zee answered for him. "We asked him to play."

Marcus looked from Zee to the others, "Well, yeah, I guess that was it." Zee and Marcus steadfastly avoided making eye contact, but Marcus was completely blown away that first Cassie and now Zee had stood up for him.

There was a long silence as they walked through the empty halls, all considering both the simplicity and the complexity of Zee's answer. Cassie broke the quiet. "I'm nervous, too."

There was no one else in the cafeteria when they arrived, so the students sat down at one of the lunchroom tables to wait. Bryant always thought the cafeteria seemed icky with no one in it. It was clean, and the tables were lined up in an orderly manner, but it felt plastic-y to him—like a place where aliens would live and not a place where they would serve real food. He considered sharing this thought, but figured it better to keep it to himself.

"Where do you suppose Clarence is?" Bryant wondered if it was still "changing the subject" if you were only talking to yourself. He immediately remembered that Marcus didn't know about Clarence.

Marcus didn't say anything, but it was clear that he had heard.

Just as Bryant was about to offer up a lame explanation, there was a commotion at the cafeteria doors as the official entourage entered. Dr. Kardashian strode boldly at the front of the group, followed closely by Mr. Unger and Mrs. Grumble with her clipboard. Mr. Rodrigues and Mr. Street brought up the rear of the group, as far as they knew, though in actuality Clarence was behind him with his own clipboard.

Toni shook her head at the sight of Clarence with that crew.

Mr. Unger saw the five students waiting and cried out loudly: "Boys and girls! I am so pleased that you are here, and I am so very honored to be able to introduce you to our superintendent, Dr. Kardashian."

The five students stood up and walked toward Dr. Kardashian, each shaking his hand in turn. Dr. Kardashian towered over Mr. Unger and was significantly rounder than the others as well. His hair was in a surprising disarray, and Cassie could not help but notice that he also had a significant amount of hair growing from his ears.

Mr. Unger turned to Marcus and asked, "Is your mother here, Marcus?

Marcus shook his head. "I haven't seen her." His response was so quiet that it was nearly a whisper.

Dr. Kardashian smiled benevolently at them and then looked on expectantly, resting his hands on the significant outcropping of his belly.

Toni cleared her throat and began, "Dr. Kardashian, it's a great honor to have you here today, and we are all very excited to have you considering Magruder Elementary School for the ACE Award. Mr. Unger asked us to join you here today to talk about how we've been trying to make recess better, making sure that it's a positive part of the school day."

Dr. Kardashian shifted slightly with this comment and cleared his throat. Toni turned and looked at Mr. Street who nodded that she was doing well, and he then gestured to Bryant, who picked up where Toni left off.

"Over the past week, we've been working with all the students to imagine the best possible recess. We drew up a map and asked everyone to imagine and draw out the best possible design to encourage everyone to play and have fun."

Dr. Kardashian was looking increasingly uncomfortable and Bryant hesitated before continuing. Sensing this, Mr. Street interjected: "If I might add, Dr. Kardashian. I have been a teacher here for almost twenty years, and I have never seen anything like this. The student response and engagement has been extraordinary." Marcus walked toward Dr. Kardashian and handed him the maps.

"These are just some of the best ones," Marcus said quietly, his voice rising just barely above a whisper.

Dr. Kardashian was looking almost flustered as he leafed through the maps. "What's this?" he asked. "Are you not teaching penmanship anymore? I can hardly make out this student's name!"

Mr. Unger looked quite stricken by the indictment. "Well, of course, Dr. Kardashian. Every student is expected to master the state framework." And without thinking, he grabbed at the maps.

Dr. Kardashian shot Mr. Unger a look of extreme distaste, clearly taken aback at having had the papers snatched from his hands. He paused for a moment to settle himself and put his index finger to his lips for a moment, regaining his composure.

"Here's the thing, Unger. I'm afraid this simply won't do." Dr. Kardashian spoke very slowly as he looked at the five students. "Children, I appreciate your leadership in this arena, but unfortunately, the school board and I have been looking at opportunities for maximizing instructional time, and we have reached the conclusion that recess represents a significantly underutilized period of the day."

Cassie was listening intently, but couldn't quite make out what he was saying. Despite her nervousness, she spoke up. "I'm sorry, Dr. Kardashian, I don't understand."

Dr. Kardashian smiled patronizingly at Cassie. "School scheduling is a complex issue, dear. We are voting on the elimination of inter-period recreational activities this coming Friday."

Cassie still didn't quite understand until she heard Clarence explain in a hushed tone, "They're going to eliminate your recess."

The four who could hear Clarence all inhaled audibly.

"But what about when we're done with lunch?" Zee asked, a note of mild horror in his voice.

"You'll go back to class," Dr. Kardashian replied tersely.

"No breaks during the day?" Bryant sounded more incredulous than anything else.

"It will give your teachers more time to teach. And we'll encourage math games in class as a substitute." Dr. Kardashian was giving no ground.

"You have got to be kidding." Toni was indignant, and Dr. Kardashian had no immediate response. There was a long pause, and Bryant shot Toni a look as if to say, "*Now* who can't hold her tongue?"

When he did respond, Toni's indignation seemed to have pushed Dr. Kardashian past his limit, and he began gesturing wildly as he spoke. "Children, recess is the most concentrated period in the day for discipline problems. Not only does it take time to go outside and play, but when students come back to class, they bring the conflicts from the schoolyard back into the classroom with them, further cutting into instructional time. As superintendent, I am being held accountable by the district to a very clear set of measures. Recess simply stands between me and achieving these standards." Dr. Kardashian took a deep breath and returned his hands to their resting spot atop his tummy.

The whole group stood stock still, stunned by the superintendent's passionate outburst.

Marcus had said nothing until this point. "But what about everything we learn at recess?"

There was a pregnant pause before Dr. Kardashian shook his head. "It's student achievement I care about. If it can't be measured, it isn't really student achievement. Is it?"

Throughout this exchange, Cassie had been closely watching Clarence. She had noticed Clarence becoming increasingly agitated as Dr. Kardashian described the assorted negative outcomes of recess, but when he damned recess by saying the learning didn't matter if it couldn't be measured, she noticed Clarence's shoulders tighten, and she knew that some sort of magical pay-back was imminent. Without really meaning to, Cassie shouted out, "No!" briefly distracting Clarence, but also bringing herself to the attention of the whole group, who collectively turned and looked at her.

Cassie stammered, uncertain how to explain her outburst. "What I mean to say is no . . . not necessarily! Maybe you should talk to some of our teachers about how kids are in class now that recess is better?"

No one said anything, and Cassie was incredibly relieved when Mr. Rodrigues stepped forward. "You mentioned that the school board is voting on this on Friday?"

"Well, yes," Dr. Kardashian conceded, though it was obvious from his tone that he was now regretting having said it aloud.

Mr. Street jumped in to support Mr. Rodrigues.

"Perhaps the students could come and present their experiences in improving recess to the board. It would be good if the board could consider alternatives to the wholesale elimination of recess."

Mr. Unger had been quiet for as long as he could be by this point. "Well, Dr. Kardashian and I will discuss what's best for the district. Look at the time! We should proceed directly to the auditorium for a closing song from the chorus. And Mrs. Grumble will be assembling the Student Recycling Club!"

Dr. Kardashian patted Bryant on the head. "Excellent! I do so love recycling!"

Clarence looked imploringly at Bryant for permission to exact retribution. But even having had his head patted, Bryant felt compelled to shake his head at Clarence. Cassie had shot him a look that seemed to say she felt strongly that zapping the jerk was a bad idea, though for the life of him, Bryant could not imagine why.

Once outside on the playground, Clarence and the four friends watched as Marcus wandered off dejectedly.

"Where do you think he's going?" Toni asked.

"I wouldn't worry, he's most likely just going to terrorize some younger, smaller kid. He's bound to be experiencing some sort of withdrawal, having been so normal these last couple of days." Bryant still wasn't entirely convinced about the Marcus conversion.

"I don't know," Cassie wasn't sure she'd ever get used to defending Marcus, but it seemed to keep happening. "Maybe the person we've seen the last couple of days *is* the real Marcus."

The friends plopped down on the blacktop and slouched against the brick wall of the school. The sense of despair among the four of them was palpable.

"This is so completely unfair!" Bryant was not a whiner, but his tone was as close to a whine as it ever got.

"I can't believe they're going to eliminate recess." Zee basically expected grown-ups to do stupid things, but this did feel extreme.

Even Toni shook her head in disbelief. "It's like we don't matter at all, you know? If you were going to set out to make school a miserable place for kids, the first thing you'd do would be take away recess."

Cassie looked to Clarence, "What do we do now?" She sounded hopeless.

Clarence, by contrast, seemed positively energized. "Game on!" he declared, bouncing back and forth from his left foot to his right.

"Huh?" Toni looked at him like he was nuts. "What are you talking about? Didn't you hear him? They're voting to eliminate recess on Friday."

"Exactly," Clarence confirmed. "And it's only Tuesday. We have four whole days to save recess."

"You have a plan?" Cassie's tone was skeptical. She didn't want to get her hopes up again after the conversation with the superintendent. She couldn't tell if Clarence's bouncing around was hopeful or the final bit of evidence that he was crazy.

"We have a plan. We're going to make recess the most outstanding, off the hook, rocking good time Magruder Elementary has ever seen!" Clarence declared.

Toni shook her head. "Why do I have the feeling I'm going to regret this?"

Cassie had a strong sense of *déjà vu*. "Be careful what you wish for . . ."

Clarence's eyes were positively twinkling. "This is going to be great! You all are going to have the best recess ever!"

Bryant and Zee looked at each other and then back at Clarence.

"OK," Zee was in. "What's the plan?"

"We go big, or we go home." Clarence was looking directly at Cassie. "We don't quit. We've seen the enemy, and he's a stuffy dude with no imagination. The only advantage he has is that he's a grown-up. We keep fighting because it's worth it, and even if we lose, we figure out a way to keep fighting because it's that important. Are you in?"

Cassie stood slowly. The other three watched her, waiting to see which way she would go. "I don't think we have a choice," she spoke quietly.

No one was quite sure what she meant—was there no choice about fighting or no choice about giving in? After a few seconds of standing there, Cassie realized that the others didn't get it. "Let's do this!" she said. "Let's show Dr. Kardashian what we're made of!"

The other three leapt to their feet and started giving one another high fives, joining Clarence in jumping around. In the moment it felt as if they were not only able to change recess, but that they had been born to change recess. It was exhilarating. Anything was possible.

The other kids out for lunch recess saw the four friends celebrating, and Aaron, Sarah, Carl, and Mary all came over to see what was up.

"Are we playing RoShamBo Rockstar?" Sarah asked.

Zee gave Sarah a high five. "We're going to play RoShamBo Rockstar and so much more, Sarah! It's going to be amazing!"

In no time flat, Clarence and the kids were teaching different games all over the schoolyard. Cassie was running a game called Giants, Wizards, and Elves in which the kids divided into two teams who secretly decided among themselves if they were going to be Giants, Wizards, or Elves. The two teams would meet at the halfway mark and then, at the count of three, would show the other team what they had chosen: the Giants stretching big and tall and beating the Wizards; the Wizards wiggling magic fingers and beating the Elves; and the Elves dancing around with their hands cupping their ears (simulating big Elf ears), beating the Giants. Members of the losing team, upon seeing the winning team show their character, would try and run back as fast they could to their home base before being tagged by members of the winning team. The losing team members who were tagged then became members of the winning team and they would repeat.

Bryant was in charge of getting Four Square going. Clarence drew out a cloud-image visual of the four squares marked A, B, C, and D, which Bryant reproduced on the blacktop using chalk. Clarence then diagrammed the game for Bryant to watch briefly. This time, Clarence's drawing had exuberant animated stick figures, one in each of the squares. The stick figure in square A began the play by dropping the ball in its square and then hit it into a different square. The four stick figures took turns hitting the balls into other squares after allowing it to bounce once in their own squares. Once the stick figure in the C square knocked it out of bounds, all the stick figures gave each other high fives, the stick figure in the D square filled in the now-vacant C square, the stick figure waiting in line jumped into the D square, and the game continued. The game moved quickly, but Bryant realized somewhat abruptly that he had been watching the whole sky visual go down with his mouth slightly agape. It was mesmerizing.

In the midst of the finger-mist visual demo, Kevin Sweeney tapped Bryant on the shoulder and said, "Dude, are we going to play this game or what?" Bryant shook himself and did his best to explain the game to the students around him who had all been waiting patiently.

Cassie kept an eye on Clarence and thought she noticed him nodding toward students when there seemed to be a conflict brewing, but she couldn't be quite sure. There would be a slight hesitation, and then both students would whip out their Rock-Paper-Scissors to decide. Cassie suspected Clarence had a hand in it, but if he did, it was subtle, not his usual heavy-handed freeze 'em style.

Zee and Toni had the Rock-Paper-Scissors games going on all over the place when the bell rang to end lunch recess. Seven different kids high-fived Bryant as they headed back to class. Carl came up to Cassie, "Man, that was the best recess ever!"

Clarence was beaming. The four friends came together before going back into class. They were tired but grinning from ear to ear.

"OK," Cassie said to Clarence. "I see how it's possible that we might actually be able to make recess better. But explain to me how this is going to make any difference with the school board?"

"Look, Dr. Kardashian had a point. When nobody pays attention to recess, a lot of bad things happen. I heard him saying that they were considering eliminating recess because that's when all the fights happen. And because when kids have a bad recess, it makes it hard for teachers to teach." Clarence looked from face to face to see if they were following him.

"We need to show Dr. Kardashian that paying attention to recess can reverse the problems. He needs to see that not only can we help stop the fights and make sure that kids come back to class ready to learn but also that a great recess contributes to learning too. I mean, even today, you all were amazing. You all did it! I only used magic once out there, and that was to briefly take away Kevin Sweeney's power of speech when he was about to call Sarah a bad name."

"You didn't make the students do Rock-Paper-Scissors?" Cassie had a hard time believing that Clarence wasn't responsible for more than that.

"Not once." Clarence crossed his heart with his index finger.

"You can't cross your heart and hope to die," Bryant pointed out. "You're already dead."

Clarence looked slightly hurt. "It's the principle of the thing," he insisted. "Every kid deserves to be as amazing as you all were out on the yard today. I think every kid has it in him. Kids just need to be given the chance to express it. You know? Like Marcus. He's been great. If we can show Dr. Kardashian and the school board how play helps students be better people at school, we're golden."

"We've got three more days. I suppose we've got nothing to lose," Zee was trying to manage his own expectations. Clarence seemed so sure this would work, but it was still hard to imagine Dr. Kardashian changing his mind because a few kids were having more fun at recess.

"Hey," Toni interrupted, "speaking of Marcus. Did any of you see him during recess?"

They all shook their heads, and Clarence looked concerned.

"Your Spidey sense telling you something is wrong?" Bryant asked.

"You all better get back to class, I'm going to go find Marcus." And with that, Clarence was gone.

larence caught up with Marcus just as he was entering his mother's office building. Marcus had been running most of the way there, past the Grove and past his house. He had considered stopping at both places, but continued on, fueled by his frustration. He wasn't quite sure who he was maddest at—his mom, Dr. Kardashian, or himself. But now that he had arrived in the big, downtown office, he was feeling smaller and more uncertain than ever. He'd only ever been there before on the weekends with his mom, stopping by to pick up papers when the building was otherwise empty. Filled with working people bustling around everywhere, it felt a lot more intimidating.

Marcus headed through the atrium and into the reception area that his mother shared with the other insurance brokers. The receptionist looked up expectantly at Marcus as he approached her. Unbeknownst to either of them, Clarence was following right behind him.

"You're here to see . . . ?" and her voice trailed off as she waited for Marcus to explain whose son he was.

"Carol Mackey," Marcus said, now thoroughly regretting his rash decision to come. "She's my mom." He had heard the assumption in her voice and felt compelled to explain.

The receptionist turned away from Marcus and pushed some buttons on her console. "Sorry to interrupt, Carol. Your son's here." The receptionist paused. "No, *here* here. In the reception area." She paused again. "All right, I'll send him over."

The receptionist looked back up at Marcus. "She's around the corner in the fourth office. She says you should go on over." And she turned her attention back to her computer.

Marcus briefly considered simply bolting. He didn't have to go in there. He didn't have to do anything. He could just take off, and no one could stop him. He thought some more about how his mother hadn't even bothered to show up at school as Mr. Unger had asked her to; how he had felt completely humiliated in front of the others. Marcus was pretty sure it was all his fault that now they were going to lose recess. He was certain that if his mom had just shown up today as she had said she was going to, everything would have turned out differently. Marcus felt himself getting angry all over again and marched around the corner to her office.

Clarence followed closely as Marcus stormed toward his mother's work space where they found her on the phone. Actually, she seemed to be on two phones, both her office line and her cell phone, and she was alternating speaking into one and then the other.

Marcus sighed audibly when he saw her. His mother's office was both cheerful and chaotic, with pictures that Marcus had drawn many years before hanging on the walls and a number of photos of him on the desk, interspersed with papers scattered about and file folders stacked up on the floor alongside her desk.

Mrs. Mackey gave her son an exasperated look as he entered her office. "John," she said into the landline, "I have a client here in the office. I'll call you back; OK?" And then turning her attention back to her cell: "Jerry? You got what you need? Great. I'll check back in tomorrow. Thanks."

She dramatically turned the ringer on her cell phone to "off" and placed it on the desk facedown. Clarence was disappointed to see that her brief inability to answer the cell hadn't had any lasting effects, but he was relieved that she was at least turning off the annoying bird call ringtone.

"May I ask what you're doing here when you should be in school?" Mrs. Mackey was clearly not pleased.

Marcus's tone was sullen in response, "You were supposed to be there."

"Be where?" Mrs. Mackey demanded, and just as soon as she had said it, she remembered and began apologizing all over herself. "Oh, shoot! Oh, Marcus, I'm so sorry! I never put it in my calendar, and the Keiths had a claim. Oh! That's so frustrating." Clarence was struck that Mrs. Mackey seemed genuinely sorry that she had disappointed Marcus.

Marcus didn't say anything.

"How did it go?" Her tone was softer than Clarence had heard it be before, and she was looking at Marcus directly. Marcus, meanwhile, was being tossed about by his own emotions in ways he didn't understand, and he felt his face flush and his throat catch as he tried to speak. Before he knew it, he was doing something he hadn't allowed himself to do in years: he was crying. Marcus slumped down into the chair across from his mother's desk and put his head in his hands.

"It was awful, Mom. Dr. Kardashian—the super-intendent—was so mean. I was supposed to show him our plans for making the playground better, but I forgot what to say. And you weren't there!" He was really crying now, and his mom rolled her office chair around closer to give him a hug.

"Oh, honey, I'm so sorry." Clarence noticed Mrs. Mackey's cell phone moving itself across the desk as it vibrated in lieu of ringing, and he worried briefly that she was going to stop hugging Marcus and let go to answer it. Clarence considered taking matters into his own hands and preventing her from answering, but waited instead. He was pleased with both himself and with her, when she saw the phone and disregarded it.

"How could you have forgotten to come today, Mom? I was so embarrassed." Marcus was still crying, and it felt so good to have her hug him, but he was mad, too.

Mrs. Mackey pulled back from Marcus so that she could look into his eyes. "Marcus, I know it's hard sometimes. I know that you would like more of my attention. But I'm just barely making enough to cover our bills. I felt terrible yesterday in the principal's office. I felt like he was judging me as a parent, and it made me so mad. He has no right. He has no idea what it's like to be a single mom. And I worry that I can't give you everything you need. I try to be mother and father to you all at once, and sometimes I feel as if I'm not succeeding at anything. But I know this: I love you with all my heart. And while I'm not perfect, no one could love you more."

Marcus wiped his eyes and his nose with his sleeve. "Can we go home now, Mom?"

Mrs. Mackey leaned back in toward her son and hugged him again. "I have to make two more phone calls, and then we can go."

Marcus looked suspicious. "*Really* two calls?" he asked.

"I promise," she said, rolling her chair back around the desk and grabbing a tissue for her son. "Here," she said, handing it to him. "Blow your nose. And can you promise me you won't leave school in the middle of the day again?" Her tone was scolding, but still affectionate.

Clarence leaned against the office wall and marveled at how seriously he had misjudged Mrs. Mackey. Perhaps he should reconsider some of the other adults he'd met here as well. The kids were going to need some additional supporters, and Mrs. Mackey's transformation suggested that there might be some other unlikely allies who could be called upon in taking on the school board.

Cassie never thought she'd say it, but she was actually pleased to see Marcus on Tuesday morning.

"Hey," she said as he crossed the street in front of the school.

"Hey," he said back. He was genuinely surprised that she was speaking with him. Marcus had pretty much decided that the other kids were going to hate him forever after the presentation to the superintendent the day before.

There was an uncomfortable silence between them as they walked up the school steps, and then they both started to talk at the same time.

"You first," Marcus insisted.

"I was just going to say that this is a big week. I mean, if we're going to save recess. And well, we were all hoping that you'd still be involved in getting the other kids playing at recess. It kind of feels like our only hope in saving it is if we can make it really awesome, you know?" Cassie felt incredibly stupid and self-conscious saying all this to Marcus. She didn't actually know if he cared at all. It seemed completely likely to her that he had left school so abruptly the day before because he thought they were a bunch of losers and the cause was hopeless.

Marcus waited to make sure she was done. "Yeah,

I'd like that," he said, completely disarming her. "I'm sorry if I blew it yesterday during the presentation with Dr. Kardashian." He thought about explaining more but decided to leave it at that.

"Huh?" Cassie had no idea what he was talking about. "You? I was worried I blew it—you seemed fine. Besides, it seemed as if he had made up his mind about recess before any of us said anything."

Marcus felt a huge wave of relief wash over him. Maybe the other kids weren't mad at him after all. "Cool. I'll meet you out at recess then." And he headed quickly into the building.

Cassie stood on the school steps for a few moments longer, marveling at how dramatically things could change in just a week. Hadn't she just been hiding from this guy, terrified that he was going to pound her into a pulp? And now he seemed like a totally normal kid . . . better than average even. She shook her head at just how weird the whole thing was.

Toni walked up next to Cassie as she stood there thinking about it all.

"It's weird, huh?" Toni seemed to be reading Cassie's mind, but nothing surprised Cassie anymore.

"It really is," Cassie agreed. It was hard to make sense of it all, but Cassie knew she was lucky to have a friend like Toni. She also knew they were pushing their luck missing as much class as they had been recently. "C'mon, we're going to be late for homeroom. We can't afford to make Ms. Swanson mad at us."

It was hard to take class seriously with all the craziness of late—an angel, Marcus's transformation, the threat of losing recess—but skipping class didn't seem like a choice, so they entered the building and headed to first period. Whatever was going to happen, was going to happen.

Clarence showed up right before the day's first recess got started. The weather was getting chillier with every passing day, and students were pulling on sweatshirts and hats as they were walking and running out onto the yard. Kids were jumping into games, continuing some from the day before, calling out what spot they had been in and the score.

Clarence came up behind Toni as she was donning her blue puffy jacket and looking around the schoolyard to figure out where the others were and where she should start.

"Walk with me," Clarence said, steering Toni out to the farthest point in the schoolyard away from the building.

They passed a couple of Four Square games that were already happening on the lines left out from the day before. A few kids had brought in red rubber balls, and Aaron had a football and was passing it around with Kevin.

"That could go terribly wrong," Clarence said as they walked by Aaron and Kevin. "They think they know the rules to football, but they don't. That almost always ends up going bad. Always better to start with a game that teaches the basics first, you know?"

"Hey, Aaron," Toni called out.

"Hey," Aaron was still surprised that Toni knew his name, let alone that she might actually talk to him.

"When more kids get out here, do you think you could help get a big game of Giants, Wizards, and Elves going?" Toni looked at him hopefully.

Aaron's look shifted from surprise to pride: "Uh, yeah, sure. I could do that." He seemed genuinely pleased to have been singled out.

"I can help, too," Kevin volunteered, clearly desperate to get in on the attention.

Toni obliged. "Great, thanks. That would be awesome." And she resumed walking with Clarence.

"You're very good at that, you know?" Clarence was amused; Toni was a natural.

She kept walking and dismissed his complement with a "pfft" noise. "What do you think our chances are?" she asked.

Clarence thought for a few moments before answering. "Honestly, I'd say you have a 5 percent chance of saving recess. One in twenty. Not terrible, but the odds are stacked against you. I'm afraid I was a little late in coming to help."

"Why *did* you show up?" Toni had wanted to ask before but hadn't really had the chance.

"It was really just like we talked about. I met Cassie

playing Capture the Flag, and then I heard her say that she wished you all didn't even have recess. I couldn't just let a comment like that go unanswered."

Toni wasn't entirely convinced. "Yeah, yeah, I know all that, but there's part of the story you're not telling. Like why you're in limbo. What'd you do? How does hanging out with us help you?"

Clarence thought about how to respond for a moment. "It's not what you're thinking. It's not like I was 'assigned' to you all and that if I do a good job I get my wings." He thought some more. "It's more like life, you know? I've figured out enough to know that the folks in charge are watching me to see if I get it. To see if I really understand who I am, and if I can use the gifts I have to do the right thing. Does that make any sense?"

Toni shook her head no.

"Look, when I was alive, I was a basically a decent person. I didn't hurt anybody or do anything really, really bad, but I didn't trust that many people either. People weren't exactly afraid of me, but I wasn't too close with that many people, you know?"

This she understood. "Does this have to do with how you died?" she figured if she was going to ask some questions, she might as well ask them all.

"No, not really. Here's the thing. Now that I'm dead, I get that how we spend our time ends up being how we live our whole lives. I know it sounds obvious, but when I was alive, I never felt like there was this big pressure to let people in because, well, I figured there'd be time. But then, all of a sudden, there *wasn't* any more time; there was just the time I had had. And now I kinda wish that I'd let people in a little closer. That's all."

"And you think *I* should let people in more?" It was pretty clear to Toni that Clarence was answering the questions because he thought his lessons applied to her. Grown-ups were always trying to do stuff like this and pass it off as a coincidence.

"You have some good friends in Zee and Cassie and Bryant. They really care about you, and you can trust them."

The two of them walked the rest of the way across the field in silence. When they got to the fence, Toni saw that there was a bag of equipment. "Was that there the whole time?" She knew it was dumb to ask, but she couldn't help herself.

"Looks like it," Clarence deadpanned.

Toni bent over and picked up the bag. "Cones and a red rubber ball. Did you have something in mind?"

"You want to try teaching everyone Gaga Ball?" Clarence clearly had a plan. "It's risky, sort of a mellow version of dodgeball. I mean, if they're going to eliminate recess altogether, you might as well go out with a bang."

Toni shrugged: "Why not? How about you explain it to me as we walk back, and then I'll get it going without the whole ventriloquist's dummy act?"

"Let me show you instead" Clarence replied, and drawing with his index finger, he illustrated a big square area marked out by four cones in the corner.

He drew a bunch of stick figures in the square, one holding a ball. The stick figure dropped the ball and called out, "Ga-ga Ball!"

Toni looked around—it was so loud. "Can other people hear that?" she asked.

Clarence shook his head and continued drawing. All the other stick figures began moving around the square, using the ends of their stick arms to knock the ball toward the other stick figures. When a stick figure would get hit below where the stick knee would be, the figure would go outside the box and stand along the boundary helping to keep the ball in play. There was no catching or throwing—the stick figures did not have hands—and Toni assumed that the same rules applied for humans. She had enough to go on.

"How do you know so many games?" Toni still had a bunch of questions she'd been meaning to ask, and she had the sense that her chance to ask them was running out. "I don't want to sound like Bryant, but it's not just because you're dead, right?"

Clarence had to laugh at that. "No, I can assure you there are lots of dead people who don't know any games like these. When I was a kid I was always outside. We'd hang out with lots of kids, and the older kids taught us all sorts of games. They taught us how to pick teams and how to even the teams out if they were uneven. No one ever said it out loud, but they taught us that everyone needed to be having some fun, or we wouldn't have enough people for a game. People would just quit, you know?"

"So, you mean other kids taught you all these games?" Toni was surprised by this. She had assumed that he must have been a teacher or a camp counselor or a coach or something.

They were almost back to the blacktop now. Zee and Bryant came walking up to meet them. Zee was breathless. "Man, this is a lot of work, Clarence."

"But it's going well," Bryant seemed unusually amped up, even for Bryant. "We've got at least seven different games going. You should have seen Aaron and Kevin with Giants, Wizards, and Elves. They said you asked them to, Toni. It was apparently a big deal." Bryant was enjoying teasing Toni just a little.

Toni refused to take the bait. "That's good. Clarence thought we should distract them from the football game for a while."

"It's true. You all may be ready for football by the end of the week, but it can be hard to get a real game going. Too much posturing and showing off and not enough playing." Clarence had once been one of those boys posturing and showing off, and he felt just the slightest bit hypocritical calling this generation out.

"Makes sense," Zee could relate as well. He scanned the field around him and smiled broadly as he looked out across the old baseball field. "Cassie and Marcus have an insane game of Kickball happening. I swear it looks like half the school is playing."

"There's still a group of third graders hanging out by the school who look like they need something to do,"

Bryant pointed out. "It's a mix of boys and girls and they seem cooperative enough, just kind of clueless."

"Clarence just taught me a new game," Toni figured that she might as well give it a shot. "It's called Gaga Ball. Come help me, you two," she knew she sounded a little forced, but she couldn't figure out a better way to say it. "I need you." Having said it, she quickly started toward the group of kids hanging out next to the building.

Bryant and Zee stared at one another, a little taken aback by Toni's declaration. Halfway to the building, she turned to check on their whereabouts and seeing that they were still standing where she had left them, she gestured for them to follow, calling out: "C'mon, didn't you hear me? I need your help."

"Uh, OK," Bryant and Zee mumbled simultaneously. Bryant turned to Clarence.

"What'd you do?"

"Not me," Clarence clarified. "I think it must be something you guys did."

Zee and Bryant looked back at each other skeptically and then dutifully trotted after Toni to help.

On Tuesday afternoon the phone in Mr. Street's art room rang. Mr. Street answered the call and then walked over to the table where Bryant was working on a collage of brightly colored tissue paper cutouts.

"That was Ms. Houghton in the office," Mr. Street explained to the boys. "She asked me to send you down, Bryant."

Zee and Bryant exchanged a look.

"Am I in trouble?" Bryant asked. It wasn't unusual for Bryant to be in trouble, but it was odd that he couldn't figure out what he had actually done. Generally he was pretty aware of his transgressions.

"She didn't say so." Mr. Street shrugged slightly. He paused and thought about it for a moment. "She did sound a bit strange, though, now that you mention it."

Zee looked at Bryant and mouthed, "Clarence."

Bryant straightened up his things and headed to

the office. When he arrived, sure enough, Clarence was standing just outside the door.

"Sorry," Clarence seemed rushed. "Mrs. Grumble is on her way here. She's on her efficiency inspection, and the office is next."

Bryant didn't know what Clarence was getting at. "And?" He could tell Clarence wanted him to do something, but he needed more information.

"The PA room! She's gunning for the mimeograph machine! We've got to stop her. It's a perfectly good machine, and I thought you said that if the machine goes, so does Ms. Houghton!"

Bryant was surprised to see that Clarence was so worked up over the old mimeograph machine. "Well, I know she *said* that, but I don't think she'd really quit. Do you?" Bryant wasn't quite sure what he could do in any case. "Did you make her call Mr. Street and ask for me?" Bryant was still a little fuzzy on what was going on.

"Yes, of course it was me. Go on in. Here comes Mrs. Grumble." And he pushed Bryant toward the office door.

Indeed, Mrs. Grumble was bearing down fast on the office, intently studying her clipboard and scribbling notes furiously. Bryant opened the office door for her just in time.

"Why, thank you, Bryant." Mrs. Grumble only looked up long enough to confirm that it was Bryant holding open the door, and then she hurried through.

Bryant and Clarence followed in her wake. Ms. Houghton looked up from her desk and looked immediately exasperated at the sight. It was clear that she was less than thrilled to see Mrs. Grumble.

Ms. Houghton greeted Bryant with a tone of deep frustration. "I'll be right with you, Bryant. Have a seat for a moment while I attend to Mrs. Grumble's needs."

"Oh, no. Not necessary. I'm just doing my efficiency evaluation," Mrs. Grumble said, her voice unnaturally high and perky.

Ms. Houghton responded by sounding even more inconvenienced. "Oh, no, Mrs. Grumble. I'm happy to show you around." And she stood abruptly from behind her desk and moved quickly to follow Mrs. Grumble as she moved around the office making notes.

"What exactly are you writing down, Erma?" Ms. Houghton was unsuccessfully trying to look over Mrs. Grumble's shoulder to read. Standing next to one another, the contrast between the two women was quite striking. Ms. Houghton was the shorter of the two, thin and wiry. Mrs. Grumble was both taller—almost a whole head taller—and significantly broader across the shoulders and hips. Mrs. Grumble's starched white uniform gave her the appearance of a rather solid wall, while the light brown cashmere sweater that Ms. Houghton wore, especially as she was trying to dart around either side of Mrs. Grumble, made her seem more like a little brown dog. Mrs. Grumble, meanwhile, was shifting her hips back and forth, working hard to ensure that Ms. Houghton couldn't see her clipboard.

Bryant watched the whole thing unfolding in horror. It seemed possible that they might actually start shoving one another. He turned to Clarence. "Should I do something?" It was clear to Bryant that he could have an extended conversation with Clarence—neither Ms. Houghton nor Mrs. Grumble was paying any attention to him whatsoever.

The two women headed around the corner in the direction of the PA room. "I think you should follow them," Clarence suggested.

"*Really?*" Bryant thought that sounded like a terrible idea.

Clarence looked at him sideways. "Why do you *say* it like that?"

"Like what?" Bryant had no idea what Clarence was talking about.

"*Really?*"

Bryant thought that maybe Clarence was doubting the sincerity of his question. "Really?"

"No, that's the word. You say *really* just like my brother used to say it."

"Oh." Bryant didn't know anything about Clarence's brother, and he didn't want to say *really* again.

Clarence looked quizzically at Bryant for another moment and then seemed to remember the task at hand. "You should check on them," Clarence instructed again, and Bryant jumped up to follow

Ms. Houghton and Mrs. Grumble around to the PA room.

When Bryant came around the corner, Ms. Houghton was the picture of impatience; her hands on her hips, holding the door open with her sensibly-heeled black shoe, as Mrs. Grumble stood just inside making notes on her clipboard.

Mrs. Grumble was talking loudly to herself inside the room. "Honestly! This is all just too much! All these wires! And this machine!" She was writing furiously, and while Clarence knew it was only a temporary fix, he nodded in her direction, just to make her stop.

There was sudden quiet. Ms. Houghton looked around to see why Mrs. Grumble had stopped exclaiming.

"Well, that's strange," Mrs. Grumble commented quietly to herself.

"For heaven's sake, Erma, what's happened now?" Ms. Houghton thought Erma Grumble was a royal pain.

"Well, it's really quite strange," Mrs. Grumble repeated, sounding more than a little unnerved.

Bryant and Ms. Houghton waited for Mrs. Grumble to explain, but she said nothing for a good long while, rifling through the papers on her clipboard instead.

"Erma?" Ms. Houghton prompted her again.

Mrs. Grumble seemed uneasy answering, and she responded slowly, piecing the words together as she spoke. "Well, it seems my pen isn't working." She paused. "And now all my notes are gone."

"Oh, Erma, I'm so sorry." Ms. Houghton could barely disguise the elation in her voice.

Ms. Houghton's tone did not escape Mrs. Grumble, who shot her a dark look and then turned and marched directly out of the PA room and straight out of the office.

Ms. Houghton looked quite pleased, and when Bryant gave her a high five, she didn't miss a beat.

The bell for recess rang.

"Ask her if she wants to come see all the stuff happening at recess," Clarence coached.

Bryant looked skeptically at Clarence and then turned to Ms. Houghton. "Ms. Houghton, we've been getting a lot of different games going at recess and well, I was wondering if you might want to come check it out."

Ms. Houghton looked at Bryant seriously. "Do you have Four Square?"

Bryant was puzzled. "We do," he answered, but it was almost more of a question the way he said it.

Ms. Houghton could tell that Bryant was confused. "I used to be the Four Square champion when I was in school," she explained.

Bryant had a hard time trying to disguise his complete surprise. "So you'll come?" he asked.

"Let's go!" Ms. Houghton was moving quickly now. She walked around to the back of her desk and got her sneakers out of the bottom drawer. "Hold on while I change my shoes," she instructed, quickly exchanging her sensible heels for a pair of spiffy black-and-purple New Balance shoes. Thirty seconds later, she was heading out of the office toward the playground, moving so fast that she left Bryant and Clarence in her dust.

Bryant stared at Clarence. "Wow, I had no idea. . . ."

Clarence didn't seemed surprised at all. "Makes sense to me. She was a kid once, right? So was Mrs. Grumble."

Bryant wasn't totally convinced. "I guess so."

"One word of advice, Bryant. Stay clear of Ms. Houghton when she's playing Four Square. I have no doubt she's fierce." Clarence was laughing as he said this, but Bryant knew he was right.

By recess, four of the school staff had joined the action on the playground, all playing side by side with the kids: Mr. Street, Ms. Swanson, Mr. Rodrigues, and Ms. Houghton. As Clarence had predicted, Ms. Houghton was a force on the Four Square court, and the kids were lining up to take her on as soon as recess began.

Marcus was overseeing the Four Square game, and he had Ms. Houghton start out in the A square to serve. He figured she was going to work her way there in no time anyhow, so it made sense to just go ahead and start her there and let the challengers line up. Ms. Houghton suspected that a good number of the students were hoping to eke out some sort of revenge since she ran detention, but the truth was that they were almost entirely inspired by her Four Square prowess.

The buzz about Ms. Houghton's Four Square skills wasn't limited to the students; it was all the talk in the teacher's lounge as well. Mr. Street and Ms. Swanson had come out to recess both to watch Ms. Houghton and also to get a better look at the playground for themselves. In just a few days, they had noticed a significant change in almost all of their students. They were coming to class in a much better mood and were involved in far fewer arguments. Ms. Swanson had witnessed two students disagreeing about who had been first in line, when they suddenly stop arguing, and quickly resolved the dispute with Rock-Paper-Scissors. Mr. Street was just generally impressed by the level of consideration that he saw students showing one another. In art class, the students' comments had shifted from "What's that supposed to be?" to "I really like the way you've drawn the shadow here" in only a few days' time.

Prompted by Clarence, Zee walked over to Mr. Street and Ms. Swanson, "I'm going to start a game of wall ball," he said. "Would you two like to play?"

Ms. Swanson looked over at Mr. Street to see if he was up for it. "You got game?" Zee was shocked to hear his homeroom teacher talking smack. The two followed Zee to the wall by the cafeteria door. There, lines of cones created a box against the wall about ten feet long and six feet wide.

"Getting these two to play might get some of the shy kids to join in too," Clarence explained. "The key is getting the grown-ups to play without having them control the game. You know?"

Zee wasn't exactly sure what he meant, but he was willing to give it a shot.

"You remember the rules?" Clarence asked. Zee nodded.

"Ms. Swanson, Mr. Street, why don't the two of you start?" Zee bounced the ball to Ms. Swanson. "Ms. Swanson, you'll start by serving. The game starts when you serve the ball toward the wall. It has to bounce one time before reaching the wall, and the player receiving the ball has to let it bounce once before hitting it back. You can then return it, Mr. Street, by bouncing it once off the ground before hitting the wall. OK?"

Mr. Street was ready. "Got it! I think we used to play this when I was a kid, but we used a small, pink ball."

Zee continued, "You keep playing until the ball bounces outside the cones or it hits the wall before bouncing off the ground or if the ball bounces twice before hitting the wall."

"And you *have* to let it bounce off the ground?" Ms. Swanson asked. Clarence suspected she was sandbagging, pretending to know less than she really did.

"Right," Zee confirmed. "Go ahead and start. It'll make sense once you get going."

The two teachers started playing, and immediately a long line of students formed—almost all of Ms. Swanson's homeroom to be precise—clamoring to get in the game.

"Line up here, behind where they're playing," Zee instructed the waiting students. "As soon as one of them gets out, they'll go to the back of the cheering line, and the player who's left will serve it up to start the next game."

Mr. Street and Ms. Swanson were playing and laughing for an extended point before Mr. Street got Ms. Swanson out on a little dinky hit against the wall.

"High five and good game," Clarence coached Zee.

Zee high fived Ms. Swanson and said "Good try," which immediately prompted Mr. Street to do the same.

"Who's up against Mr. Street?" Zee was surprised to see Mary Chen standing at the very front of the line. She smiled shyly and raised her hand.

"Right on, Mary!" Zee couldn't help but laugh. It was just like Clarence had said. Before winning Roshambo Rockstar the other day, Zee had never ever seen Mary jump into a game.

Mr. Street served, and Mary returned, defeating Mr. Street with the same dink shot that he had used to oust Ms. Swanson.

Mary and Mr. Street exchanged high fives, and the next student stepped up to play. The game was humming along when Sarah came running over. She was a little out of breath as she said: "Zee, you gotta come see this. Toni sent me to come get you!"

Zee checked to see that the game was going well and looked toward Clarence who was gesturing to Aaron, "You got this?" Zee asked Aaron. Aaron nodded, solemnly taking responsibility for the supervision of the Wall Ball game. Ms. Swanson was just about to go up against Carl, and there was good momentum and excitement.

Zee followed Sarah back toward the Kickball game, passing the Four Square court where Ms. Houghton had been dethroned, but she was currently in the C square, clearly intent upon working her way back into serving position. "How's it going, Ms. H?" Zee called as he passed by, but Ms. Houghton was too intent on the game to reply.

"You think you know a person . . ." Zee said to Sarah.

Sarah kept heading toward the end of the playground where a group was playing a lively game of Kickball. "C'mon, you've got to see this. Mr. Rodrigues is going to be up again. Last time he was up, he kicked it so high that—I don't know—I'll bet it was up in the air for almost a whole minute. He was safe at third before the ball had even come down."

Mr. Rodrigues had played with the kids before; he'd been the only adult who ever did. But there had always been something restrained about the way he joined in the games. It was as if he wasn't fully there because he felt obligated to be somewhere else. As they were crossing the field, Zee could sense that the whole school felt different. Kids were leading games. Teachers were playing. The whole place felt somehow more alive . . . and special.

"C'mon," Sarah called out. "What are you waiting for?" She walked back toward him.

Zee looked right in Sarah's eyes. He really wanted Sarah to see this the way he saw it.

He wanted to be able to share this with someone.

"Sarah, does the school feel different to you?" he

asked, suddenly completely unsure that he could explain what he meant.

Sarah nodded immediately and emphatically. "Oh, Zee, it's like it's totally changed! I mean, the kids all care, and the teachers seem so different. It's like everyone's happier. I don't even know what it is, but it's totally different!"

Zee felt a huge wave of relief and happiness combined; she got it.

They arrived to find the game in full swing. Fifteen kids were out on the field—Cassie in left field among them—and a dozen lined up waiting to take their turn at bat. The team up to bat had two outs already. The second out had been an inspired play in which Jimmy Driscoll had made a dive from second base to catch a bouncing ball followed by a no-look throw to first. Cassie marveled at the magical sense of her team being in the zone, and how much it reminded her of the dream with Clarence.

As Zee and Sarah joined Toni, Mr. Rodrigues was about to kick the ball. "Watch this, Zee," Toni said, as she pointed at the custodian. Mr. Rodrigues jogged toward the bouncing red rubber ball and with a strong kick, toe-poked the ball high into the air. It sailed toward the very edge of the school field. Everyone seemed to hold their breath watching the ball while Cassie took off running. She could tell it might be a home run. In one smooth motion, Cassie jumped up onto the chain-link fence, scrambling higher and higher until her arm could just reach out over the top. She stuck her hand out and miraculously caught the ball one handed, denying its seemingly predestined flight into Elmwood Street.

The crowd burst into cheers, and Cassie jumped to the ground unable to hide her exhilaration from the catch. Excitement and sheer joy radiated from her face.

Despite being out, Mr. Rodrigues was so impressed and inspired by the catch that he ran out to the field to swing Cassie around in a spontaneous celebration. Cassie jogged in triumphantly, high-fiving everyone on both teams just as the bell rang signaling the end of recess.

By Thursday at lunch, stories about "The Catch" had grown completely preposterous. Toni, Zee, Cassie, and Clarence were seated at the cafeteria table farthest from the front door in an effort to get a break from the steady stream of people hoping to talk with Cassie about it. Cassie was barely touching her food, but Bryant had been hungry and had gone back to the kitchen to see if he could sweet-talk one of the lunch ladies out of an extra chocolate milk.

"I just heard that you were actually flying when you caught the ball," Bryant teased Cassie as he returned to the table, victoriously holding not one but two extra cartons of chocolate milk.

"That's nothing. I heard they were making a movie earlier today," Toni added.

Cassie rolled her eyes at both of them.

The twins, Haley and Camille, came up behind

Bryant, Camille holding out her notebook. "Can we get your autograph?" Haley asked shyly.

Cassie was done. She signed Haley's notebook and turned to Clarence as the girls walked away. "Could you make it so that the kids stop doing this? At least for a while?" Cassie was begging Clarence for help. "Just so we can figure out what to do next?"

Clarence nodded out in the general direction of the cafeteria. After that, while kids would still head toward Cassie, when they got about five feet away, they'd suddenly look confused and then wander away as though they'd forgotten what they'd wanted in the first place.

"OK, that's just cool," Bryant remarked.

"Thanks," Cassie said. And then she stopped short and looked at Clarence somewhat sternly. "You didn't have anything to do with my catch; did you?"

Clarence shook his head emphatically. "Nope, I was over at Wall Ball when it happened. I didn't even see it! Though I did help out Ms. Swanson in her rematch with Mr. Street. I like him, but his use of the dink shot was getting annoying."

The four kids agreed; justice had prevailed.

"OK," Toni was bringing the group back to the business at hand. "We've got recess going pretty well. The school definitely feels different, and the kids and teachers seem psyched. But I still don't see how this translates into convincing the school board tomorrow night."

They all turned and looked expectantly at Clarence.

Clarence stroked his chin thoughtfully. "I'll admit

that this is the part of the plan that needs the most work," he began.

Bryant groaned.

"Dude!" Clarence exclaimed. "Not to fret. Here's what I know: we're going to need some grown-up allies. And you've got some: Ms. Houghton, Mr. Rodrigues, Mr. Street, Ms. Swanson. I even think we can get Marcus's mom to come talk to the school board."

The four looked among themselves in surprise.

"The cell phone lady?" The last time Bryant had seen her, Clarence had been mocking her mercilessly.

Clarence was prepared to eat crow. "She's not so bad. I think I misjudged her. But what we need are the big guns. We need Mr. Unger and Mrs. Grumble. Having them on our side would be the ultimate sign of victory. You know? They could talk about how recess contributes to achievement, cleanliness, and efficiency, and that would be an epic win."

"Cleanliness?" Zee thought he must have misheard Clarence. "How are you ever going to get them to say that recess contributes to cleanliness?"

"It's no joke. I heard Mr. Rodrigues telling Ms. Houghton that ever since you kids started making recess more fun, there has been virtually no graffiti in the boys' bathroom. It was like you said, Zee, remember? Some of the boys had been bored before and instead of going out to play, they were in the bathrooms tagging. When recess got good, they quit." Clarence looked particularly pleased with himself.

Toni had to laugh as she put down her fork. "Who'd have thought?" she asked to no one in particular. "And *efficiency?*"

"Again," Clarence was getting into a rhythm now. Bryant thought he was starting to almost sound like a preacher. "I don't think it's such a stretch. Mr. Street and Ms. Swanson were talking about how much more time they had to teach now that recess was so much better. No more arguments following kids from the playground to the classroom. I think they'd be willing to go to bat for you, but I still think for Dr. Kardashian and the school board to really hear it, it has to come from Mr. Unger."

Bryant shook his head as he put down his milk. "I think that's going to be tough. Mrs. Grumble is working him on a more old-school approach to winning this award. I was in the office when she was making plans to get rid of the mimeograph machine. I can't help but think that in her mind recess is like that machine—an idea whose time has come and gone."

Clarence noticed Zee looking suddenly distraught and followed his gaze to see Sarah. She was approaching but then paused, appearing confused.

Clarence turned to Zee, "Should I let her inside the bubble? It's not hard. I just created a zone of distraction, but I could let her through."

The offer caught Zee off guard and made him instantly uncomfortable; he hadn't realized that Clarence had been watching him.

"What?" Zee was startled to realize he had been noticed. "Oh no, it's cool."

Cassie sensed Zee's discomfort and wanted to reassure him. "I really like Sarah," she offered.

Toni and Bryant chimed in supportively as well. "Agreed. She's cool."

Zee felt himself blush a little. "Yeah, yeah, she's cool." More than anything, he wanted to be talking about something else. Anything else. "Look!" Zee called out suddenly, relieved to be able to change the subject. "There's Mr. Unger and Mrs. Grumble now!"

And indeed the two were standing side by side, right next to the end of the cafeteria line. Mrs. Grumble had her clipboard in hand, and she was scanning the cafeteria, pointing things out to Mr. Unger, and making notes.

Clarence stood watching the pair, trying to imagine what he could do to encourage their support. Cassie managed to catch his eye at just that moment and without saying a word, sent the very clear message reminding him that when it came to convincing the grown-ups, she wanted to win this one fair and square.

Clarence shifted his gaze to his feet. "Harrumph!" he said out loud.

Cassie stood up at this, "We got this! C'mon. Let's go talk to Unger." And she started across the crowded cafeteria.

Bryant looked at the others. "Doesn't it seem as if we spend a lot of time chasing after her?"

"You get us into a fair amount of trouble as well, Bryant," Toni pointed out affectionately.

Zee gave Toni a high five, and Bryant high fived them both, "True dat!" he said, and they all hurried to catch up to Cassie. Clarence was left behind, and noticing the trays the four had failed to clear away, he started to call for them to come back and bus the table. He thought about it for a second and then, looking around to determine that the coast was clear, he nodded at the trays. They immediately and discreetly bussed themselves. It was small consolation for Cassie's imposed restraint, but it put a grin on Clarence's face nonetheless.

Toni, Zee, and Bryant arrived just as Cassie was approaching Mr. Unger. "Good afternoon, Mr. Unger, Mrs. Grumble."

"Cassie," Mr. Unger's voice was hesitant, he was clearly not pleased to see Cassie bearing down on him. "We were just talking about you . . . oh, yes, and the others," he added. He seemed even less happy to see Toni, Zee, and Bryant coming up behind her. Marcus had also made his way over to see what was going on, and in no time at all, a sizable crowd of students had gathered. Mr. Unger was looking increasingly uncomfortable.

Mrs. Grumble turned to him, "You see, Mr. Unger? This is precisely what I was talking about; we can't have students suddenly organizing mass protests. It upsets the schedule."

"We're not protesting, Mrs. Grumble," Toni pointed out, though Mrs. Grumble's choice of words was like a giant red flag. "Unless, of course, there is something that we should be protesting. . . ." Toni's voice trailed off, and Mrs. Grumble shot her a look.

Mr. Unger did not like the way this was going. "Children, perhaps we should go back to my office to discuss this."

Cassie looked to Clarence for guidance, and he shook his head emphatically no. So Cassie stood her ground and continued on. "Mr. Unger, we just wanted to follow up with you about the presentation on Friday." She was clearly making no move toward Mr. Unger's office.

Mrs. Grumble could take no more. She was outraged at what she perceived as disrespect of the ACE Award. "This is not just a presentation, Cassie! This could well be the highest accolade of Mr. Unger's career!"

Mr. Unger tried to hush Mrs. Grumble but to no avail.

"Do you have any idea of what this could mean for Mr. Unger?" Mrs. Grumble asked rhetorically. It was clear to everyone present that she had no actual interest in the students' ideas about anything in this moment. "Winning the ACE is a critical step for Mr. Unger in being considered for superintendent. Dr. Kardashian is up for assistant state superintendent and the school board will be looking for someone to step in and fill his not inconsiderable shoes!"

Clarence didn't mean to do it, but without even thinking, he nodded at Mr. Unger's feet, suddenly changing them from a size 9 to a dramatically larger size 13. No one openly gasped, but a good number of heads jerked as they saw a sudden flash in the area near the bottom of Mr. Unger's pants. Mr. Unger was so concerned that Mrs. Grumble was going too far that he himself hardly noticed other than to have a slightly itchy sensation, which he dismissed in a blink to a recurring case of athlete's foot. Only later, when he got home, would he notice that all his other shoes were suddenly much too small for his feet.

Mrs. Grumble continued on her tirade like a runaway train gaining speed. "The ACE Award is Mr. Unger's golden opportunity to show the school board that he is a champion of the very values the ACE Award honors: Achievement. Cleanliness. Efficiency. If Mr. Unger is to be seen in the shining light he deserves, we cannot afford to be trifling with the obvious frivolity and chaos of recess. The school board itself has come to the conclusion that recess is a waste of valuable instructional time. It would be foolhardy for Mr. Unger to run counter to their wise decision making. As part of our application, Mr. Unger will be endorsing the elimination of recess, and I must say that your actions this week have done nothing but confirm my belief that this is the wisest course. Were you children to put the kind of thought and effort that you've invested in recess this week into important things like, like, like . . . well, achievement, cleanliness, and efficiency . . . well, all I can say is that I have no doubt in my mind that you could measure that."

And then she finally took a breath. No one said anything. Everyone just stood in total silence. Zee wondered if he had understood what she had said. Toni knew she understood. Bryant was still a little distracted by Mr. Unger's shoes.

Cassie spoke first. Very quietly she spoke five simple words: "Then we will defeat you." There was no emotion in her voice. She annunciated clearly and spoke the words as though she were reading them from a page.

Mrs. Grumble audibly gasped. "You dreadful child!" And she moved toward Cassie in a threatening way, which in retrospect was quite obviously the exact wrong thing to do.

The order of events that took place next would be hotly debated among the four friends for years, but five things definitely happened:

One: Cassie definitely stuck her arms out to defend herself from what she perceived as Mrs. Grumble lunging at her.

Two: Mr. Unger definitely yelled out: "No, Erma! Don't!"

Three: Someone, not any of the four friends but quite possibly Marcus, yelled, "Food fight!"

Four: Clarence froze Mrs. Grumble.

Five: The possibility that Mr. Unger might possibly go to bat for recess was entirely eliminated.

Chaos broke out immediately. The frozen Mrs. Grumble was pelted with tater tots, and Mr. Unger was splashed with a remarkably large serving of overcooked green beans. Cassie realized immediately that Clarence had frozen Mrs. Grumble and cried out "Clarence!" confusing many people around her. In reaction to Cassie yelling at him, Clarence quickly nodded at Mrs. Grumble, and she pitched forward, her center of balance shaken both by the experience of being frozen and the onslaught of fried potato products. And it was in this unfortunate moment that Mrs. Grumble had the experience of being hit by Cassie, while Cassie had the experience of unsuccessfully trying to catch the falling lunch lady.

Toni distinctly heard Mrs. Grumble cry out, "She hit me!" Sensing that things had gone horribly awry, Zee moved toward Cassie to try to get her out of the cafeteria, but it was too late. Mr. Unger, resplendent with green beans on his tie, his lapel, and most notably on the bald spot atop his head, pointed right at Cassie as Zee was attempting to drag her out from under Mrs. Grumble and up off the ground. Undaunted by the insanity all around him, Mr. Unger screamed, "I want to see you . . . and your friends . . . in my office immediately!" And then looking around and realizing the sheer absurdity of this, he amended his demand, "Or as soon as possible!"

Toni turned to Cassie and without thinking, spoke what she would later realize was a curse, "Well, now it really can't get any worse."

And as if on cue, Dr. Kardashian, the man who held the ultimate power over the fate of recess, walked into the school cafeteria.

"Bummer," Zee sighed.

"Ouch," Bryant agreed.

"Oh, no!" Toni exclaimed, because she was watching as Marcus catapulted a snowball-sized glob of mashed potatoes directly at Dr. Kardashian's head.

Cassie looked around, desperately hoping that Clarence was somewhere nearby and about to freeze the mashed potatoes midair, but it was not to be. Clarence was indeed nearby, but he wasn't thinking about diverting the flying white blob of carbs. Instead, he yelled out "Direct hit!" as Dr. Kardashian reeled from the blow. To Cassie's horror, Clarence seemed to be enjoying himself immensely.

The ensuing scene in Mr. Unger's office was bad. Dr. Kardashian was breathing heavily, his huge belly rising and falling in a physical display of his horror at the bedlam. Mr. Unger was pacing furiously, continuously moving in circles and muttering to no one in particular about the shamefulness of the situation. And Mrs. Grumble was unnaturally quiet. Cassie wondered if she was just stunned as an aftereffect of Clarence having frozen her, or if he had placed some additional spell on her to spare them all from having to listen to her incessant yammering. Everyone smelled more than slightly of cafeteria food, and most had visible signs of the food still stuck in their hair. Mr. Unger had a dozen or so students called into his office, but only Cassie and Marcus were suspended: Cassie for hitting Mrs. Grumble and Marcus for the assault on Dr. Kardashian. Mr. Unger had Ms. Houghton call Cassie's aunt and Marcus's mom. Both agreed to come down to the office to collect their ill-behaved charges.

Effective immediately, recess was cancelled.

Marcus's mother arrived first, and she looked quite upset with Marcus. Marcus started to explain, but Mrs. Mackey silenced him with just one look. "You will have plenty of time to explain what happened once we are home, young man."

Half an hour passed and Cassie's aunt had still not arrived. Ms. Houghton looked over at Cassie and shook her head in disappointment. "It's not like her to be late," was all Cassie could think to say.

There was a commotion at the office door, and two large men with a dolly appeared. Both men wore baseball caps and coveralls, and one had rolled up his sleeves, exposing a very colorful tattoo of a mermaid. The tattooless man spoke first. "We're here from the central office."

Ms. Houghton got up from her desk and came around to figure out what they needed.

"I'm sorry?" Ms. Houghton spoke the apology more as a question. She didn't understand why the men were there. "Mr. Unger didn't mention a delivery."

"It's a pick-up and delivery," the mermaid tattoo man explained helpfully.

"I see. . . ." The situation was becoming increasingly clear to Ms. Houghton, and she was not happy about it.

"We're here to get the old mimeograph machine and to replace it with the new Copymatic 7000."

Ms. Houghton went absolutely white. "Oh. . . ." And saying nothing else, she returned to her desk.

The two movers stood looking at each other, unclear as how best to proceed. "Um, ma'am? Where's the machine at?" When Ms. Houghton didn't even point out that it was grammatically incorrect to end a sentence with a preposition, Cassie knew that the situation had just gotten worse.

Ms. Houghton made a slight gesture with her head toward the PA room. "Back there." Unclear on the exact location of "Back there," the two men continued standing in place. "Cassie," Ms. Houghton asked quietly, "could you show these men what they want to see?"

Cassie stood reluctantly. "Yes, Ms. Houghton."

Cassie showed the men the PA room and warned them about the locking door and then returned to her seat in the front office while they wheeled out the mimeograph machine and all its assorted parts and then wheeled in the new copy machine, with its associated boxes of toner and other unidentified accessories.

When the new machine was all set up, the men emerged from the room and thanked both Cassie and Ms. Houghton. The first delivery man gave Ms. Houghton a large stack of instruction manuals related to the new machine and explained to her that the service agent would be calling in the morning.

"The service agent?" Ms. Houghton sounded thoroughly defeated.

The two men looked at each other confused, "Yeah,

you know, the guy who does the service visits and replaces your toner. . . ." It was the final blow. Ms. Houghton put her head on the desk, prompting the delivery men to back quietly out of the office.

Cassie and Ms. Houghton both sat in silence for a while, with Ms. Houghton's head still resting on the desk. Cassie thought she might have heard Ms. Houghton sniffle.

"You OK?" Cassie asked finally.

"Yes, Cassie. Thank you for asking." Ms. Houghton took another minute to compose herself and then sat upright and resumed working on the papers in front of her.

Another ten minutes passed before Clarence walked in. Cassie was surprised and confused when Ms. Houghton looked up and said, in a very serious tone, "Hello, Mrs. Murphy."

Cassie's mouth dropped open. Clarence didn't look at her, instead saying: "I'm so sorry about this. I have no idea what has gotten into her head!" To Cassie's ears, he sounded just like Clarence, but it was quite clear from watching Ms. Houghton that whatever Clarence was doing was convincing Ms. Houghton that he was Cassie's aunt.

Ms. Houghton looked around to make sure there was no one else in earshot. "Mrs. Murphy, I wouldn't be too hard on the girl. It wasn't entirely clear that she intended to hit Mrs. Grumble."

Clarence nodded, and Ms. Houghton continued.

"Honestly, I don't think the students were treated fairly. Not that a food fight is ever justified! I just think Mr. Unger should have given them a chance to make their case. And I can see why Cassie got upset."

Clarence thanked Ms. Houghton for her understanding and turned to Cassie and said, "It's time to go, dear."

They were outside the school before Cassie said a word. "What are you doing?" she demanded, her tone a mixture of a whisper and a scream. "You're going to get me in even more trouble!"

"Chill," Clarence insisted, as he led her to the puke green-colored '87 Chevy Nova parked outside by the curb. He looked around and then opened the door, "Get in quick!"

Cassie jumped in the car, and Clarence ran around to the other side, jumping in quickly as well.

"Phew! That was close," Clarence exclaimed, pointing back toward the school where Ms. Houghton stood holding Cassie's backpack.

Cassie was confused. "That's my backpack!" she said, starting to open the door.

"No, no, no! Don't do that." Clarence insisted. "The car's invisible—she can't see us when we're in it. You're going to look way too weird suddenly becoming visible. We can get your backpack tomorrow."

"This is so messed up! I am going to be in so much trouble!" She was fighting hard not to cry. "I can't do anything right. Everything is completely ruined!"

Clarence didn't know exactly what to say. He felt terrible for having made her feel like this. They sat for a while in silence.

"Look," he finally said. "You didn't do anything wrong. We can still do this. I intercepted the call from Ms. Houghton, so your aunt and uncle don't know you've been suspended. We can still make the case that recess is important to the school board. And there are still people who support everything you and Zee and Toni and Bryant have done this week. We can't quit now."

"It's not going to work, Clarence. Besides, it's not quitting if we never had any real chance of winning to start."

"So, you only play to win?"

Cassie said nothing, so Clarence continued. "Because I'm pretty sure I never said anything about winning. I'm pretty sure I said that I thought you were right, and that I thought we had a chance. But there are no guarantees."

Cassie's face was bright red, and she looked as if she wanted to scream, but she made herself speak quietly. "But if we're right, then we *should* win."

Clarence didn't laugh at this. He was serious and respectful when he answered: "That's not my experience. Being right doesn't give you power, and having power doesn't make you right. But quitting ensures that you never even have a chance."

Cassie sat up a little straighter and wiped at her eyes. She thought for a few moments before saying anything. "Clarence, if we do this, I want you to promise me one thing. When it comes time to make the actual decision, I need you to promise that it will be a real decision, not just some spell you cast on the school board so that they're brainwashed for the moment."

Clarence thought he understood her reasoning but wanted to be sure. "Tell me why."

Cassie didn't hesitate. "I want to make sure we really change their minds. You know? They don't believe that recess is important. We need to convince them, not just confuse them or trick them. It's just like everything you've taught me about getting people to play with you; you never use magic to do that. People experience how amazing it is to play, and then they *choose* it. I want the school board to *choose* play for us."

She continued: "This week, I saw how my school could be this place where I felt as if I really belonged. It's never seemed like that to me before."

Clarence knew exactly what she meant. "I get it." And he waited a beat before asking, "But I can use magic up until that very point, right?"

Cassie wanted the school board to really understand, and she was ready to concede that they might lose, but she was still playing this particular game to win. "Bring it!"

Marcus followed his mother to the car without saying anything, and they rode home from school in silence for most of the way. His mom's old Toyota was clean but showing signs of age. The beige upholstery had seen a few coffee spills, and the steering wheel was peeling in a way that didn't seem quite natural for plastic. Even though his mom was mad at him, Marcus couldn't help thinking that he'd like to get her a new car. Marcus tried apologizing, but his mother said nothing.

Marcus didn't know what else to say. "Mom, it's going to be OK."

Clearly, Mrs. Mackey did not agree. "It's not going to be OK if you get thrown out of school, Marcus."

Marcus considered this. Before they had started trying to fix recess, Marcus had felt like the only way to get attention was by being the toughest kid out on the schoolyard. He demanded respect from the other kids, and he wouldn't have cared about getting thrown out of school. But when he was given a chance to be a part of really owning the playground, everything had changed. It was stuff that he helped make happen, not just stuff that grown-ups made happen to him. He was fairly convinced that there was no way he could explain this to his mom.

But Mrs. Mackey *had* noticed that Marcus had seemed more animated about school in the last week. She just had no idea what to do to help him from getting into trouble.

Marcus wanted to explain but couldn't figure out where to start. "I just kind of went nuts when they said they were taking away recess. I mean, it was the first time I was starting to fit in, and then they were taking it away."

Mrs. Mackey pulled the car off to the side of the road and stopped. "They're taking away recess?" she repeated. "You have got to be kidding me."

Marcus was relieved to see his mom's response. It had felt completely crazy to him, and her reaction made him feel less alone. "That's what Mr. Unger said. I thought I told you before. They're voting on it at the school board meeting tomorrow. That's what started the food fight. Well, Mrs. Grumble was going to smack Cassie—that's what really started the food fight. Mom, Cassie made the most amazing catch yesterday. . . ."

Marcus was picking up speed, but his mother cut him off. "Marcus, slow down. You are still in trouble, and we are going to have to discuss consequences. But first, I need to make some calls to ensure that the other families know what's going on here. I haven't heard a word about this before. Eliminating recess at Magruder? That's insane!" And Mrs. Mackey pulled back out into the flow of traffic.

Marcus had a bunch of other things he wanted to tell his mom, but he figured that, once again, he was probably better off just keeping quiet.

The next morning Cassie got up and dressed in her jeans and three sweatshirts, just as though she were going to school. Her aunt and uncle still didn't know she had been suspended, and she was hoping to keep it that way. Cassie headed down the stairs and into the kitchen, hoping against hope that she might escape without actually having to look her aunt in the eye. Cassie didn't have much of a poker face, and she was worried that even the slightest questioning would break her. Cassie grabbed a piece of bread and spread peanut butter on it—normally she would have at least toasted it, but she was hoping for a hasty departure. She called back up the stairs to her aunt to make sure she knew she was heading out and began walking quickly toward school. Cassie ran into Bryant first and filled him in on the afternoon before, including the school district delivery guys taking away Ms. Houghton's mimeograph machine.

"Was she alright?" Bryant was worried about Ms. Houghton.

"I don't know," Cassie confessed. "I think she might have been crying."

"I'll go check in on her when we get to school," he said, as much to himself as Cassie.

"I can't go to school," Cassie reminded him. "I was suspended. Remember?"

Bryant stopped to consider this. "Oh right! You're so lucky!" He paused for a minute. "You ever think about how entirely whacked it is that, for punishment, they don't let kids go to school?"

Cassie didn't have time for philosophizing. "Right. It's insane. But in this case, I actually want to go to school."

They were just approaching the school as Cassie was saying this, and Zee and Toni came running up.

"*Here* you are!" Toni was clearly relieved to have found them. "Cassie, aren't you going to get in trouble for being here?"

"Yeah. I'm just here to fill you in. Clarence has a plan." Cassie was looking around cautiously, visibly worried about being seen. "I made a deal with Clarence. He can use his magic powers as we agreed so that we have a chance to make our case to the school board tonight. But he has absolutely promised not to use magic when they're making their decision. It has to be the real deal, or we're never going to be sure we can have recess forever. Up until the final decision, though, he can go for it. I think there's going to be a show today."

"Awesome!" Bryant cried out, dispensing high fives all around. "This is going to be fantastic!"

Toni and Zee weren't as sure Clarence's mysterious plan was going to be so "fantastic," but they were still nodding in agreement.

"The plan has three parts: B-A-D: bedlam, allies, and delay," Cassie began.

Toni had to laugh at the cheesiness of it all. It was classic Clarence. "I like the sound of it so far." And as she said this, Clarence appeared. He was wearing the fanciest sweat suit so far—neon green—and he had boldly accompanied it with zebra-striped basketball shoes.

"Bedlam, I presume?" Zee asked.

Clarence smiled broadly and replied, "At your service!" And then, smiling sheepishly, he added, "These are my lucky shoes."

Even Toni couldn't think of anything to say.

The plan was pretty straightforward. Clarence was in charge of bedlam. The kids weren't entirely sure what that meant, but he seemed confident and they were fine with leaving that part to him. The kids would share being in charge of allies, and then they'd work on delay together later in the day. They each took their individual assignments very seriously.

Bryant, Toni, and Zee were to go to class, while Cassie went to Marcus's house to bring him back to school. Bryant was in charge of recruiting Ms. Houghton's assistance, with Toni and Zee assigned to Ms. Swanson and Mr. Street. When Marcus and Cassie returned to the school building, they were to wait a few hundred feet away to avoid getting caught. The fallback plan was to head to the Grove where they had all first met if anything went wrong.

"You ready?" Clarence was excited about the plan, but he wanted to be sure the group of four were really up for it.

Bryant spoke first. "I have absolutely no idea what I am getting myself into, but I am completely ready."

"Me, too," agreed Toni.

"Me, three," said Zee.

Seeing no reason to dilly-dally, Cassie just took off running toward Marcus's house.

Clarence headed into the school office as the other three went to class. The office was bustling with excitement as Clarence entered. Mr. Unger was rushing about, clutching three pieces of paper.

"Ms. Houghton, I need you to make copies of my presentation for the board tonight." Mr. Unger stood in front of her desk, holding out the papers to be copied, but Ms. Houghton continued sorting the papers on her desk, refusing to acknowledge Mr. Unger and his request.

"Ms. Houghton?" Mr. Unger repeated.

Ms. Houghton finally looked up at Mr. Unger and exhaled sharply in frustration. "I'm not familiar with the new machine," she replied.

Mr. Unger was simply refusing to engage with Ms. Houghton's resistance. He set the papers down on her desk, his tone almost perky. "I'm sure you'll master it quickly. The Copymaster 7000 is going to make a significant contribution to our efficiency. I can feel it."

"It's a Copymatic," Ms. Houghton muttered as he walked away.

Ignoring Ms. Houghton's remark, Mr. Unger turned and began walking toward the PA Room. "I'm going to go ahead and make the morning announcements. It's a big day."

Ms. Houghton was still staring begrudgingly at the papers to be copied. She reached for the instruction manual that the men had left behind the day before and turned to the "Getting Started" page.

Clarence followed Mr. Unger into the PA closet. Mr. Unger made sure to prop the door open and then sat down at the little desk inside. Mr. Unger had agreed that the new copy machine was a good idea, but on the downside, the room was much more cramped now because it took up considerably more space.

Mr. Unger sat down in front of the microphone and swiveled to the console to turn the PA system on. He looked at his watch and at precisely 8:35, pushed down on the buzzer that signified the beginning of his announcement.

"Good morning boys and girls, ladies and gentlemen. Today is a big day here at Magruder Elementary, and I wanted to update you on the schedule for the day. Channel 2 Television will be sending a crew to interview us about our nomination for the ACE Award today at lunchtime. And as all of you are undoubtedly aware, I will be making our ACE Award presentation this evening at the school board meeting for the board's consideration."

Mr. Unger paused briefly before continuing. "As a follow-up to the disturbance we had yesterday at lunch, I am sorry to say that I have made the decision to adjust the schedule to maximize instructional time. Henceforth, we will not be allowing students to go outside after lunch or during the recess breaks. Unfortunately that kind of liberty involves a significant amount of responsibility, and it is very disappointing that a few students have spoiled it for the many."

Mr. Unger stopped again and considered expounding upon the joys of math games but decided against it. He finished, somewhat abruptly, by simply saying, "Have a nice day!" Then, just as he had a hundred times before, Mr. Unger reached to turn the machine off. This time, however, the strangest thing happened. In adjusting the knob to the "Off" position, he somehow turned it one click further to a setting he had never noticed before that read "Muzak." And sure enough, the PA machine began broadcasting an orchestral version of a song that Mr. Unger did not recognize. (Had he asked anyone, he would have been told that it was a very cheesy rendition of the Baha Men's, "Who Let the Dogs Out?")

Mr. Unger immediately tried to turn the knob back into the "Off" position, but it was stuck. He got up from the desk and stuck his head out the doorway into the office to see if the song was broadcasting on the loud speaker. Unfortunately, he found, it was.

"You probably want to turn that off now, Mr. Unger. It's broadcasting into all the classrooms." Sometimes

Ms. Houghton didn't know what to make of Mr. Unger. She suspected that he had read something about music improving the learning process and that this was just another experiment to support the ACE Award entry.

Mr. Unger stormed back into the PA room, accidentally letting the door shut behind him. He fussed with the wires and climbed around behind the big console to see if it might be possible to unplug the PA system, but it seemed directly wired into the school electrical system. With a sigh, Mr. Unger got up from the floor where he had been pulling at the plug, only to realize that he had locked himself in the PA room. Clarence stood by as a frustrated Mr. Unger banged loudly on the door, "Ms. Houghton! Ms. Houghton!" Ms. Houghton had just been walking toward the PA room to familiarize herself with the new copy machine, so she heard him banging on the door.

"Well," she said, "that was lucky. It would have been hard to hear you with that music playing if I hadn't been standing right there."

Mr. Unger stormed out without saying "Thank you" and went directly to phone the central office about sending someone to repair the PA system.

Ms. Houghton slid a box of the toner in front of the door to prop it open and moved warily toward the new copy machine. Holding the three papers to be copied in one hand and the instruction manual in the other, Ms. Houghton peered around the side of the machine to find the "On/Off" switch as the diagram in the instruction manual showed. She followed the steps listed, turning on the machine and waiting for it to warm up before loading the papers, face down, into the automatic feeder. When the "Ready" light turned green, the machine interface screen read "# of copies?" Ms. Houghton entered twenty-five and then, seeing no further questions posed, pushed the "Copy" button. The music on the PA system was still playing loudly and had switched from the Baha Men to what Ms. Houghton was fairly certain was a Cher medley. "Strange . . ." she thought to herself.

The Copymatic 7000 made a whirring noise and then sucked in the three pages from the automatic feeder. The machine seemed to scan all three pages and then began making the copies. Ms. Houghton sighed with resignation; she supposed the new machine was more efficient. She was standing by, waiting for the job to finish when she noticed that the lights on the display screen were blinking in rhythm to the music playing on the PA. She looked at the output tray and was surprised to see that there seemed to already be more than the twenty-five copies. She pulled the completed copies out to count them. Indeed, there were already thirty-five copies, stapled and collated, so Ms. Houghton pushed the cancel button. But the machine did not stop. Instead, all the lights on the display screen lit up and it seemed as if the Copymatic 7000 actually began working faster, pushing out col-lated, stapled copies with such force that they were literally flying from the sorting trays.

Ms. Houghton frantically pushed at several other buttons, hoping to end the job, but the machine just seemed to go faster and faster with every effort.

Feeling both desperate and defeated, Ms. Houghton cried out for help. "Mr. Unger!" But Mr. Unger was on the phone in his office, so he did not immediately come to her rescue. She could see him through the two sets of doors, so she waved and yelled again, "Mr. Unger! Someone!" When still no one came, Ms. Houghton went out into the office to seek assistance.

Mr. Unger was standing up at his desk, still on the phone and looking quite annoyed. He held up his hand to indicate that she should wait, but Ms. Houghton was insistent. "You *really* need to come and look at this," she said. He tried to wave her away, but she was adamant. "No, *really!*"

"Hold on just a minute. Will you?" Mr. Unger put his hand over the receiver. "What *is* it, Ms. Houghton?" In the background, a Muzak version of the Rolling Stones "You Can't Always Get What You Want" was playing.

"The copy machine is going berserk," she announced. "I need you to take a look at it."

"Surely it can wait while I finish this call," he replied curtly, taking his hand off the phone mouthpiece.

"No, it really can't," she insisted, afraid to imagine how many more copies the machine had made since she had left the room.

Mr. Unger went back to the phone: "Look, we're having another problem here I need to address. Can you send someone over immediately? It's extraordinarily disruptive having this music playing." He listened for a second. "All right then. Thank you." And he hung up. "They're sending someone over," Mr. Unger said, following Ms. Houghton to the PA room.

"I hope they know about copy machines, too," Ms. Houghton said grimly.

The machine was still busily copying, sorting, and stapling when Mr. Unger and Ms. Houghton returned. Copies were scattered all around.

"Ms. Houghton, I wanted only twenty-five copies!" Mr. Unger pronounced indignantly.

Ms. Houghton looked at him in disbelief. "I realize that, Mr. Unger. You can see on the display that I entered twenty-five." She pointed at the display, which was happily flashing the number twenty-five to the beat of the music.

Mr. Unger shook his head as he pushed the "Cancel" button. "Just because you didn't want the machine here is no reason to intentionally sabotage it. Here's the "Cancel" button." And he pushed it to no avail.

Ms. Houghton was outraged. "Are you seriously suggesting that I did this on purpose?"

Not waiting for Mr. Unger's reply, she turned and stormed out, leaving Mr. Unger in a sea of copies.

Meanwhile, having no success with the "Cancel" button, Mr. Unger fumbled around for the "On/Off" switch but just as with the PA system, the button was stuck in the "On" position. Once again Mr. Unger got down on his knees and crawled around back to try and pull the plug out of the wall but found that, like the PA system's plug, this one was also mysteriously stuck in place.

Clarence briefly considered what other mischief he might create, but decided he had done enough for now. He left Mr. Unger, rear end waving in the air, deeply engaged in a futile game of tug of war with the Copymatic 7000 power cord. Clarence was confident that the bedlam was well under way. It was time to shift his attention to recruiting allies.

The canned music was making it very hard for the teachers to teach, and quite a few had called down to the office to find out what was going on. Ultimately, Ms. Houghton stopped answering the phone calls from the classrooms because she had no good answer, and the constant cries of frustration from Mr. Unger in the PA room were making it almost impossible to focus on anything else.

The music, in combination with the sudden elimination of recess, was creating a high degree of frustration among the teachers. Ms. Swanson left her class reading quietly while she went to get more information on what exactly was going on. Mr. Street had gone in search of an explanation as well. Finding the office in a shambles, the two teachers decided to try the staff lounge in hopes of finding answers there. Ms. Swanson and Mr. Street had just walked in when Mr. Street noticed Zee and Toni at the window in the door, waving at them to come out.

(Clarence was with them, of course, but he remained invisible to the teachers.) Students were strictly prohibited from going into the staff lounge.

Mr. Street came to the door and opened it, "Were you looking for me?" he asked.

"You'd like to speak with both of them," Clarence instructed.

Zee relayed the message: "Yes, Mr. Street. We were wondering if we could talk with you and Ms. Swanson for a minute."

Mr. Street made a gesture for them to wait and then closed the door, heading, they could see, to get Ms. Swanson. The staff room was always a place of great mystery to Zee, being, as it was, a completely forbidden place. Looking through the glass in the door, one could see a battered, old mustard yellow couch and a plant that had died many years before but had never been removed. The smell of coffee wafted out whenever a teacher entered and exited, and despite its obvious dowdiness, Zee, like most of his classmates, associated the room with glamour and the promise of secret adult privileges.

"Here's the deal," Clarence quickly explained. "You're just asking if they'll come to the board meeting tonight to speak on behalf of your efforts to improve recess here. All you're asking is that they tell the school board what they've seen the past week."

Mr. Street and Ms. Swanson emerged from the lounge then. "I actually think the music is louder in there, if that's possible," she commented. And then turning to the students, clearly displeased at having been disobeyed, she said, "I thought I'd left you quietly reading?"

Zee looked sheepish and apologetic. "Sorry, Ms. S. It wasn't exactly quiet, and it was hard to concentrate."

Toni chimed in: "And we needed to ask you for your help. We're going to the school board meeting this evening to ask the board to keep recess. We were hoping that you both could tell the board about everything that happened this week." She stopped for a moment as a violin playing Elton John's "Honky Cat" seemed to peak in volume.

"Well, not everything," she corrected. "We were hoping you could talk about how different it felt when we were organizing recess and the kids were . . ." she paused again, trying to think of the right word.

Ms. Swanson found it for her: "Engaged."

"Then you'll do it?" Zee asked hopefully.

Mr. Street looked at Ms. Swanson. "Mr. Unger will not be happy," he pointed out.

Ms. Swanson considered this. "True. Though I can't help but feel that the whole way this was handled was simply unfair."

The two teachers looked at each other, and both smiled. "We'll do it," they said in unison.

"Tell them we need them to be there at five o'clock," Clarence instructed.

"Could you be there at five?" Zee asked.

"Yes. Now the two of you need to go back to class," Ms. Swanson said sternly. Zee and Toni turned quickly and hurried back to their not-so-quiet reading.

"I'm going to check on some other allies," Clarence called out after them and promptly disappeared.

Before enlisting any other new supporters, Clarence wanted to check on Marcus and Cassie, who were by now waiting just outside the school.

"It's boring not being in school," Cassie was saying to Marcus when Clarence materialized.

Clarence looked all around, assessing the situation. He immediately noticed that Marcus seemed absolutely happy as a clam to be hanging out with Cassie.

"Why don't you suggest that Marcus go try and look in the office window," Clarence suggested to Cassie. Cassie didn't immediately respond, but instead looked nervously at the school, as if thinking that Clarence's idea might not be such a hot one. Clarence could see that she was worried Marcus might be caught. "Oh, don't worry, it's such a total circus in there that they'll never see him."

Cassie turned to Marcus, "Do you want to go check if anything is going on in the office?"

Marcus looked pleased to be part of whatever Cassie was planning. He dutifully trotted over to the building and around behind the hedges to look in. When he got there, he looked in the window and called out. "Oh, man! You'll never believe it!"

Clarence spoke quickly to Cassie. "Here's the deal. I've created some initial bedlam, and we've signed on Street and Swanson as allies. Ms. Houghton is so completely ticked off that I think we can count on her both being an ally and helping with the delay." Cassie figured she understood about the bedlam and allies, but at some point she needed to ask about the delay.

Clarence continued talking before she could ask her question. "I need to go check on Marcus's mom. She's already organizing some parents—even without magic, you'll be pleased to hear—but I think I can help a little. I need the two of you to stay here and to keep out of sight. The TV crew should be arriving around 11:30 and setting up in the cafeteria. Do you have a watch?"

Cassie stuck out her wrist to show him that she did.

"I need you and Marcus to open up both the doors to the cafeteria exactly at noon—I'll make sure they're a little propped open so you can do it. Then you have to just stand there for a few minutes. Don't panic—and you have to make sure Marcus doesn't panic either. Can you do that?"

"Why are we holding open the doors?" Cassie asked.

Clarence smiled mischievously. "You're just going to have to trust me on this one," he answered.

Cassie didn't feel sure, but Clarence pushed on before she had a chance to voice questions or concerns.

"After lunch we'll meet up. I have an assignment for Marcus, and I want you to talk with Mr. Rodrigues about coming to the board meeting," he explained.

Marcus called out to Cassie again, "You gotta come see this. Don't worry; they're *definitely* not going to see you."

Cassie looked up at Clarence. The whole situation was so impossibly unbelievable. She was hanging out with a bedlam-creating angel, and Marcus was her new best friend. It was hard to say which part was less likely. Clarence gestured for her to join Marcus, and then—poof—he disappeared again. She stood there for a second. Even though he had been doing this to her for a week now, it was still disconcerting. Marcus waved emphatically for her to come, so she ran to join him behind the hedge. Marcus was standing just below the office window. He looked over at Cassie, and realizing she was too short to see without assistance, he bent his leg so that she could step up and see. She stepped up to the windowsill and looking in, saw Ms. Houghton and Mr. Unger rushing to and fro. Paper was flying everywhere, and through the window, Cassie could swear she heard an accordion playing "Stairway to Heaven."

Carol Mackey had been busy all morning. She had spent almost an hour on the phone with the school district, getting more information on the board meeting and the proposal to eliminate recess districtwide. And then she'd been calling and emailing other families. No one she had talked with knew anything at all about the proposal. And while people generally agreed that it seemed like a bad idea, the vast majority of them already had plans for the evening or had some other reason they couldn't be there. A few people had expressed the opinion that if the district was eliminating recess, the school board must have a good reason for it. And Mrs. Mackey had one very short and unfortunate conversation with a mother who thought it was about time they eliminated recess, and said she would definitely be at the meeting.

Mrs. Mackey was feeling dejected when Clarence arrived at her office. She had a sales meeting starting in ten minutes that she was pretty sure was going to last at least three hours. Clarence figured that he should start there.

Mark, the broker in the office around the corner, stuck his head in: "Hey, Carol! Great news! Smith's wife just called in to say that he's really sick. The sales meeting is canceled today!"

Mrs. Mackey turned back to her computer and opened her email inbox. A few new messages had come in from other parents who had suddenly had a change in plans or who had miraculously discovered an available babysitter. Things were looking up. Mrs. Mackey pulled up the school contact list and resumed her calling. She wasn't sure it was going to make a difference, but she was going to make sure that at least the other parents knew.

Back at school, the district's electrician arrived a little after 11 a.m. The music and copying had been going on without stop for almost two hours, and Ms. Houghton and Mr. Unger rushed toward him as he walked through the office door, exclaiming, "Finally!"

The electrician was startled by the chaos. "Whoa! Sorry to be so long. I had to stop over at the high school on my way." He paused, looking around and wondering where to start. "Um, what seems to be the problem?"

Ms. Houghton grabbed him by the arm and pulled him after her toward the PA room. They passed a pile of papers, and the electrician noted the odd strains of what he thought might be MC Hammer as interpreted by an oboe. Mr. Unger threw open the PA office door—they had been keeping it closed in an effort to contain the insanity—and the moment the electrician passed through the threshold, everything went quiet.

"Wow," he said, the overheated machines all completely silent now in his presence. "You have a real mess here!"

Ms. Houghton and Mr. Unger looked at each other in complete dismay. Ms. Houghton answered first, "Yes, he does." And she turned on her heels and left the two men standing amidst the thousands of copies of that night's presentation.

The electrician took a final account of the mess and said to Mr. Unger: "You should probably try and recycle this. Now, what was it you wanted me to fix?"

Mr. Unger gaped in disbelief first at the electrician and then at the room. Finding no words to convey his sheer and utter frustration, he, too, turned and walked silently out of the PA room, leaving the electrician clueless and confused.

In the cafeteria, Mrs. Grumble was rushing about with her clipboard. Everything was perfectly in place—the kitchen was exceptionally clean this morning, and she had even had her hair, net and all, done the evening before. Mr. Unger came through the cafeteria entrance from the school, followed by the local news anchor, Robert Roberts, the cameraman, the sound engineer, and Clarence. Robert Roberts was a former collegiate swimmer with brown hair, sprayed so that it never moved, and a perfect smile. He wore a camel-colored blazer with the KTVU logo emblazoned on the lapel. Mr. Unger was talking to him, but Roberts did not appear to be listening, looking around instead for the best place to set up.

Roberts was asking a question just as Mrs. Grumble joined them. "Why don't we shoot the footage outside?" Roberts asked. "You know? With the kids playing in the background as you talk about their healthy eating and physical activity?"

Mrs. Grumble interjected without even being introduced: "Oh, no, no! That will never do. I've got it all mapped out here," she said, showing Mr. Roberts her clipboard. "We'll open it up in the kitchen itself, and then we can get some footage of the children standing in line, and then we close with them all disposing of their waste."

The cameraman and sound guy exchanged a knowing look. This lady was a kook.

Roberts flashed Mrs. Grumble a charming but dismissive smile and turned back to Unger. "Right. We definitely want to capture the 'cleanliness and efficiency' angle that you keep talking about, but this story needs a hook. Do you have a student who was doing poorly? Someone who really hated school but then turned it around? That's what we're looking for. Tell me a story.

You've put in all these great changes, I get it. You're going to win an award tonight for the things you've been doing. But show me one child in whom I can see how those changes worked."

Mrs. Grumble and Mr. Unger looked at each other and then back at Robert Roberts. Neither of them was particularly comfortable with changing the plan, or with change at all, for that matter. It occurred to Mrs. Grumble that perhaps Mr. Roberts simply didn't understand the nature of award. "Let me show you where you can set up in the kitchen," she repeated.

Sensing that she was digging in, Roberts changed tactics: he would verbally agree while doing the opposite. "That's great!" Roberts said as he headed toward the double doors at the back of the cafeteria. "We'll get that too. But let's set up here to interview Mr. Unger." He pointed to the doors. "This leads out to where the kids play, right?"

Mr. Unger and Mrs. Grumble moved their heads in a noncommittal way. "We'll interview Mr. Unger here, and maybe some of the kids, and then we can cutaway to the kids heading outside after eating."

Mrs. Grumble was squaring up to object when Clarence realized exactly what the situation called for. It hadn't been part of the plan, but now he knew that it was absolutely meant to be. He nodded at Mr. Unger and then Mrs. Grumble, hitting them with a love spell so potent that Cupid would have been proud.

Mrs. Grumble shivered as the magic coursed through

her body. She seemed to briefly consider what she had been about to say and then dismissed it in favor of the now far-more-pressing thought. "Do you think that will be the best lighting for Mr. Unger?" she asked, looking doe-eyed in the principal's direction.

The sudden shift in tone was notable to everyone, and the sound engineer did a double-take to make sure that it was actually Mrs. Grumble who had just cooed the last question. Roberts was equally taken aback but decided to go with it. "Yes, definitely!" he assured her.

Mr. Unger moved quickly to Mrs. Grumble's side. "Oh, no, no, no," he protested. "It would be a travesty not to showcase the kitchen. It is the crown jewel of our school, and it is because of Mrs. Grumble's organizational genius that we are even being considered for the ACE Award. I insist we start in there!"

Roberts, the cameraman, and the sound guy all looked at one another, now completely convinced that Unger and Grumble were nuts. Roberts figured that the quicker they could get done with filming, the quicker they could leave.

"Excellent," Roberts said, pushing ahead. "Then it's agreed. We'll start out here and move into the kitchen to wrap up. Let's set up, boys." Roberts immediately walked away to call his producer on his cell phone and complain bitterly about the whackos she had sent him to cover.

At 11:55 the students started entering the cafeteria and lining up with their trays while Mrs. Grumble oversaw the staff bringing out the pans of hot food, carefully arranging the a la carte items on display, and occasionally sneaking loving glances in Mr. Unger's direction.

The camera and lights were all set up and Mr. Unger had his microphone clipped in place on his tie. "Let's get started," Roberts directed. "A little background noise is good, but it'll probably be too much when all the kids are in here."

Mr. Unger agreed, though the enrapturing sight of Mrs. Grumble overseeing lunch was largely distracting him.

The cameraman counted them off to cue the questioning, "3, 2, 1 … action."

"How long have you been the principal here at Magruder Elementary, Mr. Unger?"

"Four years," Mr. Unger replied, "though it really should be called Grumble Elementary in honor of our Mrs. Grumble!"

Roberts worked hard to suppress a look of complete dismay. "You're being considered for one of the district's highest awards this evening, the ACE Award," he prompted. "Can you tell us a bit about that?"

Mr. Unger nodded solemnly in agreement, "Indeed. The ACE Award stands for Achievement, Cleanliness, and Efficiency. We're very proud of the environment we've created here for our students, giving them everything they need to be able to excel." Mr. Unger looked proudly at Roberts, beaming at the eloquence of his own response.

Cassie and Marcus had arrived unseen at the back of the school while all this was transpiring. Finding the double doors just slightly ajar, Cassie had wedged her fingers in just enough to get a grip. She looked all around, hoping for some sign of the plan but saw nothing. It seemed incredibly risky, but when her watch said noon, she and Marcus did as they were instructed and pulled open the two doors, stepping to the side of them as they did, just out of sight from inside the cafeteria.

From inside, the doors suddenly flying open caught everyone's attention. Mr. Unger looked surprised, and Roberts yelled, "Cut!"

The cameraman looked up from the viewfinder, "It's actually not bad—it adds depth being able to look beyond and into the yard."

Roberts shook his head; this was a nightmare. "What else could go wrong?" he wondered to himself. "Fine. Let's keep shooting." He turned back to Unger, "You were saying?"

Unger continued, "Yes, Achievement, Cleanliness, and Efficiency." There was a noise in the distance that sounded distinctly like barking.

Meanwhile, Cassie and Marcus were standing just behind the two open cafeteria doors. Cassie's heart was beating loudly in her chest, and she was terrified that Mrs. Grumble or someone else was about to come bursting out in an effort to figure out why the doors had swung suddenly open. At least, she was initially worried about that, but other concerns quickly trumped that one. They had heard the barking, but now they could see the source: an enormous pack of neighborhood dogs was running pell-mell toward them.

"Cassie!" Marcus screamed.

Inside, Robert Roberts spun around when he heard the cry of "Cassie" from the playground. He didn't see the person who had screamed it, but he definitely saw the reason. "Oh, my heavens!" Roberts cried out, abandoning any semblance of news anchor composure and jumping up onto one of the cafeteria tables.

The dogs, all 168 of them, came running through the cafeteria doors, heading in a line directly toward the kitchen. There were terriers and Great Danes, mutts and purebreds, poodles, bull dogs, German shepherds and Labradors. Just as Roberts had done, students were jumping up onto the tables, and the dogs were stopping briefly to eat the assorted lunches that were flying around in the melee.

Mr. Unger stood statue still with his mouth wide open as the dogs ran past him. Heroically, the cameraman held his ground, capturing the whole scene on film. The sound guy followed Roberts up onto a table.

When all the dogs had made it into the school, Cassie yelled at Marcus to run for home. "Keep the doors open," she yelled, "so the dogs can get out!" They both took off running, Marcus heading for his house and Cassie back to the Grove where she figured she would wait until the coast was clear.

The dogs ran around the cafeteria and kitchen for less than two minutes, but they were the longest two minutes in Mrs. Grumble's life. There were little dogs under the tables, and the bigger ones had both front paws on the counters, happily pulling food down from the shelves. Mrs. Grumble stood by, shrieking, completely overwhelmed by the sight of utter chaos in her kingdom of order.

Once the dogs had made a complete circuit, Clarence nodded at the lead dog, a well-trained Australian shepherd whom Clarence had met on a walk earlier in the day. The dog immediately led the others back out the double doors and home to their respective houses. The students climbed down from the tables and with a nod from Clarence, they spent a few moments cleaning up their trays and the remaining debris that the dogs hadn't eaten. Roberts stood in shock as Carl, Mary, Megan, Sarah, Aaron, Kevin, and all the others quietly and calmly picked up strewn trays and upended milk cartons.

Roberts, the cameraman, and the sound guy watched as the students all filed out of the cafeteria as though nothing unusual had happened, and despite the fact that scores of dogs had just run crazily through the lunch room, the place was essentially restored to the pristine order it had been in just moments before.

Roberts turned to the cameraman, "Did you capture all that?"

The cameraman gave a thumbs-up signal that he had. Roberts climbed down off the table and walked back to where Mr. Unger was still standing. "Keep rolling," Roberts instructed, pointing in the direction of Mr. Unger. He turned to the principal, asking, "Can you explain what just happened, Principal Unger?"

Mr. Unger's tone was flat, and he sounded more like a zombie than a principal as he spoke, "Achievement, cleanliness, efficiency," and then fainted in a heap onto the blue linoleum floor.

The Grove felt unusually desolate. The ground seemed more worn, the branches more bare, and over it all, the sky hung a flat, dull gray. Clarence found Cassie sitting alone there, waiting pensively. She was sitting on one of the stumps, still resting where Clarence had moved it only the week before. He stood for a moment, watching her from the edge of the clearing. He had been feeling so exhilarated after the canine cafeteria caper, but now, seeing Cassie sitting there, his enthusiasm waned.

"Hey," he said as he walked up behind her.

Cassie tried to force excitement, but her tone rung hollow. "It was amazing! I mean, that was incredible with the dogs. Did you see Mrs. Grumble's face? And that guy from the TV station, the anchor? Standing up on the table? Totally hysterical." She was trying to sell it, but Clarence wasn't buying.

"C'mon, Cassie. What gives?"

Cassie looked down at her feet. "I'm just worried," she explained. "I guess I'm afraid it's not going to work."

She looked up at him, concerned that she might have offended him. "I mean, not your part. I know that part is going to work out. But what if my part doesn't work? I mean, if you don't use magic on the school board, and they decide not to keep recess, then we're stuck. You know? And I've gone and lost recess for everyone, when I could have made sure we had it by letting you use your powers. Why do I always have to make it so hard? Why do I have to be so different from everybody else?"

Clarence had to laugh a little. "You're way too complicated. You know that?"

She looked up at him to see if he was joking and was relieved to see that he was just playing with her.

"Cassie, everybody feels different. I'm not saying you're not different. But it's your *being different* that makes you so wonderful. It's your being different that makes you you."

Cassie considered this for a moment, but she was not entirely convinced. "I guess."

There was so much that Clarence wanted to tell Cassie, but he knew that the timing of the plan meant that they needed to get back to work. "We need to get back to school and have a talk with Mr. Rodrigues." Clarence stopped and looked at Cassie. "There are no guarantees, Cassie, but I respect your choice about the magic. And I get your being worried, because there's definitely the possibility that we won't win this round,"

She nodded that she understood. Clarence felt like a hypocrite as he said it, but he knew it was the hardest thing for him to learn, and that Cassie, cut from the same cloth, needed to learn it too: "That's the thing about getting in the game. If you want to win, you have to live with the possibility of losing."

Cassie took this in for a moment, exhaled sharply, and stood up. "Let's go talk with Mr. Rodrigues."

Cassie and Clarence drove back to school in Clarence's Nova and parked a few blocks away so that they could emerge from the invisible car unseen. School hadn't let out yet, but Cassie wanted to be sure not to be spotted, so she kept her hood up as they walked around back toward the cafeteria looking for Mr. Rodrigues.

"I'm sure he's back here," Clarence assured her. "I bet Mrs. Grumble is going to want the kitchen cleaned a dozen times to get rid of the essence of dog." Clarence had been extra careful to ensure that the dogs hadn't actually made a mess while in the school—definitely no peeing or pooping—mostly because he liked Mr. Rodrigues and didn't want to make too much extra work for him. Nonetheless, even as he had been careful, he had known that Mrs. Grumble was going to demand the custodian do multiple moppings, and he felt a little guilty about it.

Cassie and Clarence turned the corner around back of the cafeteria and looked in the window. Sure enough, there was Mr. Rodrigues. The cafeteria looked extraordinarily clean as Mr. Rodrigues ran the floor polisher for a fourth time over the linoleum. Mr. Rodrigues didn't always agree with Mrs. Grumble, but he had felt bad for her, seeing in her such a state of shock after the incident. He was happy to try and make her feel a little better if cleaning the cafeteria a fourth time would help.

"You need to knock on the window to get his attention and then ask him to come outside to talk with you. All you're doing is inviting him to come to the board meeting tonight to describe the changes he's seen this past week."

Cassie knocked on the window, softly at first, afraid that someone else might hear or see her. Clarence was looking all around. "I think you need to knock harder," he instructed. Cassie pounded harder, but Mr. Rodrigues still didn't hear her.

Clarence thought for a second. "Try it again," he suggested.

Cassie pounded her fist against the window, but this time she noticed Clarence give a little nod and Mr. Rodrigues rocked forward, as though he had been physically shoved.

He looked behind him to see what had happened and saw Cassie pounding. He turned off the machine and moved closer to see who it was. Recognizing Cassie, he came out through the back doors.

"Cassie!" Mr. Rodrigues scolded. "You're not supposed to be here. You were suspended yesterday. You're going to get into even more trouble." He looked worried and concerned.

"I know, Mr. Rodrigues. It's just that the board

meeting is tonight, and we're trying to organize it so that we can make a case for saving recess. They're going to vote tonight, and I was hoping you'd come and tell them about how you saw us change recess."

This made Mr. Rodrigues even more concerned. "Cassie, you're not thinking about going. Are you? After everything that happened with Marcus and Dr. Kardashian? I know you didn't really hit Mrs. Grumble, but she's fit to be tied, and after today, there's no way the school will win that ACE Award. Oh, Cassie, you should stay as far away from that board meeting as you can."

Cassie shook her head. "I can't Mr. Rodrigues. I can't explain it, but this is just about the most important fight I've ever been in. We may not win, but I know I have to try." She looked up and was confused by the look on his face.

She had no idea what to make of it. "You think it's a stupid idea."

Mr. Rodrigues had known Cassie since she was a baby, and he wanted so much to protect her from being hurt. "No, no, honey, not at all. In fact, I was thinking just the opposite. I was thinking how much you reminded me of your father." Cassie had known that her dad and Mr. Rodrigues had grown up together, but she hadn't spent much time with him since her parents had died. "You remember how he and I played baseball in high school together? He was amazing."

Cassie had been vaguely aware of this. Her parents

had been born and raised in this town, and it seemed like everyone had known them better than she had.

"I knew him when he was chasing after your mother as well. He was about the most determined person I ever met. The other day when you made that catch against the fence? It made me feel like I was a kid again. I swear I can remember your father making an identical catch, up against the fence when we won the division title. He climbed it like a monkey—just like you did—and people talked about it for years.

"We went to the state championship that year, and I remember your father was so caught up in it all, he was almost hard to be around. It was as though nothing else mattered. And when we lost—it was a close game, but they beat us in the bottom of the ninth—he was so quiet afterward, I was worried a part of him had died."

Cassie had never heard this story. Her aunt and uncle had told her a number of stories about her parents, but mostly about when they were children or later when they were young parents. This was a side of her dad that she had sensed but never really known.

"That night on the bus ride home, I sat next to your dad, and we talked. He told me that while winning the championship had always been his dream, he couldn't be sure which would have been worse—having his dream not come true or having it come true and having it not being everything he'd hoped for." Mr. Rodrigues stopped and looked at Cassie. "I was too young to understand what he was talking about that night, but I imagine that you understand, even at your age."

Cassie felt herself choking up. She knew it was a silly thought, but she couldn't help but think that if her father were still alive, he'd never let them eliminate recess.

"So you'll come tonight?" she asked.

Mr. Rodrigues shook his head no. "Cassie, I'd like to, but I need this job too much to risk it. Besides, the school board isn't going to listen to a custodian." He looked down at his feet and then back up at Cassie. "I'm sorry," he spoke the words softly. "Your dad would have been very proud of you."

Mr. Rodrigues put his hand on Cassie's shoulder and stood that way for a moment before going back inside to resume his cleaning. He turned, just as he passed through the door and called out, "Good luck."

Cassie and Clarence walked over to the playground and sat down on the ground in silence for a few minutes. "I blew it." Cassie couldn't help feeling that it was her fault that Mr. Rodrigues wouldn't be coming.

"Are you kidding?" Clarence demanded. "You did your part."

"I should have let you use your magic on him."

"I don't know," Clarence said. "I thought your magic seemed plenty powerful."

Cassie turned and looked at him crossly and then punched him in the shoulder.

"I'm pretty sure there are rules about not punching one's guardian angel in the shoulder." Clarence was so relieved to see Cassie looking more hopeful, he welcomed the punch in the arm.

Cassie didn't know what to think. "It just seems like some twisted joke that I got sent you as a guardian angel. I mean, you ran an army of dogs through my school cafeteria for giggles."

Clarence grinned at the very thought of it. "Just wait till you see what I did to Mr. Unger and Mrs. Grumble!"

"Oh, Clarence!" Cassie wasn't sure she wanted to know. "What do we do now?"

"Let's go find the others. We need to rehearse for the presentation tonight."

Bryant and Toni and Zee were all standing out in front of the school waiting for Clarence when he walked up. "Where's Cassie?" Zee asked when he saw Clarence approaching alone.

"In the Nova," Clarence gestured with his head back toward the invisible car.

Bryant did a double take. "The Nova?" he repeated. "Like the car?"

"That would be my car to be precise," Clarence couldn't suppress his deep pride.

Bryant remained unimpressed and shook his head in disapproval. "My uncle drives one of those. Seriously hoopty."

"Not this Nova. I think it's fair to say that this one is seriously souped up." Clarence figured the best way to prove Bryant wrong was to show him, so he started heading down the school steps and signaled for the three to follow. They had turned the corner and walked most of a long block when Clarence stopped in the middle of the empty street. "Here we are!" he announced triumphantly, but the kids saw nothing. Clarence nodded and the Nova, with Cassie sitting in the front seat, suddenly appeared.

"Whoa!" Bryant exclaimed. "It's the same puke-green color as my uncle's, but the disappearing feature definitely eases the eye strain."

The four joined Cassie in the car and Clarence launched into a review of the day. "OK, so far we have achieved bedlam and allies, but we still need to set up the delay."

Toni turned to Cassie, "You were so lucky not to be in school today. Clarence made this awful music play through the loud speakers for most of the morning."

"And way to go with making the copy machine go nuts," Bryant was deeply appreciative. "It was good to see Ms. Houghton victorious!"

"What'd you do to Unger and Grumble?" Toni asked. She had no doubt that Clarence was responsible.

"Yeah," Zee had been completely creeped out when he saw them making googly eyes at each other. "They were acting . . . well, seriously weird."

Clarence had a hard time hiding his satisfaction with that particular bit of mischief. "That was an improvisation. But I think it will help with the delay."

"What are we supposed to say tonight?" Bryant finally asked. This part of the plan was still a mystery to all four of the kids.

"Mostly, I think you should speak from the heart. And I was thinking you should have the board members play a game."

"You want to lead a bunch of grown-ups in a game? The *school board*?" Zee asked incredulously.

"No," Clarence corrected, "I want *you* to lead a bunch of grown-ups in a game. If you want this to be successful, you need to remind the school board of when they were kids. You need to make them think about what it is they really want for the students at Magruder and why they're even considering eliminating recess. I don't believe they're doing it just to be mean. I think they're doing it because they don't remember what it's like to be a kid, and they don't know what else to do. Your job is to help them remember and then lead them to another solution."

"That makes sense," Cassie could sort of imagine the school board playing. But the timing of it all was still confusing. "You keep mentioning delay. Who are we delaying?"

"Unger and Grumble," Clarence replied.

"Delaying them? Why don't we just freeze them completely and keep them away?"

Bryant didn't think having them anywhere near the place made any sense.

Clarence appreciated Bryant's perspective, but he'd been swayed by the argument that it was important for the grown-ups to actually get it. "I think Cassie's right. We can't just come up with a solution that works around them. They have to be a part of solving it; we need them to embrace recess if we want to make sure that recess is here to stay at Magruder."

Zee, Toni, and Bryant all looked at Cassie, who looked both pleased and anxious.

"Let's go rehearse in the school board meeting room," Clarence was ready to get to the next phase of the plan.

"*Really*?" Bryant asked.

Clarence just shook his head at Bryant. He was never going to get used to him saying that.

Clarence drove around the block of the school district offices looking for a place to park the invisible car so that the four kids could emerge unseen.

"This part might be tricky," he mused aloud.

They found a spot in the alley behind the district offices that seemed fairly deserted.

"So cool," Zee observed as they got out of the car. "You can park in tow-away zones because no one can see the car!"

It was 3:30. Clarence figured they had thirty minutes to practice before going to get Marcus. "Here's the deal. If someone questions why we're here, you just have to seem like you know what you're doing."

Zee, Bryant, and Cassie all turned and looked at Toni.

"What?!?" she asked defensively.

"You do the talking," Zee said. The other two quickly nodded their support.

"Sheesh," Toni muttered in response.

They headed into the district offices and not surprisingly, found no one at the front desk. The school district offices were housed in an old middle school that had been closed a dozen years before. The old lockers in the hallway looked out of place next to the mandated posters from the state detailing requirements and procedures in case of a workplace accident. The classrooms had been converted into offices and the cafeteria had been transformed into the boardroom.

Seeing no one, Clarence led the group into the old cafeteria and nodded to turn on the lights. "Let's go through the presentation."

The boardroom had been more renovated than the rest of the building, with fake wood paneling replacing the old tile cafeteria walls, and an elevated semicircle of important-looking seats at the front of the room where the board was clearly intended to sit. The space had also been upgraded with a surprisingly modern audiovisual system and a mechanized big screen in the very front of the room. Presumably the board members were intended to swivel in their big chairs to watch displays. The rest of the room was filled with rows of chairs for the audience.

Cassie was looking around trying to figure out where they would stand when an older man stuck his head through the doors. "Can I help you kids?" he asked, sounding more confused by their presence than concerned.

"I think we're all set. Thank you!" Toni said brightly.

The man stood looking, still not quite convinced.

"We're with Magruder Elementary. For the presentation tonight. Dr. Kardashian said for us to go ahead and set up." Toni didn't miss a beat and as instructed, sounded completely convincing.

The mention of Dr. Kardashian was apparently enough to convince him. "OK," he said and left them to their setup.

"Wow, you went with the full-on authority trump card. Dr. Kardashian? Last time I saw him, Marcus had launched a heaping mound of mashed potatoes at his head." Clarence was pleased that Toni had been so receptive to his coaching.

The four friends and Clarence spent the next twenty minutes reviewing what each would say and how they would ask the school board to keep recess.

"What about when Unger and Grumble show?" Bryant was still hoping the permanent freeze option might be reconsidered.

"The plan is that they arrive *after* our presentation," Clarence explained. "That's where Marcus comes in. Let's go get him before anybody else finds us in here."

"All right then!" Bryant figured that the sooner they stepped into action, the better. "Let's do this!"

Dropping Cassie off at Marcus's house, all four kids were marveling at how much had happened since they were last there just a week ago, dropping off a dazed and confused Marcus. So much had changed, and it felt as if the resolution of it all was coming down to the next couple of hours.

"I get Marcus to come with me to school and tell him to wait there till 5:30. That's when he goes inside to let Mr. Unger and Mrs. Grumble out of the PA room." Cassie was repeating her instructions aloud for herself as much as anyone.

"Correct," Clarence confirmed.

"And how do Mr. Unger and Mrs. Grumble get *into* the PA room?" Cassie was still not clear about that part—she figured it couldn't be her responsibility, but she wanted to be sure.

Clarence smiled in Bryant's direction. "I have a plan."

Bryant groaned audibly as Cassie emerged from the car, carefully looking around to make sure no one saw her becoming suddenly visible. Cassie couldn't see them, but Toni, Zee, and Bryant were all waving their anxious good-byes as the Nova rumbled off toward school.

It was only 4:20 when Clarence, Zee, Toni, and Bryant arrived a couple of blocks away from school. As they approached the school, Bryant turned to Toni and Zee and announced with some bravado, "I got this."

Toni squinted her eyes at him, "You sure you want to do this alone?" She was used to Bryant being a big talker, but this seemed a little extreme.

"Pretty sure," the cockiness in his voice seemed to be fading as he considered the situation more. "I think Ms. Houghton trusts me. You know?"

The four of them paused on the school steps, all silently considering the best next move. "Good luck," Zee said. He thought Bryant going it alone was a great idea. Bryant took a couple more ever-so-slightly hesitant steps toward the door and then turned back and pointed at Clarence "Wait, I didn't mean you! C'mon Clarence. I may need you to protect me from Grumble."

Clarence shrugged and jogged up the steps to Bryant's side. They entered through the front door and headed into the office. It was far calmer than it had been earlier in the day, but it was still busy as Mrs. Grumble and Mr. Unger rushed back and forth in their preparation for the board meeting, pausing only occasionally to stare lovingly into each other's eyes. Ms. Houghton made an exasperated snorting noise at the sight and then sighed audibly, "Good grief!"

Bryant moved forward toward the office counter, waiting for a grown-up to notice him. Eventually Ms. Houghton did.

"Bryant," Ms. Houghton sounded distinctly surprised to see him. "What are you doing here at this hour?"

Bryant shifted nervously from one foot to the other. "A bunch of us are going over to the school board meeting to support you for the ACE Award," Bryant was unconvincing at best.

But while Ms. Houghton was not buying it, Mr. Unger ate it up. "Bryant, that means a great deal to me. Thank you so much." Clarence couldn't help but wonder if love was making Mr. Unger deaf as well as blind.

Mrs. Grumble turned to Mr. Unger and gushed. "It's because you inspire them. You *really* do!"

Ms. Houghton made another nose noise, conveying utter disdain.

Bryant pushed on, "A number of teachers and other staff are still here, Mr. Unger. Are you going to say a few words to them over the PA before heading over?"

Ms. Houghton looked sideways at Bryant, tilting her head slightly like a very smart retriever. She was now clearly wondering what he was up to.

Mr. Unger looked at the clock, it was 4:30, and he was ready to leave for the school district offices. "I'm afraid there's not time for that," he replied. "We need to get going. Being prompt and prepared is an important indication of efficiency."

But Mrs. Grumble insisted, "Oh, Mr. Unger, I think it's a brilliant idea!" And she bustled him toward the PA room.

"Oh, Erma!" Mr. Unger protested playfully.

"Those two are going to try my last nerve," Ms. Houghton declared and then turned and looked at Bryant. "I don't know what you're up to, young man, and I'm not sure I want to know. But I'll tell you one thing, I don't think I can bear to hear an inspirational message from him right now. I'm going over to the school board offices. The sooner we're done with this, the better!" And she scooped up her belongings from her desk and walked directly out of the office.

Bryant looked nervously at Clarence, who pushed him gently toward the PA room. The plan was working out just as they had discussed it. But there was one last step. Bryant approached the PA room quietly. He was surprised Mr. Unger hadn't already begun speaking, but peering around the corner into the room, he saw why: Mr. Unger and Mrs. Grumble were holding hands and gazing adoringly at each other. It was all Bryant could do to stifle a shriek of utter horror.

"Now!" Clarence instructed, and Bryant shoved the box of toner that was now serving as the official door prop out of the way, closing the PA room door. Looking around to make sure no one else had seen, he bolted out of the office.

A couple of steps into the hallway, Bryant paused and looked at Clarence. "What about the PA system?" Bryant asked desperately.

"Handled it," Clarence replied calmly.

"They're safe in there, right?" Bryant was anxious that he had somehow gone too far with this particular stunt.

Clarence tried to reassure him. "Marcus will be here watching. At 5:30, he'll let them out. And Mr. Rodrigues is on duty till 6. I'll make sure they're safe."

"OK," Bryant agreed hesitantly. He was still a little unsure.

When they arrived outside, Zee and Toni were standing with Cassie and Marcus.

Toni put her hand on Marcus's shoulder, "OK, Marcus, you're on. Not before 5:30, OK? And then come over to the school board. Your mom's going to be there, right?"

"She's there already," Marcus said proudly. "I've never seen her get this worked up about anything other than her job. I think she organized like fifty parents."

The four high-fived him and headed down the stairs. Cassie turned back and waved, "Thanks, Marcus."

Marcus looked a little embarrassed as he waved back, "Um, yeah, thanks, too."

Bryant shook his head, "The whole world has turned upside down."

The five of them jogged the couple of blocks over to the Nova and after making sure no one was looking, climbed in. Clarence put the key in the ignition, but when he went to start it, nothing happened. He tried again and still nothing happened. Clarence put his hands in his lap considering what to do. Toni was incredulous, "You have a magic car that won't start? That is just so wrong."

Clarence tried to explain, "So, it's just like people, right? This car was my brother's, and sometimes it needed a push to get going. You bring all your strengths and charms with you to heaven, but you bring the other stuff, too."

Zee was putting things together. "We don't have a lot of time. Are you telling us that we need to get out and push an invisible car?"

"Well, yes, I am saying that. Unless one of you wants to drive while I push."

He had no takers. None of them were old enough to drive a visible car, let alone an invisible one. The four friends looked around to make sure the coast was clear and then got out. Clarence rolled down the window to issue instructions.

"OK," he called out the window, his head sticking out of the car in an eerie decapitated way. "I have it in neutral. Go ahead and start pushing!"

They shoved up against the Nova but were unable to get it to move.

"This thing is a boat!" Bryant complained.

"You need to get it rocking first," Clarence suggested. Toni appreciated the fact that he had the decency to at least sound apologetic as he offered helpful hints.

"On three, we push extra hard and get this thing moving," Zee instructed.

The other three positioned themselves to push.

They rocked it forward, "One!" Zee called out.

They rocked it again, "Two!" Zee cried.

And then finally, "Three!" and they shoved the Nova out of its resting place.

"Whoo-hoo!" Clarence cried out.

And then they all heard another voice clearly call out, "Bryant?" It was Ms. Houghton.

Toni whispered to Bryant. "It's Ms. Houghton; say hello. Try and make it look like we're exercising."

Bryant shot Toni a look like she had to be insane, but he waved nonetheless. "Hey, Ms. Houghton. We're jogging over to the school district offices! See you soon!"

By now the Nova had started up and rolled to

the corner where Clarence turned right. Out of Ms. Houghton's sight, they ran around and jumped into the moving car. Ms. Houghton was following, not at a jog, but at a very quick walking pace. She was expecting to catch a glimpse of the four students when she turned the corner, but they were nowhere to be seen.

"That was close," Zee observed. "We better step on it!"

Clarence turned to him and smiled. "I can do better than that!" And Clarence pulled the steering wheel back toward himself, bringing the whole big green whale of a car up off the ground and flying.

"We're flying in a car we had to push to get started?" Toni's tone clearly conveyed that she thought this a bad idea.

"This car could fly the whole time, and you're only *now* showing me?" Cassie could not believe it. She had been dreaming of flying her whole life, and Clarence had been holding out on her.

All Zee could say was, "Wow." Bryant didn't say anything at all.

The flight lasted only three minutes. Clarence knew he wasn't supposed to be flying the kids in the car, and he was hoping that he could minimize the possibility of getting in trouble with the celestial authorities if he could point to the urgency of the situation, but he knew he shouldn't joy ride. Still, ever since hearing Cassie tell the story of her dream, he had been trying to figure out a plan to get them all up in the air.

Clarence landed the car smoothly and parked on a quiet residential street a couple of blocks from the school district offices.

Toni turned to Bryant who was ashen, "You alright?" she asked.

"Not a big fan of flying," was all he managed to say.

Clarence scooted around in his seat so that he could look at all four of them at once.

"You ready for this?"

They all nodded in the affirmative.

Clarence scouted the area around the car to make sure no one would see them getting out. "Looks clear," he said and then put his hand in the middle. The others lay their hands on top of his.

"Recess rules on 3. 1-2-3!"

They all shouted "Recess rules!" and jumped out of the car, with hearts set on making it true.

The scene outside the school district offices was complete pandemonium. Marcus's mother hadn't recruited fifty parents, she had recruited two hundred. People were everywhere. Some waved signs that read "Recess Is a Human Right!" and "Play Is Child's Work!" and others were chanting. An impromptu game of Four Square had even broken out.

Toni spied Mrs. Mackey speaking with a reporter. "I am willing to admit I may have been wrong about her."

Cassie turned to Clarence. She was shocked. "Did you do all this?"

Clarence shook his head, though he qualified it: "I mean, I didn't make them all want to come, but I did help make it possible. You know, dinner meetings were canceled last minute, babysitters were suddenly available. I basically removed the obstacles, but the people caring about saving recess was all their own doing."

Ms. Houghton, Ms. Swanson, and Mr. Street were talking together and looked amused as the four friends approached.

"This is very impressive," Mr. Street said, raising his eyebrows.

Ms. Swanson was looking all around, taking in the crowd. "I haven't seen Mr. Unger or Mrs. Grumble yet."

"I guess they're inside!" Bryant said, a little too enthusiastically.

"We'll see you in there!" Toni added, and they hurried inside.

The seats in the boardroom were starting to fill up and the four friends stood near the side. There was no way that all the people who had come to express their support for recess were going to fit. The board members started filing in to their seats up front. They looked uneasy with all the attention: they weren't accustomed to a big audience.

As the starting time for the meeting approached, there was a growing commotion as it became clear that the limited space was going to mean that some people were turned away. District staff people were trying to make room for everyone, and after some negotiations, it was agreed that they would set up folding chairs and plug in to the elaborate audiovisual system to simulcast the meeting out in the hall.

Twenty minutes later, the chairs and video screen were set up in the hall and the school board chair, Sandra Willoughby, called the meeting to order. Willoughby was an unusually tall woman in her early fifties with salt and pepper hair that hung to her shoulders. After some preliminary business, the board secretary, the bow-tie wearing Jack Phillips, announced that the first order of business would be the nomination of Magruder Elementary for this year's ACE Award and the school's presentation.

There was some confusion as the school board members looked around, expecting Mr. Unger to step forward. Instead, the four students moved slowly and somewhat tentatively to the front table.

"I'm sorry," Mr. Phillips cleared his throat, "you are?"

Toni spoke up: "Toni Robinson, Miguel Zapata, Cassie Murphy, and Bryant Anderson. We're students from Magruder Elementary, and we're here to present on behalf of the students, staff, and families."

Dr. Kardashian, who was seated to the far left of the board, stood up immediately upon recognizing Cassie. "You!" he said, pointing at her.

Bryant spotted Clarence nodding at Dr. Kardashian, whose affect changed suddenly and dramatically, swinging from outraged to docile in less than three seconds. Dr. Kardashian sat back down.

"You," Kardashian continued, his tone now flat, "are students at Magruder."

Mr. Phillips seemed confused by both Dr. Kardashian's outburst and the students' presence. "Mr. Unger didn't mention this to me when we spoke today." This was a highly unusual situation, and Mr. Phillips did not like highly unusual situations.

"Nothing like the element of surprise!" Zee said, jumping up and seizing the moment.

"We actually wanted to start our presentation with a game."

The school board members looked completely taken aback.

Zee turned to the audience, sensing that they were his biggest potential supporters. "You can all participate too. We're going to start with a game called Stand Up."

There was an enthusiastic cheer from the audience, immediately quieting any possible resistance from the board.

Zee continued on, knowing that if he slowed down or thought about what he was doing too much, he could easily chicken out. "Here's how it works," he began. "I'm going to say a series of things and if a thing is true for you, you stand up. You just stay standing for a second or two and then sit back down. I'm going to say a few different things, so you just want to get into a rhythm. Here goes."

Zee took a deep breath. "If you are a parent, stand up." Almost all of the audience stood up along with most of the school board.

"You've got it!" Zee praised. "You can sit back down.

"If you're left-handed, stand up." Thirty or so people from the audience and one school board member stood up, and they cheered enthusiastically in solidarity with one another before sitting back down.

"If you have ever performed in a musical, stand up."

Easily three-fourths of the audience and all of the school board and Dr. Kardashian all stood up. Bryant was struggling with the visual of Dr. Kardashian in a musical.

"If you loved recess when you were a kid, stand up!"

Everyone in the audience and most of the school board stood up. Dr. Kardashian and the few remaining school board members all hesitated a moment, but then, giving way to the almost palpable pressure, they too were on their feet.

The crowd in the boardroom was a good mix of parents with a smattering of students and teachers. Looking out into their faces, Cassie was struck by their enthusiasm in playing the game. She wanted to believe Clarence that it was real. Cassie noticed Sarah Hechtmeyer sitting next to her dad, the chief of police, and Cassie felt a twinge of longing as she watched Sarah's dad put his arm around her. It occurred to Cassie in that moment that most of the parents had come to the meeting because they truly loved their kids and wanted the best for them. It felt like such an obvious thought, but at the same time, Cassie realized she'd never really considered it before.

Zee, meanwhile, was overwhelmingly relieved that the game had worked and that he had survived. "Great job everyone!" he said and sat down.

Toni stood and launched into her part of the presentation. "We wanted to start with a game because we wanted you to remember what it was like to play."

Toni took a deep breath and tried to remember all

the points they had decided she would make. "Scientists know that play actually shapes our brains. Play is connected to creativity, physical activity, and how we feel—both physically and mentally. Playing a game, as we just did, can also help people feel more connected to one another."

Looking now directly at the school board chairwoman, Toni continued. "I imagine that a lot of different people have come here and talked about something they cared about. I'm sure that you could sympathize with their position. But could you feel it yourself?" Toni paused for effect. "When we were playing, it was different wasn't it? You knew exactly what we were talking about because you just experienced it."

The board chair nodded in agreement. Bryant stood up and Toni stepped aside.

"We want Magruder Elementary to win the ACE Award, but not because of its achievement, cleanliness, and efficiency. It's true, the school staff make sure we have all these. But Magruder should win because it's becoming a place where it's cool to care about one another. And that's something that takes both school staff *and* students. That takes magic."

Bryant continued, "Achievement, cleanliness, and efficiency are totally fine goals, but they're not the most important goals."

The room had gone completely silent. Dr. Kardashian cleared his throat. Clarence looked at the clock. It was already 5:40, and he had hoped they would be farther along in the presentation by now. There was a commotion at the doorway, and Bryant turned when he heard someone just outside shout: "Let me in! I'm supposed to be making a presentation in there!" It was Mr. Unger.

Bryant was supposed to invite Mr. Street and Ms. Swanson up to speak at this point, but with Mr. Unger banging down the door, he was pretty sure that would be a bad idea. Making their way through the hallway crowd, Mr. Unger, Mrs. Grumble, Marcus, and Mr. Rodrigues all managed to enter the boardroom a few moments later, looking more than slightly ruffled.

Mr. Unger's disheveled appearance was soon surpassed by a looked of astonishment when he saw the four students at the front of the room. "What is going on here?" Mr. Unger demanded.

"I knew it!" Mr. Phillips exclaimed. He had thought Mr. Unger's absence highly unusual, and now he felt vindicated.

"Oh, Cassie!" Mr. Rodrigues sighed.

There was something in the despondence of Mr. Rodrigues's tone that made Cassie stand up. "Wait," she insisted, "I can explain." Cassie took a deep breath. "Mr. Unger, Dr. Kardashian, I'm sorry we weren't quite truthful with you."

"Well, I should say so!" Mrs. Grumble exclaimed loudly. Clarence promptly nodded at her, and she was not heard from again that evening.

Cassie's voice cracked a little as she spoke. "I don't know where to start." She looked to Clarence and then began. "My parents were killed three years ago tomorrow in a car accident." She turned to Jack Phillips on the board, "I believe you knew my parents, Mr. Phillips." Mr. Phillips nodded uncomfortably; this was even worse than highly unusual.

"I remember the summer before my parents died, they took me to visit one of my dad's brothers. My dad was the youngest of seven, and all his brothers and sisters and all their cousins were there, They organized the most amazing game of Capture the Flag that I had ever been a part of. In fact, I can only think of one other game of Capture the Flag that might compare.

"I don't remember how long it lasted, but it felt like days. It was out in this huge meadow. You could approach the flags by both land and by water—either swimming or in a boat on the lake. My dad told me how when he was a kid, they'd play endless games like that all the time.

"We even played in the dark. My dad and I were sitting out by the fire, guarding our team's flag, and he told me all about what it was like when he was a kid. How he had liked to win more than anything. And he told me that as he had gotten older and become a father, he had come to realize that there were things that were bigger and better than winning. He said that if you worked hard and really, really cared, that even if you didn't win in the usual sense, you won by having this amazing life, and amazing adventures, and well . . . love. "

Cassie paused again. "I didn't totally understand

what he was saying at the time," and she laughed a little. "I mean, I was eight."

The crowd had been silent up until this point, and the tension broke a little when Cassie laughed and the audience was able to laugh a little with her. Mrs. Mackey was wiping at her eyes as was Sandra Willoughby.

"When they died that fall, I went to live with my aunt and my uncle. They've raised me ever since. And they're amazing. And I have amazing friends," Cassie pointed at Bryant and Zee and Toni and even turned to smile at Marcus. "But when my parents died, I pretty much decided my dad was wrong. I decided it wasn't safe to care too much. You know?" She stopped and looked around, and Mrs. Willoughby nodded. A lot of the grown-ups were nodding.

"So, I basically stopped hoping. I mean, I did OK in school, but I didn't put myself out there too much." She paused again. "Except, maybe, when I was playing something. There is something about playing that feels so different. Like, when we're out on the field, the way you can know what another person is thinking, and how you might move to a spot because you would just know that was where that person was going. I know this sounds crazy, but I remember thinking, 'I bet this is what heaven feels like.'"

Someone sniffled in the audience, and Cassie took a deep breath to make herself keep going. "But the older I got, the less I got to play. And then this year at school, even recess broke down. We couldn't seem to get any games going; nobody was getting along. It was as if nobody cared.

"Until last week. That's when everything changed. We made recess fun again, and everyone wanted to be a part of it. And it was as if we were all responsible for it. We were all a part of the school. And I didn't mean to, but I started to care.

"Recess was pretty bad before we fixed it. But I need you to understand that when we started making it more fun, it meant so much more than what you might think. It meant that we were a part of making Magruder an amazing place. And more than that, when we started to care about recess, it meant we started to care about one another. And really, there's nothing more than that."

Cassie had been tough for as long as she could, but now she started to cry. "I started to care again. And so I'm here to ask you . . . to beg you . . . not to take away the thing that means so much." Clarence, Bryant, Zee, and Toni all stood up and walked forward to gather around Cassie. And behind them, all of the audience began to stand, and everyone, even the people standing outside in the hall began chanting, slowly and quietly at first: "Recess! Recess! Recess!" The chant got louder and faster, and the pressure mounted so that it felt almost explosive.

Mrs. Willoughby banged her gavel on the table: "Ladies and gentlemen! Ladies and gentlemen! I'd like to remind you that we are currently discussing the nomination of Magruder Elementary for the ACE Award."

266

This brought the crowd back somewhat under control. There was still some rumbling, but people were quieting down. Mrs. Willoughby addressed Mr. Unger: "You have some very impressive students here, Mr. Unger. Is there anything you'd like to add?"

Mr. Unger looked somewhat uncomfortable and turned to Mrs. Grumble, who was uncharacteristically quiet.

"Well . . ." Mr. Unger began. But then he, too, was interrupted by a commotion at the door. This time it was Robert Roberts who came rushing in through the now open boardroom doors. Given everything that had already happened, no one was quite sure what to expect. Mr. Roberts marched to the front of the room, holding a video cassette.

"Can we help you?" Mr. Phillips was now being openly hostile. The situation had gone beyond highly unusual and moved fully into completely unacceptable.

Mr. Roberts turned on his best broadcaster voice. "As a concerned citizen, I felt it essential to share this important footage with you before you voted on the ACE Award," he announced.

Mrs. Willoughby was confused. "Isn't the more normal protocol that you air things on television?"

Mr. Roberts was dismissive in his response, but his tone conveyed a certain frustration as well. "We had some technical difficulties with the camera and were only just now able to remedy them so that we could share the film."

The four friends all looked at Clarence, who shrugged in a way that conveyed, "Imagine that!"

The school board members looked at one another, and Mr. Phillips made his usual noises about how this was quite unusual and out of order. Seeing, though, that the crowd would not be satisfied otherwise, he took the cassette from Mr. Roberts and popped it into the player so that the board and audience could watch.

What happened next caused the entire audience to gasp. The film clip opened with the footage of the cafeteria and Mr. Unger discussing the ACE award, only to be interrupted by a pack of marauding dogs running into the cafeteria. The cameraman was right in the middle of it all, and nothing about it cried out cleanliness or efficiency. It was a zoo!

But then, there caught on film, was Mr. Unger springing into action. The camera captured him leaping to lift a child up out of harm's way and onto a cafeteria table. And then in the next moment, Mr. Unger sprang, cat-like, in front of a dog that was bearing down on yet another child, forcing the animal to run in a different direction. The video caught Mr. Unger leaping and springing ninja-style all over the cafeteria, ultimately seizing on a miraculous, albeit unlikely, piece of T-bone steak that he flung out the back door, leading all of the dogs out and ridding the cafeteria of its peril. He finally leapt back into his original position, said "Achievement, cleanliness, and efficiency," and collapsed into an altogether understandable heap.

After a moment of stunned silence, the crowd once again broke out into spontaneous cheers. "Unger! Unger! Unger!"

Mrs. Willoughby turned to Mr. Roberts: "Thank you so much for sharing that, Mr. Roberts! That was extraordinary reporting!"

Mr. Roberts was completely dumbfounded by the footage, his mouth agape. Only after a few seconds was he able to recover enough to mumble, "Well, as a concerned citizen, I thought you should know."

Mr. Phillips seized the moment to move things along. "Well, given this, Madame Chair, I think we should call for a vote!"

"All in favor of awarding the ACE Award to Magruder say 'Aye!'"

"Aye!" the board unanimously called out.

"Students, Mr. Unger, congratulations!"

There was cheering and more chanting of "Unger!" until Cassie was finally able to be heard. "Madame Chair?"

The boardroom quieted down and all eyes were once again on Cassie.

"What about recess?"

Mr. Phillips cleared his throat again, and Bryant made a note to himself to always be careful of throat-clearing grown-ups. "Perhaps we should put off the vote tonight. We've had so much excitement."

"Oh, no you don't!" It was Mrs. Mackey who, leaping to her feet, called this out from the audience. "You're just hoping we won't be able to muster this big a crowd again. This school board is an elected body, and we want to see you vote on this issue. We want to know where you stand on recess!"

Cheers followed Mrs. Mackey's declaration, and the chant of "Recess!" began to gain momentum again.

Mrs. Willoughby banged her gavel loudly. "Ladies and gentlemen, surely we can display the same civility in the boardroom that Cassie so eloquently described the students creating on the playground." She turned to Mr. Phillips. "Jack, I do believe you initially brought the idea of eliminating recess to the board. Can you give us some more background on it?"

As boos and hisses erupted from the crowd, Mr. Phillips shot Mrs. Willoughby a withering glance, clearly miffed that she had so openly betrayed him. Mr. Phillips looked to Dr. Kardashian for support, but he was actively avoiding eye contact in an effort to distance himself from the now unpopular proposal.

"The issue is . . . frankly, I thought Cassie described it well. Recess has been extraordinarily disruptive at many of our schools—the highest concentration of discipline problems, kids coming back to class too riled up to settle down and learn. Frankly, it's been cutting into instructional time."

"And what would it take to fix it?" Mrs. Willoughby had little patience for people who talked about problems but offered no solutions.

"Money, I'm afraid. What these students have

accomplished is amazing, but it seems as if we would need a lot more support for staff to teach the kids at all our schools how to play well together, how to make recess time good again. It's not like when we were growing up. We came to school knowing these things already. And right now, I don't see where that kind of money would come from."

At this, Mr. Rodrigues stood up. The crowd turned and silently watched as he stepped to the front of the room. "Jack . . . uh . . . Mr. Phillips. You and I grew up with Cassie's dad. We grew up playing Capture the Flag in the Grove; you remember?"

Mr. Phillips nodded. His capacity for handling the unexpected was exhausted and his impatience reared its ugly head. "Yes, that's true, Mr. Rodrigues, but what does that have to do with our challenge here?"

"I was thinking that maybe we could pull together a Murphy Memorial Capture the Flag Game. Make it a giant fund-raiser to help with recess. We could sell food and have a cakewalk and do all the things our parents used to do when someone needed help. Do you remember?" Mr. Rodrigues was speaking to everyone now.

People in the audience started calling out things that they would do to help but then Mr. Phillips asked what was inevitably going to be the question that killed the idea: "But when are we going to do it? We need the money now!"

And the enthusiasm went out of the crowd like air from a popped balloon.

Mr. Rodrigues was not daunted. "Why not tomorrow?" he asked. He did not need to point out that it was the anniversary of Cassie's parents' accident.

And once again, Clarence nodded.

"I can do it tomorrow," Mrs. Mackey cried out.

"I can do it tomorrow," Sarah's father, the police chief, called out. "I can do it!" "I can do it!" Thanks to Clarence's scheduling help, it was miraculously a crowd without any commitments the following day.

Mrs. Willoughby banged her gavel victoriously. "Excellent. Do I hear a motion to protect recess for our elementary schools?"

Several board members cried out at once, "So moved!"

"And I'd like to move that henceforth we will celebrate the power of play each year with the Murphy Memorial Capture the Flag Game," Jack Phillips added, now smiling at Mr. Rodrigues and relieved to be back on the good side of the crowd.

"All in favor?"

The board responded with a unanimous and enthusiastic, "Aye!"

"Game on!" Mrs. Willoughby declared, "and meeting adjourned!"

The Murphy Memorial Capture the Flag Game turned out to be a huge success. Hundreds of families showed up for the picnic beforehand, and the day flowed with an abundance of food and celebration and generosity. Mrs. Mackey had organized a cakewalk with fifty cakes. Police Chief Hechtmeyer had borrowed the dunk tank from a neighboring police department, and they had raised $700 before noon with Mrs. Grumble being the star dunk tank attraction. Toni's mom had organized a big picnic lunch and Aaron Zimmerman's dad manned the barbeque for at least four hours. Mr. Rodrigues and Mr. Phillips laid out the boundaries for the Capture the Flag game just as they had when they were kids. Bryant and Zee watched in astonishment as Mr. Phillips tied a bandana around his head like a hippie. Cassie divided everyone into two teams by having the January to June birthdays on one side opposing the equally fierce and shockingly balanced July through Decembers.

The game started up in the afternoon. Everyone— parents, kids, teachers, board members, even Mr. Unger—participated, playing hard and having fun. Just as dusk was starting to settle in, Cassie found herself alone in the Grove. She had followed a parent in, thinking it was someone from the opposite team, but she had a sense once she arrived that it had been Clarence who had led her to this spot.

"Clarence?" she started to shout, but then she realized almost immediately that he was standing right next to her.

"That totally freaks me out when you do that!" she complained, but there was a lightness to her tone, as though she had let down her guard a little.

Clarence was happy to come upon this more relaxed version of Cassie. "You have a good day?" he asked.

"Oh, Clarence, it was amazing. I think my dad would have been so proud!"

"He was." Clarence knew he was overstepping, but he wanted her to know.

Cassie stopped short. It had never occurred to her before that Clarence might actually *know* her parents, let alone that he might actually be communicating with them.

"*Are you saying*?" Her tone was incredulous. Cassie didn't even know where to begin.

"Look, there's not a lot I can say. They love you

very much. They're insanely proud of you." Clarence nodded, and the same logs they'd sat on that first day moved in so that two were close together. "And I have to say good-bye now."

"What?" This was too much. "But we just fixed it so that it's good." Cassie had assumed that Clarence would have to leave at some point, but still, she couldn't believe he was saying this.

"Exactly," Clarence agreed. "And I think the powers-that-be feel that I've learned a lot and that if I hang about any more I'm going to be pushing my luck."

"So you *were* on probation?" Cassie had suspected as much from the beginning.

"Well, sort of. Look, you and I have a lot in common. We're stubborn; you know? Last night when you were talking . . . I don't know, I guess it felt as if you were talking directly to me. I learned something from you yesterday, Cassie."

Clarence looked down at his feet, uncertain how to say the next thing. "I died in a car accident, just like your parents." Clarence's tone was soft, and he looked bashful as he spoke. "My brother was driving."

"The Nova?" Cassie was more than a little horrified.

Clarence couldn't help but enjoy the moment. "Yeah! Man, would it piss my brother off if he knew that I got the Nova in the afterlife. He *loved* that car."

"Clarence!" Cassie wasn't as shocked as she tried to appear, but she really didn't get Clarence's sense of humor.

Clarence remembered what he'd wanted to tell Cassie and his tone shifted back to serious. "We had just been playing basketball, and my brother was driving us home. We'd lost, I was in a bad mood, and my brother was just giving me all this grief. I lost it, you know? I told him I hated him. And he looked at me, and he said '*Really?*'— just the way Bryant always says it."

Cassie looked stricken as Clarence continued. "And I meant to say 'No,' but in that moment, that's when we hit the other car. And I was an idiot and didn't have my seat belt on, and I went flying through the windshield. I died instantly. It didn't hurt. And the Nova was totaled. My brother was all shaken up, but he had his seat belt on, and he wasn't seriously injured."

They sat in silence for a while before Cassie spoke.

"So you know, right?" Cassie's tone was flat. Clarence sat quietly, not saying a word, so Cassie continued. "The last words I said to my parents before they left me to go to the party?"

Clarence was still quiet, but Cassie could tell that he knew.

"I've never told anyone that the last words I said to my parents before they died were 'I hate you.'"

"They knew you didn't mean it," he said quietly.

Cassie was crying as she spoke, but her words came out clearly. "They wouldn't let me go with them, and I didn't want to stay with the babysitter. I'd give anything to take it back."

"Consider it done."

"Oh, Clarence." Cassie let loose with huge, heaving sobs and Clarence scooted in closer to give her a hug.

"Look, here's what I can tell you. Your parents never gave it a second thought. They were both just so glad that you hadn't been with them that night."

"But if I had come, maybe it wouldn't have happened." Cassie had always wondered if that might be true, but had never said it out loud. She'd never ever felt safe enough.

"It was their time, Cassie. It was an accident, but it happened."

It was all completely unsatisfying to Cassie, and now Clarence was leaving, too. "I hate this! I don't want you to go. What if it all falls apart again?" Cassie wanted to jump up and down and have a temper tantrum the way she had before her parents had died.

"You know how to fix it now." Clarence's tone was patient and calm. "I'd like to say goodbye to the others and to leave you all together; OK?"

Cassie didn't know what to say. It wasn't OK, but she knew better than to try and resist, and being frozen while saying good-bye seemed embarrassing. She nodded her assent, and the three other friends came walking into the Grove. Cassie had no doubt that Clarence had led them there, just as he had led her.

"Here you two are! We've been looking all over for you," Zee was clearly relieved to have found Cassie. The day before had been very emotional, and he was feeling very protective of her.

"Marcus captured your team's flag," Bryant said to Cassie, his tone ever-so-slightly mischievous. And then turning to Clarence, "Couldn't we freeze him just one more time?"

Toni looked closely at Cassie, and seeing that she'd been crying, turned to Clarence.

"You're saying good-bye. Aren't you?"

Bryant and Zee were caught off guard. *"Really?"* Bryant said. And Clarence turned to Cassie and laughed. "You see?"

"You're really leaving?" Zee was surprised. He'd been suspicious of Clarence in the beginning, but now he'd gotten used to having him around.

"It's time for me to go, but I did want to say good-bye. You all were fantastic last night!"

"We couldn't have done it without you." Zee stuck out his hand to shake but instead, followed it up with a hug.

Bryant hesitated for a second. "I don't mean to be ungrateful or anything . . . I mean, it's all amazing and everything. But Unger and Grumble aren't going to remember I locked them into the PA closet, are they?"

"We're all good on that score," Clarence confirmed, and then he and Bryant exchanged hugs.

"I was getting kind of used to you telling me what to say," Toni teased. But then very sincerely she added, "I'm going to miss you." Clarence said nothing but gave her a hug as well.

Finally he turned to Cassie. "You gotta keep it going now. OK? You gotta make sure that it doesn't just stop at Magruder. Maybe one day, every kid in America will get to play every day just because of you."

Cassie hugged Clarence tight and whispered in his ear, "Tell them I love them . . . OK?"

Cassie felt Clarence nod, and then he was gone.

The four friends all stood quietly for a few moments, looking at one another and not knowing what to say. Their whole world had completely changed, all because of a sweat suit-wearing, Nova-driving, mischief-causing angel named Clarence.

After what seemed like a long while, Cassie finally broke the silence. "Marcus didn't really capture the flag, did he?"

Bryant smiled sheepishly and shook his head. And then Cassie opened her arms wide enough to hug the other three all at once.

"C'mon, then," she said. "We got a game to play!"

EPILOGUE

Dear Cassie, Toni, Bryant, and Zee,

I know you probably won't need this, but I wanted to leave this playbook behind for you, just in case. I figured it might be helpful if you get fuzzy on some of the rules, or if you're trying to teach the younger kids how to run the games before you all go off to middle school. It's also good if you have any grown-ups trying to help out—grown-up brains like to see things written down, you know?

And I know it sounds like overkill, but you just want to get in the habit of reviewing the rules out loud really quickly **every time** before you play. That way nobody has to fake knowing the rules when they really don't, and new kids never have to feel left out.

I can think of so much more that I wish I had told you, but mostly you know it all anyhow. If you make sure everyone feels as if they're welcome and that they belong, you can't go wrong. I couldn't be more proud of you,

Clarence

RoShamBo

- Two players; all ages
- No equipment is required.

How to play: The ultimate problem solver,

RoShamBo (aka Rock-Paper-Scissors) is played by two people who stand opposite one another, count out "Ro-Sham-Bo" while rhythmically and gently pounding their

fists into their open hands, and on "Bo" throw out either a rock (closed fist), paper (flat out hand), or scissors (sideways peace sign with index and middle fingers sticking out). Rock crushes scissors, scissors cuts paper, and paper covers rock. In the event that both players throw out the same thing, they repeat until a winner is determined.

Variations: I don't mean to seem rigid, but I'm a RoShamBo purist. No variations, I don't even really approve of two out of three—I think it muddies the game—best just to abide by the first throw.

Switch

- At least five participants; all ages
- No equipment required, though cones for marking the corners can help if you don't have chalk to draw out the square. You can also use an existing Four Square court.

Before you start: Make sure everyone knows how to play RoShamBo.

How to play: The game begins with five players

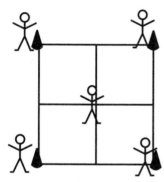

on the court—one on each corner and one in the middle. Play begins when the person in the center calls out "Switch," signifying that everyone needs to go to a new corner (with the middle no longer being an available space). If two players arrive at a corner at the same time, a quick game of RoShamBo is played, and the winner stays. If more than five people are playing, the first person in line goes to the center and begins the next round.

Variations: Switch can be played on courts of different shapes and with different numbers of corners. You can also enlarge the size of the court, making for longer runs.

RoShamBo Relay

- At least eight participants; all ages
- Cones for marking out a U shape to race around

Before you start:

- Make sure everyone knows how to play RoShamBo.
- Divide the participants into two even groups.
- Set the cones out in a U or horseshoe shape 20 to 30 feet long—you can also use half a basketball court.

How to play: The goal of the game is for a player from one line to make it to the start of the opposite line. The two teams line up with one at either end of the horseshoe. Play begins when the leader calls out "Go!" The first players on each side racewalk toward each other (you must always have a foot on the ground to make it racewalking, absurd hip-swiveling is encouraged). When the two opposing players meet up, they play RoShamBo to determine who continues

racewalking toward the other team's starting point, while the team of the defeated player sends out another representative from the starting point. Again, when the players encounter each other, they play RoShamBo until one player wins. The game continues, with each team earning a point each time one of their players makes it all the way around the horseshoe.

Variations: You can make the horseshoe longer or shorter and add obstacles to the course.

Movement Name Game

- At least ten participants; all ages
- No equipment is required.

Before you start: Have the group circle up.

How to play: The Movement Name Game is a

 great way for a group to learn one another's names. The game begins when the first person says his or her name and then makes a silly motion to go with it—a jumping jack or a distinctive wiggle. The group repeats the person's name and the motion, and then the person to the right says his or her name and adds a new motion, continuing on through the circle until everyone has gone.

Variation: After everyone has said his or her name and demonstrated a motion, you add a ball, with the thrower required to say the intended recipient's name and make his or her motion before throwing the ball to that person. The group works together to see how quickly they can pass the ball to everyone.

RoShamBo Rockstar

- At least ten participants; all ages
- No equipment is required.

Before you start: Make sure everyone knows how to play RoShamBo.

How to play: Group players into pairs. Each pair

plays RoShamBo to determine the winner. The winner moves on to play another winning player while the player who has been defeated becomes the winner's cheerleader, following that person and rooting for him or her to win as they continue to play. After each round, the winner advances to play again, with the defeated player and all his or her cheerleaders joining the winner's cheerleaders in an ever-growing throng of support. The game continues in this way until only two players remain with the whole group cheering for one or the other.

Wah!

- At least ten participants; better for grade 3 and up
- No equipment is required.

Before you start: Make sure everyone knows the three motions: becoming a tree, chopping down a tree, and having a tree fall.

How to play: Have everyone stand in a circle facing

one another. Play begins when a designated player raises both arms overhead with palms together to form a "tree" and says "Wah!" The two players on either side of the tree make a chopping motion toward the midsection of the tree while also saying "Wah!" (they don't really touch the tree) When the tree is chopped, it falls by lowering its arm and bending at the waist, pointing at anyone in the circle except the people directly next to him or her. The player pointed at immediately becomes the next tree by raising

288

both arms and crying out "Wah!" The game continues until someone hesitates in being a tree or chopping a tree, or if the wrong person says "Wah!" That player then steps out of the circle. Players outside the circle cheer on the trees. The game continues until only four players remain, and they are declared victors.

Variations: Don't eliminate players and work together to keep the game going as long as possible.

Gaga Ball

- At least ten participants; all ages
- Equipment: A ball that bounces, cones to mark out a circle roughly 15 feet wide

How to play: To start the game, everyone stands on the outside boundary of the circle. The

leader drops the ball in the center of the circle, allowing it to bounce three times and saying "Ga-ga ball" as it bounces. Players then move into the circle and use their hands to bounce the ball toward the other players. If a player is hit by a ball from the knee down, they are out and must then go to the boundary line where they help keep the ball in the circle by acting as a wall. The ball can be hit only with an open hand—no throwing, catching, or holding the ball. You can hit the ball only once before it either hits a boundary or another person. Play ends when there is one person left or time has run out.

Four-Square

- At least five participants; all ages
- Equipment: A playground ball and a 10-by-10-foot square on the ground broken into four smaller 5-by-5-foot squares labeled 1, 2, 3, 4 or A, B, C, D

Before you start: One person stands in each square, and extra players wait in line.

How to play: The game begins when the server (1

or A square) drops the ball once in her square and then hits the ball into a different square. The ball can only bounce once in any square and players can hit the ball into another square using any part of their body after it has bounced once in their own square. If the ball hits a line or goes out of bounds before it bounces, the player who last hit the ball returns to the waiting/cheering line. There is no holding or catching the ball and a player can't let the ball bounce more than once in a square before being hit. Finally, you can't hit the ball before it bounces in your square.

As players move out of the game and back into line, the person at the front of the line moves into the D or 4 square and everyone else advances toward A or 1 to fill out the squares.

Variations: For younger students, you can start out by letting the players catch and release the ball. For older students, you can also include more students by using two adjacent 4-square courts for a game of 8-square.

Giants, Wizards, and Elves

- A large group, ten or more; grades 3 and up
- No equipment is required, although cones for marking the corners can help if you're not using a defined field or a basketball court with existing lines.

Before you start: Make sure everyone knows the three motions: Giants stand very tall with hands over their heads crying out "Aaargh!" Wizards stand with one foot in front of the other, arms extended to the front, fingers wiggling, and make the sound "Hsssssss!"

Elves squat down and cup their hands to make big elf ears while making the raspberry sound with their lips. Explain that Giants beat wizards, wizards beat elves, and elves beat giants. Divide the group with each half on either side of the middle dividing line.

How to play: Before the game begins, each team huddles on their side of the line and chooses a first and second character to be. Each team then moves to the middle line. The game begins when the leader yells: "One, two, three—What's it going to be?" Each team then flashes their first choice, with all acting out the giants or the wizards or the elves in unison. Whichever team is dominant then chases the other team back to the rear boundary line. Anyone tagged before getting to the rear line becomes part of the opposing team. If both teams show the same first choice, the leader again calls out "One, two, three—What's it going to be?" again, and both teams flash their second choice. If the second choice is also the same, the teams regroup and pick two more characters for a new lineup.

Kickball

- At least twelve participants; better for grades 3 and up
- Equipment: A kickball and markers for bases are required. It is easiest to use an existing baseball or softball diamond. A regulation field measures 60 feet between bases.

Before you start: Teams should play RoShamBo to determine who has first ups. The kicking team determines their kicking order, and the fielding team determines their field positions.

How to play: The game begins when the pitcher

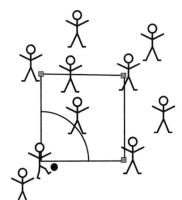

rolls the ball to the person up to bat, the kicker. Play stops when the ball is thrown to the pitcher. Teams switch sides after three outs or nine runs. Outs are granted when:

- the kicker kicks a ball that is caught before it lands
- the base player has control of the ball and a foot on the base before the base runner reaches the base

- a base runner is tagged with the ball while running to the base
- one base runner passes another
- a base runner intentionally interferes with a fielder trying to recover the ball

Note: A player on base can tag-up when a ball is caught, meaning that he or she must wait until after the ball is caught before attempting to advance to the next base. Also, if a base runner must advance because of another runner or the kicker behind, it is a force out, and the base player need only tag the bag. If no runner or kicker is forcing a runner to the next base, it is not a force out, so the player must be tagged with the ball.

A runner can advance only one base on an overthrow to a base player. A run is scored for the kicking team when a base runner touches all four bases, in order, without being called out at any time. If the ball is kicked and rolls out of bounds before going past first or third base, it's a foul. Four fouls equals an out. If a member of the fielding team touches the ball before it bounces, it is a fair ball.

Three-Lines Basketball

- At least nine participants; best for grades 3 and up
- Equipment: Basketball, three cones, basketball court

Before you start: Place the three cones along the half court line—one in the middle and one on either side, roughly 10 feet apart.

Divide the players into three roughly equal-size groups, each lined up behind a cone.

How to play: To begin the play, the first player

from each of the three lines steps out into the court and turns around to face the people in line, becoming the first group on defense. These players will be playing half-court basketball against the next three. The group facing the basketball hoop is offense, and the game starts with their middle player in possession of the ball. That player passes the ball to one of his/her teammates, and the object is to score a basket.

If a player shoots and misses, either team can rebound and shoot immediately. When a point is scored, the team that scored stays on to face the next set of three players. The team that did not score returns to the end of the player lines. If a foul is called, the player who is fouled gets to throw the ball in from out of bounds. If the leader determines it is taking too long, they begin counting down "Ten, nine, eight . . ." If no shot has been made before zero, the two teams play RoShamBo to see which team stays. If a team wins three games in a row, that team returns to the end of the player line.

Variations: Players cannot dribble. They can move the ball only by passing.

Wall Ball

- You really only need two people to play, but it's more fun with people rotating in and out. Best for grades 2 and up.
- Equipment: Bouncy ball and either cones or chalk to mark out the boundary

Before you start: Make sure everyone knows the boundaries on both the wall and the ground.

How to play: The game begins when one player serves the ball by bouncing it once on the ground before hitting the wall. The ball can

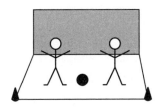

be hit with an open hand or fist. The receiving player must let the ball hit the wall and bounce once on the ground before returning it. The player can then return it by bouncing it off the ground and hitting the wall again.

Play continues until the ball bounces outside the boundaries (including hitting the line), hits the wall without bouncing on the ground, bounces twice on the ground before hitting the wall, or is not allowed to bounce. When a player stops the play, she or he goes to the end of the line, and a new player comes into the game. The remaining player is the server and begins the new game.

Capture the Flag

- At least ten participants; best with grades 3 and up
- Equipment: Each side needs a flag and eight cones or two hula hoops to create the flag zone and a holding zone for players captured from the other team.
- A field or other large space with good boundary lines (for example a gym) that can be divided in half

Before you start: Make sure everyone knows the boundary lines and how to tag safely. (Use a light touch like butterfly wings, on the back and shoulders, being careful not to cause someone to fall.)

How to play: The game begins with each team on its own side of the field. The goal is to try and take the other team's flag and return across the line without being tagged. If a player is  tagged while on the opponent's side, that player is taken to the holding zone on the opponent's side. If a player in possession of the flag when tagged, the flag goes back to the flag zone. Teams can guard the flag or the holding zone, but players must stand at least 2 feet away from the zones. A player can be freed from the holding zone when a teammate crosses the center and tags them; both players then receive a free walk back to their side. A player can free only one teammate at a time. If a player gets to the flag zone without being tagged, she can stay there safely (i.e., players can't be tagged in the flag zone) until she attempts to run back to her own side.

Jill Vialet is the CEO and founder of Playworks. Jill has won a number of awards for her work with Playworks, including the Ashoka Fellowship, the Forbes 30 Leading Social Entrepreneurs, the James Irvine Award and the Women's Sports Foundation's 40 for 40. Jill grew up in Washington, DC where she played in epic games of Capture the Flag as a child. She now lives in Oakland, California with her family. *Recess Rules* is her first book.